In Her Defence

Jan Edwards is an award-winning author with titles that include *Winter Downs* (winner of the Arnold Bennett Book Prize) and *Sussex Tales* (winner of the Winchester Slim Volume Award). She has also been awarded the BFS Karl Edward Wagner Award.

Her short fiction can be found in crime, horror and fantasy anthologies published in the UK and USA. She was a script writer for the Doctor Who DVD and its accompanying book *Daemons of Devil's End.* Jan is also an anthologist with the award-winning Alchemy Press, co-owned with her husband Peter Coleborn. A native of Sussex, Jan now lives in north Staffordshire, UK.

https://janedwardsblog.wordpress.com

Also by Jan Edwards

Bunch Courtney Investigations

Winter Downs

In Her Defence

The Things You Were (coming soon)

Other Titles

Sussex Tales

Fables and Fabrications

Leinster Gardens and Other Subtleties

In Her Defence

A Bunch Courtney Investigation

Jan Edwards

Published by
The Penkhull Press

Published 2019 by the Penkhull Press by arrangement with the author

FIRST EDITION

ISBN 978-0-9930008-9-8 (print edition)
ISBN 978-1-9164373-1-9 (eBook)

Published by The Penkhull Press
Staffordshire UK

www.penkhullpress.co.uk

Dedication

To the memory of my Pop and to Aunt Jean, for passing on their war-time anecdotes and their knowledge of all things rural and Sussex.

Acknowledgements

I spent many happy hours poring over internet pages and shelves full of books, gleaning fascinating snippets on life and death in the 1940s; so I send many thanks via the ether to that numerous hive-mind. Thanks go to the Renegade Writers for poking holes in the rubbish bits so that I could build a better book. Much appreciation to the horse-nuts Lindsey Russell, Raven Dane, Sue Burns and Bev Adams for correcting me on all things equine.

Huge debts of gratitude are owed to the Penkhull (and Alchemy) Press crews: Mike Chinn and Jem Shaw for their infinite knowledge of guns and trains and planes; Debbie Bennett for tips on policing matters; Misha Herwin for her unstinting support in beta reading and for those many mornings of coffee-shop brain-storming; and last but never least, the lovely Peter Coleborn for his editorial genius and design magic.

Friday 3 May

Bunch Courtney leaned against the top rail of the stock pen, enjoying the sensation of unseasonably warm May sunshine on her back, and perused the pair of Jersey heifers she had purchased at auction. The cows stared back with their soft-doe eyes and quietly continued their munching.

When a trio of fighter planes swooped across a clear sky it was Bunch who broke that peaceable contact, shielding her eyes against the sun to watch the aircraft dwindle into the distance. 'Fourth flight we've seen in under an hour. Something's up', she said. 'Were those Hurricanes or Spits? What do you think?'

Roger raised his head hopefully and thumped his tail in the dust, and she reached down to scritch the top of the dog's head, finding comfort in the gesture. The planes were a dark reminder of what lay a mere hundred miles to the south; Bunch offered up a silent prayer of thanks for the English Channel. She wondered for how much longer market days could possibly survive. *Or anything else for that matter,* she thought. *No, I refuse to even contemplate the possibilities.* She stretched across the rail to give her Jersey maids a final pat and pushed away from the barrier. There was a lunch appointment to keep and she was already late.

A few minutes later she stepped into the dim oak-panelled

confines of The Marquis Inn's saloon bar, where the smell of roasting meat and Friday fish, mingling with the ever-present pall of smoke and beer fumes, closed in around her. Every white-clothed table was occupied and she searched the room for her luncheon partners without success until Daphne waved to her from within one of the window bays that overlooked the market. Daphne was grinning at Bunch, as she wove her way toward the table, tapping at her watch.

The perfect English rose in her red and blue florals. And Mother would love that spiffy little pillbox hat. Bunch adored her sister but was constantly aware of how unalike they were. She was the sporty, tall brunette; her sister the golden blonde, slight and delicate despite her pregnancy. Bunch leaned down to kiss her sister on the cheek. 'Yes I know, I'm late as always. Hello Dodo, you're looking well. Positively blooming.'

'Thank you Rose, darling. So glad to see you. We were beginning to think you'd forgotten us.'

Bertram Tinsley got to his feet and pulled out Bunch's chair. 'Good to see you, Rose.'

'Thank you, Barty.' Bunch nodded to Dodo's father-in-law as she slid into her seat and laid her slouch hat on the vacant chair beside her.

'My pleasure.' Barty took a mouthful of beer as he settled back down, wiping his extravagant moustaches carefully with a napkin. 'Good auction?' he asked.

'Excellent, thank you.' Bunch waved Roger beneath the table out of harm's way. She took a sip from her schooner of sherry that was over-sweet and did nothing to quench her thirst. She wished it was a beer but, knowing how the old-fashioned Tinsley disapproved of ladies with pint pots in their fists, she said nothing and poured herself a glass of water.

'Busy out there today,' Barty continued. 'You'd think with everything going on people would be terribly cautious about being out and about.'

'They are trying very hard not to consider the alternatives,' Bunch replied. 'Parsons even thought prices were a little up on last month. Though we won that pair of in-calf heifers for next to nothing.'

'The little Jerseys? You were the only person seriously bidding for them. Speaking of which, I thought Parsons would be joining us.' Barty jerked his head at the fourth setting reserved for the Courtney's estate manager.

'The old boy sat with me through the auction but he left the moment my bid was in.' Bunch looked at the vacant chair. 'He was feeling unwell. I must speak with Daddy about letting him retire gracefully. I'm very fond of Parsons and I'd feel so dreadfully guilty if anything happened to him.'

'Didn't he travel here with you? How will he be getting home on his own?'

'I gather Dickie Bale is giving him a lift.'

Barty snorted derisively. 'I hope Parsons has that right because Bale was in here not twenty minutes ago. Didn't spot us, I'm glad to say. He's a bit of a nincompoop, if you ask me.'

'Can't say I know Bale that well. He and Parsons seemed quite chummy.'

A roar of good-humoured jeering attracted their attention toward the bar and the gaggle of Canadians gathering there.

'Damned bad form. Should be in the four-ale bar if they want to kick-up.' Barty glowered in their direction. 'No discipline.'

'They're very young,' Bunch replied. 'And a long way from home.'

Barty grumbled some retort but Bunch had ceased listening.

A young woman seated alone, just a few feet away from the raucous drinkers, had caught her attention. A sturdy girl in her early twenties with light-brown hair scraped up beneath a red hat. Her clothes were worn though of good quality, and plainly not English by their cut. Whether it was her obviously foreign air or that she leaned on the bar top with her head in her hands that made her a source of curiosity, the girl had attracted attention from others in the room. Some were inquisitive glances, a few of them lecherous, others hostile in varying degrees, each seeing what they wanted to see in a woman drinking alone. For Bunch, it was the way she wore her sadness like a halo. Obviously ill at ease, perhaps even in pain from the way she stared fixedly into her half-pint of pale ale, oblivious to the noise and bustle all around her.

Lost, Bunch thought. *That's the only word for her. Probably waiting for somebody who never turned up. And she's so obviously unwell. Poor little wretch.*

The woman was lost to view as the crowd shifted and Bunch's attention drifted back to Dodo and Barty. Her sister was, as she had already observed, positively blooming. Barty, she noted, was a more considerate man: no longer the blustering martinet he had been before the crushing events of earlier in the year.

Hardly surprising, she thought. *With all the stiff upper lip in the world, one doesn't lose one's wife, son and reputation without some kind of change.*

The trio chatted on about this and that for some minutes and had placed their orders for lunch when a sharp cry sliced across from the bar. A strangely liquid shriek. *As though,* Bunch thought, *someone was crying from beneath water.* Bunch swivelled in time to see the young woman snap forward, with both arms clutched around her midriff, making no attempt to save herself from crashing to the floor where she writhed, screaming for help in English and some other language that was Germanic to Bunch's ears, yet not the German she recognised.

The room broke into panic as diners rose to their feet.

Some rushed toward the girl and as many backed rapidly away. Bunch was forced to elbow her way through the gathered watchers, to where the girl flailed at their centre, uttering wordless sounds on a tide of vomit and foam.

A tall man, a travelling salesman Bunch guessed by his shiny suit, brought his arm down to bar her way. 'Keep back, Miss. She needs a doctor.'

Bunch eyed him coldly. 'I've some training as a nurse,' she snapped. 'Stand aside please.' He withdrew the offending limb with poor grace and stood back to allow her through. Bunch knelt by the woman to examine her at close quarters and found no immediate signs of injury, yet the woman's pain was obvious. 'Move back please. Give her some air.' She looked around the jostling circle of bystanders ogling the scene. 'Will somebody please fetch a doctor? Now. And telephone for an ambulance.' She gripped her patient's wrist searching for a pulse and frowned to feel it race beneath her finger tips.

The girl gasped in agony and then struggled to regain the breath she wasted on it, her mouth gaping as she fought to suck in air.

'Steady old thing. Help is on its way. Where does it hurt?' Bunch murmured and leaned down to catch the woman's words. *Definitely not German,* she thought. *Danish? Or Dutch, perhaps? Hard to tell when she can barely speak.*

The patient arched her back, her blue eyes bulging and twitching rapidly from side to side. Then she inverted violently to a foetal crunch.

'Hush, hush,' Bunch crooned as she checked the girl's pupils, and her pulse once more. Neither was even close to normal. Bunch's training with the FANY had been thorough, as far as it had gone, but was incomplete when she switched to ATS. She did not mind admitting to herself, at least, that she was out of her depth. 'We'll get you some help very soon,' she said.

The sick woman howled, bending and straightening and continuing to claw at her belly. Her breath came in heaving gulps as she struggled to take in sufficient air to remain conscious.

'Is it a fit?' The landlord crouched beside Bunch and cast furtive glances around the watching crowd.

'No, not a fit.' Bunch felt the girl's forehead and shook her head. 'And no sign of fever. I don't believe it's any kind of contagion. What has she eaten since she came in here, Mr Vernon? Or drank perhaps?'

He jumped up with hands out, flapping them toward Bunch as if he could batter her words into the vomit-strewn carpet. 'She's not eaten in here,' he said, and louder for the benefit of the crowd, 'nothing she's had from here, Miss Courtney. I can't have you sayin' that.'

Bunch looked him up and down. The man was more concerned with being blamed for bad food than for this sick woman, and it disgusted her. 'Never mind the reputation of your kitchen,' she snapped. 'This woman is seriously ill. Fetch a doctor. Right this instant. And get these people away. Clear the room, in fact.'

'The whole room? But 'tis market day. We've—'

'You honestly want people eating in here while this poor creature is vomiting on the carpet?'

Ted Vernon took a few moments to weigh his options and reluctantly began to call for people to 'Give the maid some air. Plenty of room out in the garden.'

'Can I do anything, Rose?' Barty fought his way through the crowd and crouched beside her.

Bunch looked down at the girl who was still writhing and struggling for breath. Despite her chiding Vernon for his selfish acts, she could not be certain that whatever had this woman in the throes of something deadly was not some ghastly disease. Her first thought was for Dodo and her unborn child. 'I can deal with this, Barty. Get Dodo home. And take the dog as well. Please.'

Barty drew breath to argue and for a moment Bunch thought she saw *Tinsley: Bertram A, Colonel (retired)* fighting to resurface. But when Dodo appeared at their side, her face ashen at the sight of the stricken girl, her obvious distress seemed to decide him on the best course of action. He nodded to Bunch and called the dog to heel as he hustled his daughter-in-law away.

Once they had left the room Bunch breathed relief. There were any number of illnesses that could account for these symptoms and she could only pray that the lack of fever ruled out more exotic choices. She was still betting on food poisoning and considered whether an emetic to eject whatever remained of any such substance was a good idea. When her patient retched once more, heaving a tiny trickle of pale-yellow froth across Bunch's jodhpurs, she realised the time for that had passed. 'Your gut has to be empty by now,' she muttered.

The victim's struggles were already weakening to twitches and spasms, her agony subsiding into whimpers and groans, whilst tears seeped down her face.

Bunch gathered the girl across her lap to raise her up a little, hoping to ease that frantic choking for oxygen, all the while trying to give what comfort she could with physical contact, but feeling increasingly helpless in the face of a life ebbing away at a terrifying pace. 'Where's that damned quack?' she shouted.

'Doctor Ashton to you, young lady. If you'd just move aside?' A bulky man with greying hair knelt beside Bunch and gently took the body from her.

Bunch sat back, unabashed at his rebuke, and watched as Ashton began an immediate examination, his expression giving little away though his movements were increasingly rapid. 'What has she eaten?' he demanded.

'Nothing.' The Landlord's ruddy cheeks flushed as deeply as his veined nose. 'My food's all good. Ask anyone.'

'She was drinking when I came in,' said Bunch. 'Pale ale was it?'

The landlord nodded. 'She did, aah. She only 'ad a half though.'

'And coffee.' His wife, now at his elbow, added. 'Before the beer. Asked for it black, she did.' Maude Vernon screwed up her face. 'Asked for some aqua-something or other to go in it. An' I told her, we never 'ave 'ad furrin stuff in 'ere.' She half turned her head, watching from the corner of her eye as the prone woman ejected another noisy dribble of bile and foam. 'Furriner,' she added, 'bringing some unkering sickness over 'ere.'

'She's gravely ill,' Ashton replied. 'I can't say what's causing it, precisely, but something taken by mouth is highly likely.' He looked down as the girl moaned a few words at him. Her breathing was becoming more laboured and she only managed a rattling croak. 'Don't try to talk my dear.' He patted her arm. 'The ambulance will be here soon.'

His patient's eyes rolled back, her mouth working soundlessly.

'I doubt the poor creature will last that long,' he muttered. It was obvious to them all that the woman's struggles for air were rapidly weakening. 'Let's get her chest raised a little more to ease her lungs, shall we?'

Between them they held her half upright and the patient gasped in a half-lungful of air before she sighed deeply and sank back, her head lolling against the doctor's shoulder. He felt quickly for a pulse and bent to listen to her chest before shaking his head at his self-appointed nurse. He lowered the dead woman gently to the floor, closed her eyes and respectfully folded her arms across her body. 'Not long at all.' Ashton got slowly to his feet and pulled the publican to one side. 'Ted, could I trouble you to use your telephone?'

~~~

Chief Inspector William Wright lifted the rough blanket and gazed at the corpse's pallid face. He lowered it again and got to his feet, dusting his knees as he did so. 'You shouldn't have let anyone leave the scene, Mr Vernon,' he said. 'I hope you at least saved the items she drank from?'

'She broke the beer glass when she fell.' Ted Vernon shrugged, his expression mutinous. 'Are you saying my beer killed her?'

'According to Doctor Ashton, her death is unlikely to be from natural causes,' Wright replied. 'He's reasonably certain the victim was poisoned. And, so far as we know, yours was the last establishment in which she ate or drank.' He stepped a little closer to the sweating landlord. 'I rather feel a little more co-operation would be to your advantage?'

Vernon threw a furtive glance at his wife. 'We was busy. Market day y'see. An' Maudey keeps a tidy eye on the crocks. Clears en off, tidy.'

'No cup?'

'I already washed en,' Maude replied. 'Can't have slabby cups about the place.' She met Wright's eye more levelly than her husband, defying even this law keeper to disagree with her in her own fiefdom.'

Wright pursed his lips, his gaze fixed on the broken shards of glass around the corpse. 'Collect those up,' he said to the constable taking notes. 'The ambulance can remove her once the coroner has viewed the body.'

'When'll that be?' Vernon demanded. 'I 'as to open up again in an hour.'

'I'm very sorry Mr Vernon but that won't be possible,' Wright replied. 'Not until after the coroner has been. I suspect that will not be for a few more hours yet so I doubt you shall be opening this evening. Perhaps tomorrow. Meanwhile, we shall require a full list of people who were on the premises today.'

'All of en?' Vernon shook his head. 'Can't be done. Not everyone as comes in here on a market day. In an' out like flies, they are. Place was fair shackled. Public bar were even worse. Had half the Cannucks in from Fryern Hall. Noisy baggerin' yafflers.'

'If they were not in this room then they needn't concern us,' Wright replied. 'Let's hope your clientele are more observant than you.' He turned reluctantly to Bunch. 'Miss Courtney, I would say it's a surprise to see you here but somehow it isn't. You have a nose for trouble.'

Bunch unfolded her arms to spread them in a slow shrug. Until that moment he had not acknowledged her beyond a curt nod and this formal address was a shock to her. She was somewhat gratified to have his deference yet at the same time he was being insufferably patronising, even insulting. She and Chief Inspector William Wright had not met since they had investigated the violent deaths at Perringham at the turn of the year. She had thought they'd become friends back then. *Apparently I was mistaken.* 'Good to see you after all this time, Chief Inspector.' She laid a heavy emphasis on the final two words. 'You do know that I've called you at the Station on several occasions?' she said. 'Messages were left.'

'Have you? I mean were there? I'm sorry. I didn't get them.' Wright looked down at his notebook, flicking idly through the pages as if he might find the missing missives there. 'My apologies. Notes that aren't related to a case tend to get mislaid before I even see them.'

Bunch could not tell if that was the truth or not. She did know that when she had not received a return call she concluded their friendship had been nothing more than camaraderie under fire. She had not telephoned him a third time. Here, in this saloon bar with glass crunching under foot, facing each other across yet another cadaver, their relationship was reignited by death. His long lined face and a lean frame were disarmingly ordinary. *Not my type at all.* He was regarding her quizzically apparently expecting an answer. She shrugged. 'I'm a farmer. This is market day. Where else would I be?'

'I meant in here,' he said. 'I wouldn't have seen this as your sort of place. It's not exactly the Ritz.'

'The Ritz is rather a long drive just for luncheon. Even further than Brighton. I suppose there are good restaurants down there. Should one have a good reason to look?'

'I imagine there are,' he replied. 'I don't have much time to spare for dining out.'

'Because there's a war on.'

'Something like that.'

Another tweak of his lips broadened into a smile and Bunch began to laugh. 'Take my advice, Inspector. As the poet said, "Gather ye rosebuds" because life is not going to get any easier at any point soon. Now, if you don't need me for anything else I need to get my new stock home before dusk. I don't want to be herding them into their stalls in the pitch dark.'

'Understood. Before you go, is there anything else you can add about today's events?'

Bunch thought for a moment, casting her mind back to the minutes leading up to the girl's collapse. A clear image of the young woman sitting at the bar was burned into her retinas. 'Her body was … lax. Shoulders drooping, and she was holding her head. She was obviously in pain. A headache? No, gut more like.'

'Was anyone sitting close to her?'

She tried to expand her memory a little further. 'Not close. I remember the Canadians because they made so much noise, but the rest were just a jumble of people. Apart from her looking unwell I didn't notice anything odd. I say … this girl,' she said, 'de Wit? Where was she from?'

Wright consulted his ubiquitous notebook. 'Janine de Wit. A Dutch national according to her papers.'

'Dutch.' Bunch gazed across at the body-shaped mound of army blanket. 'I thought she could be.'

'What was she doing when you arrived?'

'I've already told you everything I know. She was hanging on to her head for grim death, if you'll excuse the term. That was what made me notice her. Sitting all alone in crowded bar and utterly oblivious to her surroundings. Not exactly the place for a quiet think— I did wonder if she'd been let down by some chap.' Bunch lowered her head to look at Wright from under her bobbed fringe. 'They do that, you know, these chaps.'

Her jibe had no apparent affect on its target. 'Was anyone paying her particular attention?' Wright asked. 'Was she approached by anyone?'

Bunch shook her head. 'Couldn't say. I'd barely had time to sit down before she collapsed, and our table was way across the room. I doubt I'd have been physically able to see more than I did because it was so rammed in here. If Barty hadn't booked a table we'd never have had a chance of lunch. Which, I might add, I never did get.'

'I'm sorry, I won't keep you for much longer. Go on.'

'Not a lot else to say. She – wailed. That's the only word I can come up with. An awful sound, truly awful. Then she bent over. Or maybe pitched forward is more precise. Snapped over like the bar on a mouse trap and simply fell off her chair.'

Bunch blinked slowly to clear the image from her mind. 'Then she went into convulsions. Screaming like a mad thing. By the time the quack arrived she was all but dead.'

'Ashton suspects poisoning.'

'Presumably administered by persons unknown.' It was not a question. Bunch nodded. 'That had occurred to me. Something pretty damned potent, whatever it was. Not suicide. I think we can be pretty certain of that.' She smiled apologetically, recalling the last time she had said something almost identical to Wright. 'Without wishing to tell you your job, I really do think I'm right.'

'You do? And why would you be so certain?' Wright lifted his chin to view her through narrowed eyes.

'Well, you haven't mentioned that she left any note.'

'We haven't found one,' he replied. 'So far.'

'Then she was obviously killed. Nobody bumps themselves off in the middle of a crowd unless they have some grand point to make. And so far as I heard there was no dying declaration. Unless she left a note in her rooms, wherever they are, I'd lay certain odds that she did not die at her own behest.' She waited for Wright's verdict on her theory, unconsciously holding her breath.

'I concur.' Wright nodded slowly. 'According to the Vernons, the de Wit girl had been staying here for the past three nights. She spoke good English but with a heavy accent. She didn't meet with or speak to anyone that they ever saw.'

'Yet somebody apparently knew her.'

'Or else it was a stranger who did not have her best interests at heart.' He snapped his notebook shut and gave the corpse a long stare. 'I don't think I need delay you any longer. I shall have your statement typed up and send it with the local PC for you to sign, if that is agreeable?'

'Oh— Right.' Bunch left a gap for Wright to go on but all

she received was a professional calm. 'I shall be off then, Chief Inspector. Toodle-oo.'

'Miss Courtney.' He shook the hand she held out warmly enough, and she was certain something unspoken was lurking behind that blandness that she could not quite pin down. But right there and then she felt too drained to care about much beyond getting home.

Monday 6 May

Bunch blinked at the bright sun streaming through the windows of Perringham Dower House, along with the heady scent of wisteria and just a hint of the stable yard.

Seated across the expanse of pristine starched linen, Beatrice Courtney sipped at her coffee and eyed her granddaughter frostily as she listened to the clipped accents of the BBC droning out the morning news.

Edward Courtney had insisted on a radio being installed in the room so that he could hear the news with his breakfast, and even when he was absent Beatrice had gained her son's habit of listening in for the latest broadcasts on the war.

Bunch paid it little heed. Her attention was fixed on small bubbles jostling around the edge of her cup. Her dark bobbed hair fell across her cheeks causing her to sweep it back every few seconds. Despite their differing approach to early mornings, no one could doubt she and Beatrice were blood kin, with their lanky frames and angular features and a certain set to their jaws.

When the door opened it was Beatrice who looked up.

'Good morning Madam. Miss Rose.'

'Ah, Knapp. Are those the newspapers?'

'Yes, Madam. I apologise for not bringing them in sooner. I

gather the trains were running late again this morning.'

'I quite understand. It's unconscionably early for any of us to be up and about.' Beatrice took the neatly pressed *Times* from the housekeeper and rattled it open, ignoring the front-page headlines of fighting in Norway in favour of items far closer to home. 'Still nothing about your little Dutch girl, Rose,' she observed.

'I imagine that's because there are bigger things going on in the world,' Bunch replied. 'And I'm sure Daddy would rather my name wasn't making the headlines.'

'True. We'd quite obviously prefer the family wasn't in the papers. But one might have thought a murder would warrant a few lines, if only to give a date for the inquest.'

Bunch smiled distractedly. The doings of the previous Friday were not something she wished to discuss. Having a young woman die in her arms had shaken her, though perhaps not as much as her run-in with Wright.

'I hardly think the doings at Storrington market are a high priority for *The Times*.'

'No, certainly not.'

She scooped a fork-full of kedgeree into her mouth and poked through the stack of correspondence that lay beside her plate, hoping her grandmother would take the hint and drop the subject. Formal manila envelopes for the Estate's business were set to one side and of those that remained Bunch paused at a pale-blue rectangle.

It was not receiving personal correspondence on cheap stationary that caught her attention, though that was cause enough; it was the familiar handwriting that made her sit a little straighter.

And with a local postmark, she thought. *How odd.*

She slit it open and extracted the single sheet of pale-blue paper to read its brief missive with care.

3 Green Lane, Chiltwick
30th April

Dear Rose,

I hope this letter finds you well or as well as can be in such times. The last time we spoke you were setting off for France, and as you can see from my address I am now in England and very close to Perringham House.

We have been friends for too many years for me to beat about the bush, so I will be honest and say that I need to beg a favour. If you can bear to see me I shall be at the tea rooms in Chiltwick on Monday afternoon at three o'clock. I would very much like to have a chat for old times sake if nothing else.

In anticipation and with fondest wishes.
Your friend
Cecile Benoir

Bunch turned the sheet over and back again and checked the envelope but found nothing more. 'Well this is a turn out.'

Beatrice looked up from *The Times* to peer at her. 'Beg pardon, dear?'

'I've had a rather odd letter from an old school chum.' Bunch flapped the single sheet as evidence. 'Cecile Benoir has never been exactly chatty, but this must be the oddest correspondence I've received from her yet.'

'Do I know Cecile?'

'Of course you do. Cissy and I were at Château Mont-Choisi together.'

'Ah, yes, Lavinia Hepple's daughter.' Beatrice let the paper rest on the table for a moment. 'She was an odd girl. Spent all her time at Perringham in the library, but then she took after her mother in that respect. Lavinia's marriage caused quite a stir, you know.'

'Why was that?'

Beatrice looked up at the chandelier as if searching for memories amongst the crystal droplets. 'Lavinia was something of a blue-stocking, so nobody was surprised when the object of her affections was an academic. Benoir was well enough bred. The family have a Chateau just east of Nancy, but he lacked personal fortune. We thought it terribly romantic until her father cut her off. I was somewhat surprised when the child was sent to be finished but I'm reliably informed that her grandmother insisted the girl went to Switzerland, even though Munich was far more fashionable at the time.'

'I'd much rather have gone to Germany. They have better stables. And Mother is usually so keen to be *a la Mode*.'

Beatrice laughed. 'That was your father's doing. He didn't want you loose in a fast city like Munich risking diplomatic incidents.'

'That's hardly fair.'

'You think so? Who, in her final term at school sneaked out to the circus one afternoon and had half the county's constabulary searching for her until well past midnight?'

'They had liberty horses.' Bunch grinned despite herself. 'Anglo-Arabs. Totally gorgeous and far more interesting than Latin prep. But we're not talking about me. Cissy, however—' she tapped the letter '—followed her parents in the brainy stakes.'

'She would need to earn her own living. I can't imagine her father's post offering anything like enough to attract a good marriage for her.'

Bunch sighed and nodded. Despite her past dealings with suffrage, her grandmother could be so very Victorian at times. Her recall of pedigrees and properties, however, was often nothing short of encyclopaedic. 'Yes, that would fit. Then they moved to Paris in '38 I think? And we rather lost contact.'

'And now she's here?'

'So it would seem.' Bunch pursed her lips and stared through the tall wide windows into the gardens beyond. 'Wonder when she arrived? I can't believe she's been living here under our noses and never said a word. And now, suddenly, she wants to meet up for tea. Today of all days.' She glanced at the envelope. 'This was posted on Friday.'

'Then she's lucky it reached you in time. Nothing is working properly these days.' Beatrice peered at her over the paper. 'Are you going?'

That is a very good question, Bunch thought. She examined the single sheet of paper carefully as if it might give her a hint of Cecile Benoir's motives for remaining hidden from her. It was hard not to feel slighted under the circumstances. Theirs had been an especially close friendship in those final months. Curiosity and a sense of obligation to that relationship, and to the old school, were powerful reasons to find out what was afoot. She finally set the note aside and applied herself to breakfast. 'Do you know, I rather think I shall. It's only a couple of miles,' she said. 'And it's a lovely day.'

Beatrice nodded. 'As you wish. Let somebody know you will be out.'

Bunch paused, her fork between plate and lips, to eye her grandmother as calmly as she was able. 'Granny, I appreciate your concern but the estate is not going to fall apart if I take an afternoon off. I may cycle however. I used up my petrol coupons driving over to the Pitman's for dinner last weekend. I could ride of course but people do seem to get rather upset when one hitches a horse up outside their premises. I can't imagine why.'

'I imagine it's because they don't wish their garden perennials to become horse fodder,' Beatrice replied. 'That ugly brute of yours has no manners. Don't be too long. If you get the chance perhaps you could call in to see Parsons. Mrs P sent word that he was not well enough to come in this morning.

'He seemed fine yesterday.'

'He's not a young man. Or a well one.'

'No older than you – and you're organising the WVS campaign. And aren't you also on the Hunt Ball committee?'

'That's very true, Rose. But I was never in the trenches breathing in gas like Parsons and the rest of Lowther's Lambs. Please remember that.'

'Yes, Granny. I'm sorry.' Bunch adopted a sudden fascination for her breakfast plate. Since the MoD's requisitioning of Perringham House the enforced sharing of the Dower House with her grandmother was proving every bit as fraught as she had feared. Her redoubtable relative was autocratic, impatient and stubborn to a fault, which created clashes, as Bunch had known it would. Yet she was extraordinarily fond of Granny, often feeling closer to her than her own parents. *I know she has the good of estate at heart,* she thought, *and I was frightfully rude. But it would so much easier if we had a little more elbow room. It would be so much easier if Daddy was here. So much easier if the bloody Germans hadn't waged war on the world at large. Easier…* She glanced in the general direction of Perringham House though her old home could not be seen from where she sat. It may as well have been a continent away. *Pull yourself together, old girl.* She fed Roger a forbidden crust beneath the table and scritched behind his ears.

A rustling of the paper drew her back to the present. 'You will make that dog fat.'

'Silly old thing deserves a treat or two.' Bunch brushed toast crumbs from her thigh and smiled at the canine nose and eyes peeking from under the cloth and tried to ignore the whitening of her dog's muzzle. He had aged so rapidly since the winter. The bullet he had taken in her stead, when they'd encountered rustlers in the new year, had shattered two ribs, pierced his lungs and nicked his shoulder blade. His hunting days were over but she could not bring herself to put him down, as several people had suggested she should, merely because he could no longer fetch a bird or two.

'I rather enjoy the return to horses,' Beatrice went on without looking up. 'We've all got so used to rushing hither and yon. Not for people in power to dictate, however, though we also have to get used to them taking liberties I suppose.'

The ice in her grandmother's voice was unmistakable. Somebody or something had provoked her ire and of course Bunch was expected to know what it was. She tried to be casual in her reply. 'Did you have anyone particular in mind?'

'There is a new chap in charge at the House.' Beatrice turned to the front of *The Times* and perused the headlines. 'Regular army by all accounts.'

'What happened to Colonel Kravitz?'

'Not a clue. I gather he left several weeks ago.'

'You'd think they'd have told us.'

'I have no doubt they informed the FO and they would have informed Edward's office. But with Edward away that is as far as it will have got.'

'Hardly neighbourly.'

'Very military. When your grandfather and I were in India the officers were always the last to know anything.'

'How did you know this?'

Beatrice smiled. 'The same way anything ever gets found out. One of your Land Girls told Cook when she brought in the milk. Cook told Knapp and *voila*. Careless talk, however. You may want to mention that to those girls.'

'Really, Granny, I seriously doubt either Cook or Knapp are harbouring Nazi spies in the pantry.'

Beatrice lowered her paper and frowned across the table. 'We had a violent criminal working in our sheep pens. And that boy was born on this estate.'

'Very true. What else did she say?'

'What did who say?'

'Don't be obtuse, Granny. What else did Kate say to Cook?'

'That a new CO took up his post at the House last month and by Saturday he had his chaps laying barb-wire around the Lower Nitch.'

'That's not part of the leasing agreement. He has no right.'

'I assume that is why your girl told Cook, who told me to tell you.' Beatrice snapped her paper upright to hide her face as she added. 'In my day we had boot boys to deliver these messages.'

~~~

Having decided that arriving at Perringham to beard the new CO on a bicycle was not an image guaranteed to impress, Bunch then found she had to forgo her beloved Fell pony Perry. The Fell was on almost permanent harness duty, pulling the pony cart, since petrol rationing had begun biting ever harder.

It was on her father's hunter Robbo that she set out shortly after lunch. She took him at a brisk trot to the barrier strung across the entrance to Perringham House where two sentries emerged from the guard post before she brought Robbo to a halt.

'Miss Courtney to see Colonel Ralph.' She took her identity card from her pocket and leaned down to the younger of the soldiers who stepped forward, took it without a word and handed it on to the sergeant.

The sergeant took his time in perusing it, making a point of glancing at Bunch as if to assure himself that it was indeed her likeness though she would have laid odds that he knew exactly who she was. He double checked his clipboard before he handed the card back. 'One moment, Miss.' He stepped into the wooden hut and she could see him talking into a radio handset and hear his one-sided conversation to the House. He was watching her all the while with a well-oiled Lee-Enfield rifle resting comfortably against his hip. He was an older man, with the remains of a long-standing tan that only came from working in a far warmer clime than England or even Europe. His sergeant stripes were well washed on a uniform that was perfectly turned out but far from new. And that military strut had not been learned in six-week basic training. *Regular army*, she surmised. *Curious for someone of his rank and experience to be standing guard duty. Rather below him I'd've thought.*

Bunch waited, trying not to get annoyed at the gatehouse as she invariably did whenever she passed by on the lane. The hut, now daubed in khaki paint, had started life as a charming powder-blue summerhouse overlooking the carp lake, and had been relocated to the lane almost from the moment the military had arrived. Somehow it had come to symbolise the entire alienation from her family home. To have the army as unwanted tenants was one thing but rearranging the fixtures and fittings was quite another.

Deep in her cogitations she jumped when the sergeant emerged from the once-summerhouse. 'The Colonel is expecting you, Miss Courtney. Private Aimes will escort you up to the House.'

'I do know the way,' she snapped. 'It's my house, dammit. Or it was.'

'Sorry Miss. All visitors are to be escorted when entering the estate grounds. Express orders of our new CO.'

Bunch breathed in slowly, exhaled, swallowed down her temper and wondered briefly whose nostrils were flaring wider – her horse's or her own. 'Do you know who I am?' She enunciated slowly, staring unblinking at her antagonist.

He stared back. 'Yes, Miss. Sorry, Miss. Orders, Miss.'

'Poppycock. I rode straight in just last month.'

'New orders, Miss.'

'From your new CO. So you say.' Bunch eyed him up and down.

He hefted his Enfield rifle and returned her glower with a respectfully insolent mask.

Bunch wondered if she were losing her touch. She also wondered how far she would get if she just popped Robbo over the barrier rail. The hunter was more than capable of taking such an obstacle from a standing start.

As if divining her thoughts, the sergeant leaned forward and caught hold of the bridle. Robbo sidled away but he held firm.

Stupid notion. This chap looks far too comfortable with that rifle of his. 'Steady Robbo, steady boy,' she muttered. 'Sergeant, is that absolutely necessary?'

'Sorry Miss, but you can't go without an escort.'

For the briefest of moments she thought he was joking. 'I am expected.'

The sergeant's bland expression did not falter beyond an almost imperceptible twitch of his brow. He reminded her of a M'aitre D at one of the better hotels faced with a gaggle of rowdy young men fresh from their day at the races. 'Sorry Miss. Orders. Most of our visitors come by motor. You can wait for me to call for a staff car if you'd prefer.'

'I don't have time to wait.' She pocketed her papers and waited for the barrier to rise before nudging Robbo forward. Entering the grounds under armed guard irked her even more than the re-planted summerhouse. She set off at a walk through the tunnel formed by the small woodland, quietly fuming at the indignity of it all.

The private kept pace with long strides, not looking at her but holding firmly onto the reins beneath Robbo's jaw. Robbo was a well-mannered creature and well-schooled against most situations but still his ears twitched back and fore. Bunch could feel his irritable chomping and pulling at his bit. He was not happy at any stranger's touch and smell. Bunch knew she only need squeeze her calves and ankles lightly against Robbo's flanks and utter a quiet clicking of her tongue for him to pick up his gait. She glanced down at her guard. He was grinning at her and shortening his grip on the reins beneath Robbo's jaw, slowing the hunter to a steadier pace. The man was plainly used to horses.

As they moved out from under the trees the change in the frontage of the House made her heart miss a beat in shock. It was less than two months since she'd been here last but it was all too clear that the spring growth in hedges, shrubs and borders had gone unchecked, though she noted that grass had been mown. *It is*, she thought, *like visiting a totally foreign land.*

Bunch glanced at the soldier at Robbo's head. Irrational, she knew, but somehow it was easy to view him as culpable. War made pawns of them all. She kept to their easy walk through the shaggy box edgings and up to the sweeping twinned steps before the front doors. Two guards came to attention on the upper level, one of them bringing his rifle around to a low firing position, casual but controlled. The other descended rapidly to meet her, taking the steps two at a time. He took over the reins as he reached the bottom and then flipped Bunch a salute.

Bunch ignored him and stared around the short stone and brick perrons, which swept up to the front terrace from either side. The absence of the ancient twin posts that had always stood at the base made her swear under her breath. In the days of the motor car hitching posts had become obsolete, she realised, but those ornate pieces had been a feature. The snaggle-toothed space where they had recently stood came as a shock. A slightly nauseous feel was stirring in her gut. Close up, the broken balustrade and one beheaded stone figure were a greater jolt. It made sense that the army, or whoever it was who occupied Perringham House, would not care for the place as did her own family, but she had not expected wanton damage. She slid from the saddle.

'Miss Courtney?' The soldier saluted again and shortened his grip on the reins. 'I shall take care of him. The Colonel is expecting you in the mess. I think it used to be the library?'

Bunch hesitated. Her shock at the changes around her made her wary of handing the animal over to a stranger but the way in which he slapped at the creature's neck and urged him into the shade of the House reassured her. She took the steps slowly and paused at the door to take a breath before she stepped into the hall, expecting the worst and relieved to see that huge notice boards had been erected to protect ancient plaster work and panelling. She hurried across to the library and paused for a moment, chagrined that she had almost been about to knock.

'Ridiculous,' she muttered, 'that would be just too much.'

She knew that the bookshelves had been emptied of books and the pictures and furniture mothballed, because she had supervised it herself. But the deterioration of the room since then appalled her. The motley assortment of armchairs and tables were to be expected but the make-shift bar that had been thrown up against the farthest corner made her wince. A dartboard was fixed to a section of panelling by the window furthest from the bar. Even at that distance she could see a stippled patina in the surrounding walnut where stray missiles had found their mark – like the ravages of a particularly voracious colony of woodworm. For a moment she could only stare – and shuddered at the very notion of what her father would make of it all. *Or worse still, Granny. It's only been six months since the MoD laid claim. What in hell is going to be left after this is over?*

'Miss Courtney?'

She turned slowly to meet the speaker, with a long stare. 'Colonel Ralph?' She looked him up and down quite openly, keeping the query from her tone in favour of arctic disdain.

'Yes, I'm Everett Ralph for my sins. I can only apologise in advance.' A lean fair-haired man emerged from the depths of a club chair and bounced toward her with right hand outstretched. 'Pleased to meet one of the family. I've heard a lot about the Courtneys, especially you. All good, I hasten to add. I knew a cousin of yours at Sandhurst. Mortimer? Frightfully good chap. He used to talk about you all. But none of it does you justice.' He grinned. 'I'm babbling. Terrible habit. Please do sit down. Would you like coffee? Or tea perhaps? A little early for sherry but I don't doubt—'

'Thank you but no,' she replied. 'It will not take long to say what I need to say.'

'Oh.' His smile fell from beam to chagrin. 'Now you sound like Matron. Am I in terrible trouble?' He stepped between the chairs to stand not merely within touching distance but close enough for her to inhale his waspish blend of soap and cigarettes.

Bunch took a casual step to one side putting enough distance between them for another suitable glare. She expected someone far older, a desk-bound martinet or grizzled veteran of the Empire, not this slightly fey creature with his wide-set eyes and disarming mouth. She cleared her throat to cover the certainty that she was staring, just a little. Ralph's apparent youth and undeniable charm were disconcerting, distracting even. *Steady old girl,* she told herself. *He might be a keen little pip but rein it in.* She had seen his type throughout her life. The London clubs and polo fields were full of them. Handsome young chaps full of bon homie and studied charm, except that those slender features held something far more than the usual puppy-dog enthusiasm.

Ralph lowered his head a little to gaze at her from beneath a very unmilitary fringe that flopped across his brows. His pale eyes held a great deal of humour and intelligence as he tilted his head to one side. 'Now how may I serve, dear lady?'

Bunch noted how his smile, disarming though it was, formed radiating lines around the corners of his eyes, which only came with years spent beneath a bright sun. *This chap's far older than he looks*, she thought. 'Quite easily,' she said aloud. 'Your troops have been laying wire along the Lower Nitch copse. You do realise that it's not part of the grounds that go with the House?'

'Is it not?' He looked at the floor, hands joined behind his back, as he rocked on his heels. 'Oh, I say, that's not good, is it?' He looked up straight into her eyes. 'Do you need it?'

'Pardon?'

'That particular wood you mentioned. The Nitch, I think you called it? Do you need it for anything? It's not suitable for grazing or arable so I didn't imagine you had much call for it.'

'Well…'

'Only it is terribly useful to us, don't you know? I did hope you'd be a real friend over it. It's not being farmed, after all.' That electric smile widened. 'If you could see your way clear to letting us borrow it for a bit?' He had a personality that was as charming as it was disarming.

Bunch was annoyed at herself for weakening very slightly. 'I agree we don't use it for food crops. But we do coppice that section for wattles and such. And then there's firewood, given that coal is so damned expensive. So yes, we do need it.'

'That could prove a little tricky.'

'I don't see why. Just move your barbed wire and we shall say no more of it.'

'Ah, yes, the thing is – we have a little ordnance laid down. Nothing full scale but enough. Clearing it would be tricky not to mention a little inconvenient. Rather dangerous for any of your people to go wandering about.'

'You've mined my woodland? Ye gods, man. Are you insane?'

'Hmm, well I hope not. It's for training you see. Need our chaps to get the feel of that kind of stuff.'

The bumbling Colonel facade did not seem quite right to Bunch, coming from this fresh-faced Eton old-boy, who appeared to be just a few years senior than herself. *He'd look far more at home punting down the Isis.* She eyed him up and down, hoping to anticipate his next move and realising she had no idea. 'What kind of s*tuff* would that be exactly?'

Ralph made a few small noises of uncertainty in his throat as he looked down once again at his savagely polished boots.

For a moment Bunch was reminded of Johnny Frampton, gentle affable Johnny with his hidden core of steel – but gone these six months and still missed. *He's bluffing,* she thought. *Johnny was never unsure of himself in his life and neither is this chap.* 'Can't say any more?' she said. 'I can understand that. But you're still trespassing. I want those woods cleared by the end of the month or I shall be putting in a complaint to the War Office Estates Department. Now if you will excuse me I have another pressing engagement. Good morning Colonel.' She shook his hand briefly and wheeled away before he could reply. It was the only method she knew of dealing with his type: hit and run. Land your demands and beat a retreat before the shock waves could begin to spread.

Bunch was prepared for him to call after her, even follow her. She wasn't sure how to feel when the only noise that accompanied her exit was the clip of her own riding boot heels on the hall's marbled floor. As she strode toward the front entrance the door to the main drawing room opened and a large dark-haired man in civilian clothing emerged. Bunch glimpsed several young people, men and women, seated in semi-circle before a large chalk board; and then the door closed on a few snatched words of perfect French.

Without breaking stride she hurried out to the front steps and stood at the very edge of the estrade to catch her breath. The view was so achingly familiar and yet currently so very alien.

She rushed down the steps with eyes averted from battered masonry to find Robbo already waiting for her. She stepped into the stirrup, nodding a curt thanks, before wheeling the horse around and setting off down the drive at a brisk trot and was so angry that she barely registered the car shadowing her progress down the drive. She had not expected to be bosom pals with anybody involved in the government's legalised theft of Perringham House, as she saw it, but that man was the limit. 'He was flirting with me, Robbo,' she said. 'Can you believe that? Of all the damnable nerve.'

~~~

The Jenny Wren Tea Rooms & General Store was quiet, which was not unusual on a weekday. The village of Chiltwick was off the beaten track, even for the wilds of Sussex, and its population was both sparse and scattered. Some claimed calling it a village at all was a misnomer, that it was technically a hamlet. Just a few dozen houses straggled around a pub and the Jenny Wren, which also doubled as the Post Office.

The ride from Perringham House had calmed her somewhat and she tied Robbo off under the trees, well away from the garden hedges and edges. She slapped his neck heartily as he bent to crop at the grassy verge. 'I shall get you a drink on the way back.' He nodded his head vigorously at the sound of her voice, trailing long strands of greenery that he had tugged from the hedgerow, and chewed contentedly, green foam already gathering around the bit rings. She sighed and laughed. 'That tack's going to take some cleaning. I just hope you enjoy it. Behave yourself out here you greedy old lump.'

She turned to cross the road and pushed open the door, ducking to avoid the low lintel, standing on the threshold for a moment to allow her eyes to adjust after the brightness of the outside.

The place had changed little in all the years she had been using the shop. Left turn would take her into the small general store with its Post Office counter tucked away in the far corner. Turn to the right and she would enter the tea rooms. Bunch noted the usual half-dozen tables covered in familiar faded-green gingham table cloths, all flanked by the same hoop-backed chairs that had graced the floor for at least twenty years. The familiar antique copper samovar was steaming noisily at the end of the glass topped counter. Beneath that scratched cabinet top she could see a small plate of scones, an oblong chunk of pound cake, and half a Victoria sponge. Bunch felt a moment's disappointment not to see one of the cream-smothered rhubarb streusels that had been the elder Miss Mann's speciality, and then smiled wryly. *I suppose continental desserts may not be as welcome these days.*

Two elderly women were seated at one of the tables, whom she recognised as Miss Lewis, the GP's sister and secretary, and the local worthy Mrs Bale. Both glared at Bunch disapprovingly and for a moment she wondered if she had spoken out loud. The women had lowered their voices but she caught the words 'Perringham' and 'murder', doubtless by intent. It was inevitable. She'd been the subject of gossip since Johnny Frampton's death and she had hoped they might have found some other topic by now. *I suppose Miss De Wit's demise has put paid to that.*

'Ladies.' Bunch smiled and nodded, and both women looked away with a muttered 'good afternoon'. She knew neither of them well and, as their opinion mattered little to her, she paid them no more attention and wove between the tables to the door on the far side of the room overlooking the courtyard garden. She held back in the shade of the cafe to assess the only occupant of the garden. Had she not been here to meet Cecile Benoir she would have not known the exotic creature in the tea garden as her old school chum.

The woman seated in the May sunshine was slim, elegant, showing not a hint of the slightly gauche sixteen-year old Bunch recalled from school. Had the outfit she wore been less faded, this woman would have been the height of Paris chic. Her trademark mass of dark hair was tamed beneath a saucer hat, tendrils escaping to flutter around her face in a frame of tiny ringlets. Cecile Benoir was twining one of those coils around her forefinger, her expression pensive as she gazed at an ivy-covered wall.

Bunch strode past the empty tables toward her old friend and bent to give Cecile a brief hug. 'Hello there old thing. On you own I see.'

'Hello Rose. To the point as always.' Cecile stood to greet her friend, taking her by the shoulders and kissing Bunch on both cheeks in the continental manner.

Bunch leaned into the gesture a little self-consciously, remembering a time when their kisses had been far less formal. As she sank into a vacant chair she took off her hat, which she felt was rather mannish against Cecile's net-and-feather concoction, and finger-combed her own hair dishevelled by the ride.

Hilda, the younger of the Miss Manns who co-owned the Jenny Wren, came to stand close to them, a tattered notepad in hand. 'Good afternoon Miss Courtney. Would you like tea?'

'Yes please, Hilda.'

'Cake?'

'No, thank you.' Bunch smiled brightly and watched Hilda Mann pocket the notebook untouched by the pencil nub and hurry away. Bunch always had liked the sisters and would not offend them for the world, but something told her the old lady would be far better off not knowing whatever it was Cecile had to say. 'It'll take her a while to fetch it,' she murmured to Cecile. 'Now. To what do I owe the pleasure? Spill the beans. What's brought you to sunny Sussex?' She leaned back in her chair and gazed steadily into Cecile's face. 'Why didn't you tell me you'd arrived here before?'

'We've not been here long, honestly – a few months.' Cecile blushed a little at the contradiction. 'And we would still be in Paris but for the war.' She wrapped her arms around herself and gently rubbed her elbows, a visible shudder running through her.

'We can sit inside if you prefer.'

Cecile glanced toward the open door and the two women craning necks to see who 'that Courtney girl' was with. 'I'm perfectly fine here. It seemed to be the best place to wait for you – in a little peace.'

'Safe from prying ears out here. Those old gorgons would hate the breeze cooling their tea.'

Seconds ticked past in awkward silence and it was Cecile who broke it. 'I am sorry for not writing to you before' I truly am. Papa forbade me to talk with anybody because of his work. And you know how he was. I've barely spoken to a soul here. That kind of women, they always ignored us. I don't think they much like a foreigner in their midst. Especially Papa. He had such a strong accent.'

'Had?'

Cecile paid a sudden attention to the clasp on her clutch bag. 'Papa died,' she said. 'Last Friday.' Her serenity did not miss a beat and Bunch was at a loss at how to react.

'I'm very sorry to hear that. Please accept my condolences.' The formality of those phrases was expected but seemed so inadequate. In the face of Cecile's lack of emotion Bunch floundered for a new line to take. 'Was it sudden?'

'Very. Papa was not a young man, as you know, but he had always enjoyed good health.' Cecile scrubbed at the back of her left hand with the right, a frown creasing between her eyes. 'This is why I called you. I did not know who I could trust.'

'Of course you had to call on me. What was it? His heart?'

Cecile allowed a bleak smile to light her eyes. 'One might say that. His heart failed from a large dose of some toxin. The police have not named the poison yet but we do know that he was murdered.'

The silence between them was punctuated by bird song and the distant droning of village gossip from within the café, as Bunch sorted through her slender repertoire for a suitable reply. Nothing she could think of seemed remotely adequate. 'Oh, I say,' she murmured finally. 'Are you sure?'

'Quite sure.' A moment of panic was clear in her face. 'In Berlin poisons were a large part of our research. I am certain that the coroner will confirm that Papa's life's work also turned out to be his death.' Cecile fixed Bunch with a ferocious stare, her dark eyes made darker by the rings of fatigue that powder could not quite conceal at close quarters. 'The police are investigating but I have the distinct impression they are not looking so hard or very far.'

'Surely they don't suspect you?'

She spread her hands, a gallic moue pleating her lips. 'But of course. In such cases it is most often those who are closest that commit such crimes.'

'How awful.' Bunch touched her hand to her lips to stifle the somewhat unladylike expletives that sprang to mind. She had barely known Cecile's father and what little she recalled of him had not been a fond memory. Whether because he did not care to know his daughter's friends, or that Cecile kept them from him, she had never quite decided, but she felt deeply for her friend's loss, nevertheless. 'I'm so sorry,' she said. 'I really do mean that. I suppose there's no chance it was an accident?'

'None. I am a Doctor of Chemistry now. Did I tell you that? I qualified just before we left Berlin. But I have no certificate, so…' She scowled. 'No matter. I know how my father died.'

'I am sorry,' Bunch said again. 'That seems such an inadequate word.'

'Thank you. It still has not really sunk in. I don't doubt it shall in time.' Cecile took a deep breath. 'Meanwhile, my immediate problems are a little more prosaic. The cottage was rented in Papa's name by the people that he worked for.' Her lips formed into another breathy pout. 'The upshot is that now he is gone I am left in desperate need of two things. A new home and a job.' She gave a small chuckle. 'Just the smallest of things. But being a foreigner it is almost impossible to find either.'

'Surely you have a British passport as well as a French one? And France is still our ally.'

'For how long?' She shook her head. 'Yes, I have all my identity papers and I did believe they were all in order. But it appears that though Papa is officially French the fact that he lived so many years in Berlin made him a resident alien. I think that was the term I was given? It has everyone terribly confused.'

'The people he worked for must have been aware of this? And it can't apply to you, can it? You're only half French.'

'You would think so. I was told that because I have living English relatives here I am not the concern of the government. Except that they will not yet grant me a work permit as a citizen because of Papa's status.'

'What a nightmare. But you do have family in England?'

'Grand-père Hepple forbad them all to speak with my mother. Even though he passed away a long while ago it seems I cannot lean back on their hospitality.' She spread her hands. 'Until I can sort out Papa's affairs I am effectively stateless, homeless, and without any way of making a living. It is why I turn to you, Rose, to ask that favour. Your father is in the government. Could he possibly put in a word? Get some temporary papers on my behalf?'

'Daddy is away.' Bunch smiled an apology as she steered Cecile from her father's whereabouts as a matter of habit. 'I'm not sure when I shall see him next. I'm so sorry old thing. It's beastly that those people are not doing anything to help you. Surely they owe you some sort of loyalty for his sake?'

'For Papa? It is almost as if they were relieved to see him go.' She laughed sharply. 'He was brilliant – but he also had a knack of making himself very unpopular. I do believe they would have preferred it if I had drunk from the same bottle.'

'Tell me what happened. Was it—' Bunch turned at the rattle of a tray and nodded with a hearty '—why Miss Enid, how nice to see you. Thank you so much.' She waited for the elder Miss Mann to lay out the tea and grumble her way back indoors before she spoke again in a low voice. 'Enid never waits tables. Shoved her sister aside to come out and see who you were, I'll be bound,' she said. 'I love those old darlings to pieces but they do have this desperate compulsion to know what's going on. I dare say it's an occupational requirement. Now. What have you been doing? Tell me all.' Bunch lifted the lid from the pot and stirred vigorously with the over-large spoon provided. 'If it's not too awful for you, obviously.'

'All of it? You know we left Berlin in haste?'

'It was unexpected. I rather assumed it was down to some family duty.'

Cecile emitted a grunt that may equally have been a laugh or a sob but dipped her head to hide her expression. She unclipped her clutch bag with shaking fingers and retrieved her cigarette case which she offered to Bunch. Bunch slipped a cigarette into her cigarette holder that she took from her pocket before accepting a light. All done in what seemed like slow motion and in silence, broken only by the clatter and chatter within the cafe.

Bunch blew smoke into the clear air. Observing her old friend at such close quarters she could see the shadows beneath her eyes and the sharp hollow at her throat. She watched how Cecile's fingers twitched in rapid succession against the cigarette case, as if fingering minute piano keys. She was wound tighter than the seven-day case clock that had once stood in the billiard room at Perringham House. Bunch took another slow inhalation of smoke, held it for a moment and breathed out, steadying her own nerves. Losing her home to the government had been a wrench. She could only imagine what losing everything else would be like. She smiled at Cecile and took a sip of tea, allowing the woman all the time needed to gird loins.

'Papa was approached by his faculty in Berlin to head a special and highly secret project. They made it very clear to him that he was to work directly for the Reich.' Cecile drew sharply on her own cigarette, the tip showing brightly despite the sunlight.

'Was he unhappy about that?'

'He complied. He told me that we were being watched. That our mail was being intercepted. Our phone calls listened to.' She drew a breath and then took a sip of tea. 'We were hardly alone in that, of course. Most academics were under scrutiny. Anybody who was not a party member, in fact. The SS have eyes and ears everywhere. I cannot tell you how awful it is knowing your every move is being monitored and calculated.'

'Sounds perfectly beastly. Did you tell the university?'

'Hardly. So many of the faculty were moved on. Especially the Jewish professors. Most of those with foreign links were let go and the people who replaced them were all party members. Papa joined the party to protect himself, and me I suppose, but I don't know how he held onto his post as long as he did.'

She gave Bunch a rueful smile and Bunch nodded. 'I'd heard things of the sort. A lot of the county crowd were mixing with Mosley's fascist party back then. You must remember Diana Mitford? She "finished" the same year as we did?'

'I do. She and Bobo were very popular amongst the Munich and Berlin sets just before we left there. I didn't quite move in those circles, of course. I might have been better off if I had.'

'You think so?' Bunch snorted. 'You've had a bad time but you're home now.' She covered Cecile's hand briefly with her own. 'I shall make sure you're safe. It's what we old girls do.'

'Thank you, I do appreciate it considering we rather lost touch these past few years. Papa insisted I stop writing because my contacts with England should not come to the attention of officials.'

'We've only just started to realise how things were in Berlin for people who did not agree with the Chancellor. According to Daddy a lot of people that did run with his party have realised their mistake and came streaming home last summer. And so many people we both know who thought Moseley's BUF party was the flag to follow changed their minds rather sharpish when they realised how things were moving. Though you wouldn't think so to hear Chamberlain and his appeasers.' Bunch took a mouthful of her own tea, eyeing Cecile shrewdly before she continued. 'How did you finally get out of Berlin?'

'That was all so very sudden. Papa had not shown any hint of wanting to leave though I begged him time and again. And then one day – poof.' Cecile snapped her fingers. 'He came home from an unscheduled faculty meeting. One that he had not told me of, though I was supposed to be his assistant. He said that we were in danger and that we must go. I don't know where that came from and I didn't press the point because I was so glad to hear him say we were finally leaving.'

'So you moved to Paris?'

'Not straight away. It was hard to gain travel documents. Well, for most people it was impossible by late then. I am certain we would have been arrested had we'd tried to simply go. Papa insisted that he had contacts in the right places and he obtained some travel passes for us both, totally without warning. I gathered all I could in a couple of suitcases and we snuck away in the dead in night, like a pair of alley cats.'

'That sounds perfectly rancid.'

'It was. We had to abandon most of our belongings. And once we reached France, Papa was furious to find that our German bank account had been closed. I was not surprised but he seemed to think…' She shook her head. 'Papa said it was perfectly clear we were not welcome at le Chateau.'

'Why?'

'I am not entirely certain. My Uncle Frederick was the elder, you see, so the estate was all his. There was no common ground. It was why Papa moved to Berlin. Back then, Germany was a very different place of course.' Cecile tweaked the bleakest of smiles. 'Papa was a very conservative man. He fitted in with the Party quite well.'

'He was a Nazi?'

'No— At least—' She took a deep breath and lit yet another cigarette, her fingers shaking as she fought for composure. 'Papa may as well have shot the President of le Republique at very least for all the welcome my uncle gave us. Fortunately, quite out of the blue, Papa was offered a post at Le Sud by an old colleague. I don't know how or why that happened but it was a life-saver. We moved to Paris in January of '39 in time for the new semester.' She hugged herself once again, her face set into a blank mask. 'Before very long it became obvious how things were moving and we fled Paris for England just as war was declared. You do know that Hitler will walk into France very soon now? He has already attacked Hollande— And Belgique. After that it is only a matter of time before he looks across *la Manche*.' Cecile's voice rose an octave, fear bleeding through the old-school reserve and accentuating her alienness for a moment.

Bunch glanced toward the open door but nobody seemed to have noted her friend's excitement. She made a show of pouring tea, allowing her companion's emotions to level out. Her own brief sojourn in France the previous year, even the death of her brother-in-law, had not brought the shadow of the enemy as close as it was at that moment. 'How did you come to be here? In Chiltwick I mean.'

'Another of those lucky co-incidences. We had barely been in London for a month before Papa brought us here.' She smiled an apology. 'You had gone to France by then with your BEF. So funny to think we could almost have waved to each other from our ships going opposite ways.'

'But I've been back for ages.'

Cecile nodded. 'Papa had become paranoid about secrets. He would not let me even write to you. And then he no longer wished me to help him at the laboratory. It was a strange time.'

'Do you think your father was murdered because of his work?' Bunch asked quietly. 'Did he feel he was in danger here?'

Cecile freshened her own cup and took a sip as she asserted a level of control. 'He had no reason to fear.'

'And yet? How did he come to be poisoned?'

'I cannot say.' Cecile stared at the ivy-strewn wall for a

moment. 'I was preparing supper. Because we have no staff you understand. I had become both secretary for his work and his housekeeper. I could not get work elsewhere. Being foreign is one thing, though I hold a French passport and not German. But being foreign *and* a woman.' She shrugged.

'This has been a difficult year for you.'

'It has been a hard few years. But that night Papa was almost happy. I know he came here to this cafe that day, as he did now and then.'

'I bet the locals loved that.' Bunch glanced at the women within the tea room and chuckled. 'Gave *them* something to think about.'

Cecile gave a dismissive *pfft* 'He would not have noticed. He was in good humour because he had a bottle of pastis. One of his favourites and not something seen in England very often, so he was looking forward to sampling it. I had poured us both an aperitif but I did not drink right away because I smelled burning and I went to rescue our supper.' She glanced at Bunch and blew out her cheeks. 'I am not a cook, you know.'

'None of our circle were exactly domesticated,' Bunch said. 'Go on.'

'While I was in the kitchen I heard the noises but when I reached him— It was terrible. I ran to call for a doctor of course, but it was too late. The poison had done its deed.' She allowed a solitary tear to mark a dark track through the powder on her cheek. 'Such agony. I know what poison can do but reading about it and seeing it played out before your eyes...'

Bunch laid a hand on her friend's arm. 'I'm truly sorry. But it could so easily have been you with him. What a lucky escape.'

Cecile nodded with the ghost of a smile. 'I don't *believe* I was the target but yes, I was lucky. Saved by the burning of *les pommes de terre*.' Her laughter held little humour but Bunch smiled dutifully at the effort.

'Where did the wine come from?'

Cecile shook her head minutely as she drew frantically on her cigarette.

'And the police also have no idea who did this? Or why?'

'*L'inspecteur* was such a charming man. A gentleman in fact. Not how you expect a policeman to be. But he tells me that there is little chance of finding anything until we know who sent the wine. The officials at … where Papa was working … said they had not seen him taking anything home that night.'

'I didn't know there were any laboratories around here.'

'Few do.' Cecile raised the cigarette holder to her lips once more, contemplating the curling smoke for a quiet moment. 'Chief Inspector Wright was here once again this morning. And now he has gone back to Brighton.'

'Wright, you say? Tall chap?' Bunch took a sip of tea, avoiding her friend's eye. 'Fortyish? Brown hair?'

'You know him?'

Bunch nodded, annoyed at the jolt the name had given her. Annoyed even more that he had come so close to Perringham and not so much as dropped in to say hello. 'The Chief Inspector and I have a chequered history.' She took a mouthful of the rapidly cooling beverage and considered the problem at hand. It was a macabre kind of synchronicity that brought all these things together. A friend in need, a crime, and a perfect opportunity to torture the elusive Inspector Wright. 'We shall have to tackle him over his total inadequacy,' she said. 'But first thing is to get you settled. Daddy is away so no chance of help in getting those papers changed right now. We shall just have to let the gears of officialdom grind away as slowly as they do. If it's a job you need in the meantime, then I do believe I can help. It won't pay very much but you will get full bed and board.'

'That would be simply marvellous. What would I need to

do?'

'Personal secretary not beneath you, is it? You being a blue-blooded academic.'

'If it pays a wage the post of secretary will be very welcome. Who is it for?'

Bunch grinned as she got to her feet and placed a few coins on the tea tray. 'If you think you can stand it, then come and work for me.'

'For you? At Perringham House?'

'Yes ... well, not at the House. Daddy handed that over to the bloody army so I'm running the estate from the Dower House.'

'Is your Grandmother still with you? Won't she mind you just inviting me to stay?'

Bunch pulled a face. 'She'll grouse and gripe because she can. But it's all family property and my home now. Plus—' she grinned suddenly as a great irony hit her '—Granny is master-minding the local WVS drive to support refugees, so she can't in all honesty object now, can she?'

'If you're sure. I shall need to pack but would Thursday be too soon?'

'Thursday will be perfect.' She handed Cecile a card. 'Here's my telephone number. When you have your camel train loaded give me a ring and I shall come and fetch you in the shooting brake.'

'That's good of you, Rose. But I shall get a taxi.'

'No arguments. And we have bags of room.'

'No. Save your fuel coupons and your time. I have some things to deal with and I don't know how long it will take.'

'Do you need help to pack?'

'After two moonlight flits?' Cecile laughed, head thrown back to expose her slender neck. 'My belongings are few.' She began her hair twirling, twisting a ringlet round and round her right index finger once again.

A nervous habit, Bunch decided. *Which is understandable.* Her own parents were hardly ever at home but if they were not there at all, if anything happened to them, she would be at such a loss, too.

'If you are sure that your family will not object,' Cecile murmured, 'then I shall go to pack. *Jusqu'à la,* Rose.

Bunch returned her friend's embrace. 'Yes, until then.'

Thursday 9 May

Beatrice adjusted her hat before the hall mirror and gathered up her bag. 'I do apologise for not being here to welcome your friend, Rose. We're relocating the last of the evacuees to the western counties this weekend and we are up to our necks in red tape.' She paused at the door, a vague frown settling around her eyes. 'I trust Miss Benoir has a ration card? Cook will have a fit if she doesn't. Forged cards are top of our WVS agenda for next week.'

'Do you know, I hadn't thought to ask. I assume she must, or she and her father would have starved by now.'

'Well, please do check.' She turned to the housekeeper hovering near the door. 'Knapp, should anyone call I shall not be back before tea. Oh, and Rose, Parsons wanted to speak with you. I told him you would be in the office all morning. Now I must go.' She gave Bunch a light tap to her shoulder and sailed out into the sunny morning.

Bunch glanced at her watch. It was past nine already and she knew there would not be time to take Perry out for a spell. She'd had little time to exercise him in the last for days and the lack of pure physical exercise irked her. He had been far from idle however since Parsons had disinterred the pony cart from the darkest regions of the stable block.

She headed across the yard toward the estate office squeezed between the stables and the house kitchens. When the running of the Perringham estate had first relocated to the Dower House, Beatrice had allocated the use of attic rooms for office space. In the months that followed she was disapproving of outside staff tramping through the house, even when they used the staff stairwell, and had eventually allowed a stable-yard storeroom to be converted.

It not been Bunch's first choice, with its tiny window and ill-fitting door, but once the telephone had been rerouted and a couple of paraffin stoves moved in, she had found it tolerable enough. She unlocked the newly fitted ledge-and-brace door, leaving it ajar to allow sun and air to flood the interior and for the ever-present paraffin taint to escape. She would have left the window open at night, but security had become a real issue. Locking an outbuilding in daylight hours, even when nobody would be in the yard, was unheard of a few months before. That was before Guest and his rustling; before there had been so many outsiders passing through; before meat rationing made any farm office a lucrative target. *It seems such a shame that trust is in such short supply. But at least I can work without coat and gloves now that it's warmer.*

An untidy stack of invoices lurked in the tray on the left of the desk waiting her attention. She rifled through the heaps to extract the most urgent and dealt with them quickly enough. The teetering heaps of Ministry documents were something else entirely. With her father away on Foreign Office business, and Dodo now mistress of her own domain, the running of the Courtney estate fell to her. *And paperwork has never been my strong point.* A glance at the wall clock showed it was almost ten and Cecile would arrive any time soon, under her own steam despite all of Bunch's offers of help. She pushed papers around for a while before there was a tapping on the door.

'Good morning Miss Rose.'

She spun the chair around to face the lean figure outlined against the open doorway, round-shouldered with age but still tall. Parson's hazel eyes held an unusual wariness. He appeared to be deciding on whether or not to enter the tiny room and such vacillation was unusual. As Estate Manager he was as much a part of Bunch's life as the estate itself. Little went on around the Perringham farm and its grounds that he was not aware off, nor willing to comment on.

'Good morning.' Parsons tipped his hat and ambled in to ease himself into the office's only other chair. Bunch could hear his lungs squeaking protest at the exercise they were being asked to perform and wondered again at her father's decision to persuade the old chap out of retirement. 'And are you well?' she asked. 'Granny said you weren't earlier in the week.'

'Just the old trouble.' He patted gently at his chest.

'If it's all too much please do tell me. I can't have you making yourself ill.'

'Nothing urgent. If I take my time.'

'If you're sure?'

'I am.' His tone ended the query without question. 'I thought you would like to know the shearing is finished.'

'Already?'

'We've half the flock we had last year,' he replied. 'I've moved them up the coombe. We've also had the first hay cut off Hem's Corner and we should be done by end of today.'

'Excellent. If this weather holds we'll have it turned and stooked by the end of the week.'

'I hope so, Miss.'

'Good to hear. I shall be here all morning if needed. I am waiting in for a guest to arrive. More than a guest as it happens. You will need to meet her because she will be helping us out with the clerical duties.'

'I heard. A Miss Benoir, so Mrs Knapp tells me.' He huffed sharply. 'Do we need her?'

Parsons seldom used more words than strictly necessary but his face could convey a speech worthy of Churchill himself, and she could not help but gain an impression of disappointment, disapproval even. It was fleeting and gone the instant that she saw it, but disquieting. He was not a man to question the family in anything other than agricultural matters. *His imagination is running amok,* she thought. 'We have a heap of paperwork from a dozen Ministries. More than you and I can get through. Father intended to be here, of course, but his FO post must take priority. He dragged you out of retirement to do all of this in his absence but that was before this damned form filling trebled, so it's only fair I get in some extra help.'

'I was led to understand the elder Mrs Courtney was taking some say in the running.'

'Granny isn't half so robust as she likes to think. Anymore than you are, and I worry for you both. The extra pair of hands will ease things all round.'

The chair creaked as Parsons shifted impatiently. 'We can manage. I hear this Miss Benoir lost her father very recently. It seems hard putting her to work already.'

'It was Cecile who came to me for work.' Bunch smiled. 'I think she needs our money far more than our compassion, and you were only asking me a few days ago if you could borrow one of the Land Girls to help out with filing.'

'Your father would have consulted me first before he took somebody on.'

His challenge came as a huge surprise, perhaps even a shock. Parsons had ticked her off many times in her childhood years. He was a quiet man with measured opinions, yet he looked deeply troubled and she wondered what lay behind his obvious concern. 'I'm sorry, Parsons. You're perfectly right and

I do apologise. No slight was intended, I assure you. We need someone to make sense of all this red tape, however, and Miss Benoir was a research assistant for her father for many years. Attention to detail is her speciality.' Bunch could see that a small war of loyalties going on behind the man's eyes. She scratched gently at the centre of her forehead with one finger nail. 'I am sure she will fit in perfectly well.'

Parsons shifted awkwardly as he pondered his reply. 'It's not that your Miss Benoir can't do the job. It's who she is. Or maybe I should say, what she is.'

'A scholar?'

'A foreigner,' he said.

'That bothers you? The French are our allies. And they are going to need all the friends they can get if the news is to be believed.'

'You know me better than that. You know this doesn't bother me one jot.' His eyebrows creased, pulling a deep V toward the bridge of his considerable nose.

A sure sign for Bunch that he was about to drop a bombshell. 'Do I detect a *but*?'

He raised both hands in exasperation. 'I've known you all your life and you're like my own child, so you know I'm saying this for the best of reasons.'

'Do spit it out, man. You obviously have something to say, so say it.

'Very well. Her arrival is bothering some of the staff,' he replied. 'The whole place is buzzing like a skep of bees and we can't afford to lose the ones we still have. Especially if the MoD enlarge the call up, as they've said they will.'

'Come now. I can't see people giving notice simply because of Miss Benoir. And I'm told Ag Labs will be exempt from enlistment.'

'Perhaps not but it can and has caused ill will. It may give them the incentive to enlist.'

'But why?'

'There's a rumour that her father was German.'

'Cecile's father was a Professor at a German university for some years it's true, but he was French. And Cecile's mother was as English as you or I.'

'That is all well and good. I know you have the best intentions but people are willing to listen to all kinds of tittle tattle. If Mr Churchill has his way over internment camps it will only get worse.'

'Not for the French. Even if they are overrun it won't come to that.'

'The papers are full of invasions because the government want people stirred up to fight. Anybody who is the least bit different will be a target for all of that. They may even be murdered.' He nodded slowly and held her gaze to emphasise the point. 'It happened last time and it *will* happen again. If it hasn't already. Once people get an idea into their heads there's no shifting it. They're frightened and not without cause when we have the Hun back on our doorstep.'

It was a long speech from a man she always knew was one of few words, yet he was not telling her everything. That was perfectly obvious from the way he avoided looking her in the eye and the flushing pink of the lined skin around his collar. 'It's not like you to repeat idle gossip,' she said. 'Who told you this?'

Parsons met her gaze this time around. 'Several sources,' he replied. 'As I said.'

'Staff?'

'Some.'

His manner puzzled her. Guilt, perhaps a little anger, all engulfed by a large dose of sorrow. 'Miss Benoir is a friend who has asked for my help.'

Parsons nodded. 'I do understand and it is your decision, of course. You know I have the family's best interests in mind.'

'I never expected anything else.'

The warring of his thoughts was obvious to her and she waited for more, but he only got to his feet – abruptly, considering his rheumatic joints. 'Remember that I warned you,' he said and left Bunch to gape after his retreating back as he crunched slowly across the yard into the farm lane.

She had known the man to be forthright but never judgemental. She wished she'd insisted he tell where the rumours had come from. *Why tell me half the story? Did they come from a relation and he wants to protect them? Or perhaps he honestly doesn't know? Once the Chinese whispers begin in a village like ours there's no knowing where it started.* She thought about the women taking tea in the Jenny Wren and remembered that his wife was a friend to both of them. *No guesses it was them.*

Bunch shrugged the thought away. There were far more pressing things to worry about than the ill humour of a few locals, Cecile's imminent arrival being one of them. The railway wall clock above the desk showed it was past eleven o'clock. Late in the morning for Parsons to be dishing out the day's workload, which was a further anomaly. *The poor man is obviously finding the tug out of retirement more of a trial than he's willing to admit – and I'm not sure I've the heart to retire him again even for his own good. I'll have to hope Daddy is home soon.*

The chaos on her desk reclaimed her attention and she filtered out the sounds of staff coming and going across the yard and of Land Army girls clattering back from their breakfast break. She barely registered a car pulling off the lane and was still engrossed in shuffling papers when a silhouette stepped into the slanted block of sunlight from the open door.

'Rose?' For a moment she was the Cecile of school years, taller and more slender, yet still the same gauche awkward girl, and then she moved into the office and the only shadows remaining in her face were those beneath her eyes.

'You're here.' Bunch launched out of her chair and clasped Cecile's hands. 'I wasn't expecting you until lunch time.'

'The taxi arrived and he did not want to wait.' She waved a hand at the suitcase and a pair of battered trunks out on the yard. 'Packing was simple. It's mostly Papa's books.'

Bunch went to the door and frowned at the luggage. 'The taxi just brought you to the rear gate and left you? I will have to speak with him.'

'Oh don't. Please. I told him I was starting a new job here in the estate office.' Cecile grinned and picked up a wad of papers scanning them quickly and looked at the shelves littered with box files. 'No time like the present, I think.'

'Don't you want to settle in first?'

'I am sure whatever space you have for me will be perfect. After the tiny apartment we rented in Paris my expectations are not high.' She pulled up the second chair. 'If someone can put my trunks somewhere inside I shall be fine. I need to be busy.'

'I can see that. Any fresh news from the police?'

'Nothing at all. They won't even tell me when they are to release Papa's remains for burial.' Her tone was neutral, devoid of emotion, as if the subject of her only relative's interring was unimportant.

Bunch was not fooled for a moment. 'Leave the damned filing. It's already been waiting for months. I hardly think a few hours or even a day will make the slightest bit of difference. Have you had breakfast?'

'Yes.'

Bunch smiled, recognising the uncertainty in Cecile's manner as she looked away. 'Well I'm hungry so let's go and have some coffee and perhaps one of Mrs Westgate's excellent scones, if she has some to spare. And after that we'll get you settled in your room. All this—' she dismissed the desk and its clutter with a flick of her hand '—all this can wait.'

~~~

Bunch sat on the edge of the bed and watched as Cecile unpacked the trunks, which took a depressingly short time. Once the books had been set aside there was very little left. Her few dresses and outfits were lost in the solid double-sided wardrobe and only two shelves in the matching press were utilised for a half dozen blouses and jumpers. Bunch noted their quality but also how worn those things were. It told her far more than words that Cecile had not been living in any kind of comfort for some considerable time.

'Sorry we don't have a maid to unpack for you. We have almost no staff left. I hope you like the room,' Bunch said. 'It's not very big but it's cosy in winter.'

'It's lovely, Bunch. Please don't trouble yourself. I don't expect to be treated like a guest.'

'You thought we'd put you up in the attic with the maids? Not that we have any.'

'I don't expect to be treated differently to the rest of the staff.'

'Stop that, Cissy. You're my friend. Friends don't put friends in spider-strewn attics.' Bunch gave her a wry smile. 'Enough of your excuses. Our next job is to go shopping. You need kitting out.'

'No, please. I don't need so very much.'

Cecile's face settled into a wary blandness that lacked expression beyond a polite half-smile and Bunch cursed her own legendary lack of tact. 'Sorry, that was thoughtless. I realise you had to travel light. We don't have much of a social round these days but Granny still insists we dress for dinner. And we have tennis parties and the odd race meet. We might even go up to Town now and then for a show. In fact we should go up to Town next week. Take Dodo because she has far better fashion sense than me.' She plucked at the counterpane, avoiding her friend's blushes. 'If it's the money that bothers you I can give you an advance on your wages. I can't imagine you have been able to sort out your father's accounts yet.'

'Could you? That would be rather useful.'

'My pleasure. And I am sure I can persuade Dodo to lend you a few things. You're about the same size, or you were before she started expanding. She won't be wearing a lot of her things until after the sprog arrives.' Bunch got up and crossed to the door. 'We shall have to take the cart. We've absolutely no petrol for the jalopy and even if I had the coupons, which I don't, Granny has taken the Crossley today. Or would you rather ride?' She looked hopefully at her friend and then sighed. 'We'll take the pony cart after lunch. Dodo will be grateful for the visit. She hates not being able to gad about like she's used to.'

A tap at the door preceded the housekeeper. 'Chief Inspector Wright is here to see Miss Benoir. He says he needs a private word so I've put him in the Drawing Room.'

'Thank you, Knapp. Tell him she'll be down directly.' Bunch arched an eyebrow at Cecile. 'Didn't take him long to track you down did it?'

'I can't think that there can possibly be a question he hasn't asked me ten times already,' Cecile replied. 'Would it be terrible if I asked you to go down with me?'

Bunch pursed her lips, deciding how forthright she should be. Wright had not spoken to her since the events at the Marquis and she was fairly certain he would not be that keen to speak with her now. He had made it very plain that he thought she should not become too wrapped up in events. *A problem that is his alone*, she thought. *And this is my home.* She shrugged lightly. 'If you want me to, then of course.'

~~~

'Miss Courtney, sorry to intrude.'

Bunch studied Wright carefully as she'd not had time to do so in the Marquis. She noticed how his brown hair was that bit greyer at the temples and in desperate need of a trim; how the bags under his eyes were that bit darker; how his suit hung loose from shoulders and hips. *He's lost weight since the New Year,* she thought. *And God knows he couldn't afford it in the first place.* 'Chief Inspector Wright,' she murmured. 'What brings you here? We can't offer you a hot meal for luncheon, I'm afraid. Cook has made some scones. And I believe we have some cold pie.' Chief Inspector Wright grinned, and she noted how his features lost ten years in a broad smile.

'Thank you but no. I've came to speak with Miss Benoir.'

'How kind. Do take a seat.' She ushered them to the pair of small sofas flanking a low table in the bay window where Roger lay basking in a patch of sunlight. 'If you won't stay for a meal, perhaps coffee?'

'No thank you. I must get back to the station for an urgent meeting. I just wanted to bring Miss Benoir the results of the post-mortem.'

'Which is?'

'The coroner was able to confirm acute poisoning,' he replied.

'The same type of poison as Miss de Wit?' Bunch demanded.

'We can't say yet whether the two are the same. I rather think Miss de Wit has not been a priority case for him.'

'Perhaps she will be now. Seems damned queer to have two poisonings and not be connected.'

Wright shook his head. 'Death by poisoning is more common than you might think. Either by accident or design. The coroner doubts they are the same at this stage, but we can't rule it out. Cyanide is almost certainly the murder weapon in Professor Benoir's instance.'

'Which was as I suspected.' Cecile's reply was little more than a whisper.

She was staring out at the garden directly in front of the window. Bunch doubted her friend even saw the twin borders on either side of the lawn foaming with early summer blooms – all that had survived Beatrice's order to 'dig for victory' across the rest of the grounds – or the tiny pale-cream summerhouse at the far end, or the undulating Downs beyond. She reached out to touch her friend's arm.

Cecile patted Bunch's fingers and smiled ruefully. 'I told them my father was poisoned. And I told you the same thing when you came to see me after.'

'Your statement has been filed,' Wright replied. 'It will all be dealt with in due course.'

'Dealt with? My mother was British, *Monsieur Inspecteur*,' she said. 'Yet I cannot work when the authorities have chosen not to recognise my qualifications or even my nationality.'

'Ah,' said Wright. 'Your father was French but also registered as a German resident, without question.'

'My mother was not. My papers will prove that. Both she and I were born here in England.' The young woman's attention returned to the view beyond the window. 'But you are correct about Papa. I received a letter this morning. It seems that because our documents showed both Berlin and Paris addresses, it has complicated matters.' She shot Wright a fleeting glance. Her neck flushed pink and the rigid veins in her temples showing blue against the paleness of her face as she turned back to Bunch. 'I am so sorry. It puts you in such a position and that will cause you embarrassment. I shall leave, of course.'

Bunch gently stroked the hair from Cecile's face and

laughed. 'Don't be so bloody ridiculous, Cissy. You shall be my house guest until we can get this sorted out.'

'Your father will not mind?'

'Father is not here. And you—' she glared at Wright across the occasional table '—Inspector Wright, I thought you would know better.'

'I'm merely a humble Chief Inspector,' he said, with a marked emphasis on his rank. 'Whatever decisions the worthies of Whitehall choose to make are way above my level. That aside, until Miss Benoir's papers are brought to order she is obliged to inform the authorities of any changes in domicile.'

'I informed the constable in Chiltwick. He assured me that he would make a report.'

'And he telephoned the Brighton station for advice. You do know that you require permission before you relocate? Strictly speaking I should arrest you for breaking regulations.'

Cecile's chin dropped to her chest and her gaze fixed in her clasped hands. 'Yes.'

'You can't possibly consider arresting her. For God's sake man, she's been through hell these past few months. She's here because her landlady was evicting her, and she can't go anywhere else because she doesn't have a job.' Bunch put an arm around Cecile and glowered at the policeman. 'I can personally vouch for her nationality. Isn't that enough?'

'No.' Wright passed his hand over his hair and exhaled. 'Her landlady reported her to the local internments board. As I understand it, the cottage in Chiltwick is owned by a local family but was let through an agent who omitted to tell that owner that her tenants were not British.'

Cecile looked from one to the other. 'It was not Papa who took the cottage. It was found for us.' She hesitated, her attention switching between Bunch and Wright and back again. 'His employer was the British government,' she said at last.

'Does that not count for something?'

Wright consulted his notebook though Bunch had the distinct impression he knew exactly what he was going to say. 'The lease has been traced back to Whitehall, which is precisely why I've been authorised to backdate the relocation. Professor Benoir had some influential benefactors.'

Cecile gazed at him for a long moment before slowly bending forward, her hands covering her face to stifle a sigh.

'You are an absolute rotter,' said Bunch, 'letting this poor girl think she was about to be thrown in jail. That was such a horrible thing to do.'

'I had to be sure her story fitted the facts to hand.' He looked toward the door and lowered his voice as he added. 'There are plans already being made for the internment of German citizens should France fall. Or perhaps I should say, when.'

'Should you be telling me that?'

'Probably not but you ought to be aware of the facts.'

Bunch flashed Cecile a confident smile, far more confident than she felt. This was the second time that somebody had warned her about the dangers of German connections and she would be lying if she thought it was not something to be concerned about. Her father would have opinions on it, she was sure. His views on the antics of the Mitford girls had been pithy, to say the least. But ten years ago – five, two even – so many of the fashionable people in the fast Munich set, which included so many of the British upper classes, had been fascinated by the German maestro. *Cecile is different, surely?* she thought. *If Professor Benoir had been employed in some secret project, then he had been decreed safe by whatever Whitehall potentate rubber stamped these things? So who is Wright to argue?* She turned her smile on him. 'I am sure Mr Chamberlain would not allow that to happen. He's essentially a man of peace.'

'I doubt we shall have Mr Chamberlain as our Prime Minister for very much longer. His health is poor and Mr Churchill is baying in the kennels.'

'Dogs of war?' she said.

'You don't think much of him?'

'I don't think anything. Churchill is as he is, and he does talk some sense. It will not make a great deal of difference which of them holds the reins if Herr Hitler does not stop at Calais.' She picked up her coffee cup and hid her irritation behind its rim. 'We're at war despite all Chamberlain and Halifax could do.'

'It was Chamberlain who conceded points back in September.'

'England did not have a great deal of choice,' Cecile murmured. 'And they may have fewer choices still by the time September comes around again. Not against the Reich. The Inspector is quite correct. Anyone who has lived there as long as I did will be suspect. When Mother's family wanted nothing to do with me … I can perfectly understand if you prefer I find another lodging.'

'I would not hear of it. You will stay here and they can ask all the questions they like.'

'Thank you.' Cecile grasped Bunch's hand. 'I shall be the best secretary you ever had.'

'Of course you will be, darling. Now then Chief Inspector. Is there any news on how the poison found its way into the wine?'

'Not yet. We do know that there are only two sets of fingerprints on the bottle. The Professor's – and yours, Miss Benoir.' Wright looked to Cecile with little emotion showing in his face. 'I shall keep you informed of any developments. In the meantime,' he continued as he got to his feet. 'I would appreciate your not leaving the estate until further notice.'

'At all?' said Bunch. 'That's a little harsh.'

'It's far more lenient than was first suggested,' he replied. 'The only reason Miss Benoir is not currently under house arrest, or else sitting in the cells, is that you and others have vouched for her.'

'I vouched? When?'

'Just a few minutes ago.' He smiled at Cecile, turning his hat between slender fingers. 'You have good friends – or you might have been taken into custody.'

'Surely you don't believe Cissy killed her father?' said Bunch.

'I have no opinions on the matter. My position as an officer of the law can make them rather inconvenient. The details of the case against Miss Benoir could be seen as compelling by some. Her prints are all over the wine bottle containing the poison. A bottle that nobody else can recall seeing. Nor can anybody else be placed at or near the scene.'

'Cecile did not kill her father,' Bunch growled. 'I will stake my own life on it.' She smiled at Cecile and touched her arm with two fingers.

'If you vouch for her then I am willing to believe that. My immediate superior may need to be convinced.'

His eyes met hers with one brow raised. What he meant by it she could not be sure but it explained his reluctance in speaking with her until duty dictated. *Duty be damned*, she thought. *You do think she did it!* 'I should tell you we are planning a ride over to see my sister. I assume you are not going to arrest us half way there?'

'I am releasing Miss Benoir into your care,' he replied. 'If you have any questions or you come across any information the police should be aware of you know where my office is. Good morning ladies. I shall see myself out.'

Bunch pulled a face after him. 'He didn't have to be such a crumb about it,' she growled.

Cecile did not reply for a moment, her attention apparently

fixed on the garden. Her left arm was hugged protectively across her chest. The shuddering pleating of smoke from the lit cigarette in her right hand was the only outward sign of her trembling muscles. 'He is doing the best he can.' Her voice crept barely above a breath. 'He is giving a great deal of ground to you. I thank you for that.'

'Perhaps. But…'

Cecile rose suddenly, grinding her cigarette into the glass dish. 'I need some air. Some time to think. Perhaps we could delay our outing?'

Bunch watched Cecile exit the French windows and stride rapidly along the stone path toward the Dower's summerhouse. She squashed the impulse to follow, at least for that moment, letting her hand rest on Roger's head. He leaned against her legs sensing her mood, anxious in turn. There was a downside to the people around her being so self-contained: life could be a constant guessing game. She understood Cecile's need to be alone however. Grief for her father was bad enough but knowing she was effectively under house arrest was enough to send anyone into a tail spin. *Wright though, he's another matter, with his enigmatic comments. Was he excusing the distance he had placed between us all this time? Or warning me against it?*

Friday 10 May

The warm dry spell was holding and it was a great day for riding out, but Bunch reluctantly conceded that Cecile was not experienced enough to ride the mounts she had available. Perry was headstrong and apt, in her opinion, to play silly buggers with the unwary. Whilst Robbo, though steady enough, was prone to ignoring a novice rider and would quite calmly and without malice make his own way home. *Cecile has enough to contend with already without being dumped into a ditch by either of those monsters.*

The pony cart, which Parsons had dug from the depths of somewhere on the farm and treated to a coat of fresh red and green paint, was the best option. Bunch backed Perry into the shafts and then set off at a moderate walk. Now that they were on a quiet stretch she flicked the reins to gee Perry into a smarter pace, clicking her tongue and calling at him to trot on. The Fell pony leaned into the harness and moved up to a brisker walk. Not the trot she had requested but Bunch allowed him some leeway when his harness skills were somewhat rusty and he was, she admitted, on the small size for the vehicle. Pulling two adults was not that great a load however and he showed willing. She still slapped the reins gently across his rump as a reminder of who was in charge.

Cecile's fingers whitened as she took a tighter grip on the seat edge. She was staring directly ahead, silent and solemn and had barely said three sentences since they had listened to the BBC's news broadcast over luncheon. Bunch could understand that. Alvar Lidell's measured tones delivered so much for the nation to think about. Almost too much to take in on a single day.

'Fighting in Norway continues and reports are coming in of a German march through Holland, Belgium and Luxembourg...' 'The Prime Minister Mr Chamberlain is expected to step down in favour of Mr Churchill despite a strong show of support by Lord Halifax...' 'The House is awaiting word from Clement Atlee on the formation on the expected coalition...'

They listened with mounting gloom. Almost overnight the quiet war which had been happening 'somewhere else' ever since September was becoming a gaunt reality. *It's as if the entire island is holding its breath. And its nose*, Bunch told herself.

'I've run ahead of them twice now,' Cecile said. 'Where could I even run to now? America?' She laughed, a sharp guttural sound without a hint of humour. 'I'd much rather we should make a stand.'

'We shall,' Bunch replied.

Cecile's lips parted and she drew breath as if about to reply then closed them and gazed straight ahead once more.

Bunch saw her friend's jaw line tightening against the temptation to say far more. She knew the look. *What she's keeping to herself God only knows. The dear girl's been through enough but that is a stiff upper lip if ever there was one. She'll spill when she's ready.* Another flick of the reins to the pony to keep pace and she settled back against the seat rest to watch familiar sights roll by.

The back lanes between the Perringham estate and Banyard

Manor had always been quiet but the lack of petrol rendered them deserted, beyond tractors and delivery vans, and the occasional military vehicle lost in the winding back roads since the removal of signposts.

The air was thick with the scent of cut grass as farm workers scurried to make the most of the weather and rushed to get the first cut of hay into barns, or stack and thatched into ricks, for the coming winter. May and blackthorn added a cloying sweetness ahead of an encroaching blanket of wild clematis and honeysuckle vines. Larks spiralled, loud and distant in a blue sky that was dotted with high white cloud. They passed verges frothing with parsley and ox-eye daisies and willow-herb and the more shaded banks still held evidence of spring primroses.

It was a time of year that Bunch rejoiced in yet one, she realised, she had taken for granted for most of her life. Yes, she would far rather be riding Perry across the Downs than watching his stocky rump and unruly tail as he hauled the cart through the lanes, but she was glad to be sharing this land of hers with a close friend when the news was so dark, albeit shared in a slightly awkward silence.

When they arrived at Banyards they were shown to the loggia at the rear of the house where Dodo lounged on a well-cushioned steamer chair, her slender legs covered by a light blanket despite the sun.

'Hello old thing. No, don't get up.' Bunch dodged forward to plant a kiss on the top of her sister's head. 'You remember Cecile Benoir? We were in Switzerland together. Cissy, this is Daphne. Dodo to me and you.' She eyed her sister darkly. Dodo could be touchy about who was permitted to refer to her by the diminutive, but Bunch did not want Cecile to feel like an outsider any more than necessary.

Dodo got the message. 'Pleased to meet you again Cecile – Cissy.' Dodo held out her hand and shook Cecile's warmly.

'Excuse me for not getting up. My back is aching like billy-o and the District Nurse has ordered me to rest.'

'No need to apologise. Good to meet you again, Daphne.'

'Dodo, please.' The reply was instant. 'Do sit down, both of you. I asked Cook to send up tea when you arrived.' She smiled at Cecile. 'My condolences on your father's passing. I understand you have few people here? If there is anything I can do you only need ask.'

'Thank you,' Cecile murmured. 'You are too kind and yes I shall.'

'I mean it. Losing people closest to you is simply horrible. You will be sick of people offering good wishes and sympathy after a while but be glad whilst they still do.'

Bunch eyed her sister with the suspicion of a frown creasing her forehead. Dodo was not given to bitterness or even self-pity and she wondered what had prompted that caustic aside.

If Dodo noticed the questioning look she chose to ignore it. 'No Roger today?'

'No, poor old chap finds it impossible to jump into the cart these days.'

'What a shame.'

'Well he's not a pup any longer. And in the same vein—' Bunch looked around '—no Emma?'

'Took the train to Guildford. Some academic meeting or other. She'll be back later. Emma gets rather bored being cooped up here. I think I'm too stupid for her.'

'Don't take it personally. Everyone is stupid compared with her,' Bunch replied. 'She doesn't mean to, but she makes me feel like a complete duffer.'

'I know. But some company would be nice. Family I mean. And our family is shrinking by the day it seems. Has Granny told you about Rupert Berry. Remember him? Second cousin? Third, perhaps. I can never work it out – Granny would know.

I'm not sure where he was killed. Norway, I assume.'

'I hadn't heard. Of course I remember Rupes. Poor chap. He did the season with Cissy and me. Dull as ditch water but a decent sort.'

'Granny told me she will write to his mother for us all.'

'I should add a note.' Bunch sighed. 'I don't suppose he'll be the last before this thing is over...'

Dodo broke the ensuing quiet. 'How long will you be staying at Perringham, Cissy?'

'Rose has been very kind and offered me some work and a roof over my head while my papers are sorted, which is more than I expected. I shall probably be here for a little while.'

'Has she indeed?' Dodo frowned at her sister. 'How like Bunch to take people for granted.'

'*Bunch.* I had forgotten we called you that,' Cecile murmured. 'And Dodo is correct. It troubles me that I am imposing on your grandmother's hospitality. The Dower is her domain, after all.'

Bunch helped herself to a biscuit and crunched noisily by way of reply. Her younger sibling was right, at least in so far as moving semi-permanent guests into the Dower House might be viewed as something of an imposition. Years of constant shifting of guests in Perringham House, where it was seldom that all the bedrooms were occupied, had made such invitations of no consequence. The Dower House had fewer rooms and two of those were allocated for her parents when they returned from the Far East. Bunch knew Dodo was perfectly correct but having her younger sister 'in the right' was, in her opinion, inherently wrong. *Or at the very least somewhat inconvenient.* 'Granny is quite all right about it. Told me it was the least I could do,' she said at last. 'I couldn't see Cecile on the street when her father has just died. Under what have the police are calling "suspicious circumstances". I can't do much with Daddy still abroad – but I do have some contacts.'

'I am sure that won't be necessary.'

Bunch reached across to touch Cecile's arm. 'I know you don't have anyone else to help out. I shall do what I can to get to the bottom of all this.'

'Having the chance to play detective once again is mere happenstance,' Dodo observed. 'As if you don't have enough to do without taking up lost causes.'

'Daphne Tinsley, that is incredibly unfair.'

Dodo glared, irritation clear in her expression, and Bunch sighed. They had been Bunch and Dodo since their nursery days. Using their given names when speaking to each other in earnest was a verbal blow. *And on this occasion, it was*, in Bunch's opinion, *totally uncalled for.*

'Forgive me Cissy,' Dodo said. 'I don't mean to offend.' She eased her gravid body back in the chair and studied her sister carefully. 'But we should leave the police to investigate.'

'That all depends,' Bunch muttered. 'It does feel most awfully bad luck for Cissy and her father to have gone through all they have only for him to be poisoned right here in England.'

'Was it poisoning?'

'Oh yes, the coroner was very plain on that point.'

'Well I hope the professor being French does not hold up things. One hears such terrible things about cases being allowed to slide in favour of the national interest.' Dodo held her hand up to stem Bunch's tart rejoinder. 'If your Inspector Wright is on the case, however, I am sure you don't need to be worried.'

'I know.' *When*, Bunch thought, *did she grow up? This time last year my sister was a giddy bride and before that she was a giddy debutante. And now she is the one handing out advice.* 'Enough of gruesome subjects. Not suitable for a mother in waiting. How are you?'

'Apart from the back? Quite well as it happens. I have an

appointment with Doctor Ephrin on Monday.'

'In Harley Street? Are you sure you want to travel all the way up to Town? The trains are absolutely bloody right now. Full of troops.'

'Not in first class,' Dodo replied. 'Can you come up with me? Bring Cissy. We can have tea at Claridges. It will be rather jolly.'

The younger woman's face was wistful, almost pleading. Bunch knew how lonely Dodo had to be and felt a jolt of guilt at neglecting her only sibling. Telephones were all very well but when the social round had all but ground to a halt it was easy to become isolated. House parties were few and far between and dinners non-existent. Not only because of petrol being hoarded for absolute need but with the fresh round of foodstuffs being added to the ration books dinner tables of all levels of society were starting to look a little Spartan. Not to mention the small fact that having a murderer in the house, even way back in the winter, had made Dodo something of a social pariah. 'Doesn't Nanny want be with you?' Bunch said. 'I will go of course but Nanny might feel it's her territory.'

'She probably does but Granny has persuaded her to stay where she is with her sister in Shropshire. We're winding her gently into retirement.'

'Oh? You are not having her look after your sprog when it arrives?'

'God no, she's eighty-five. Apart from anything else the old love can hardly see her own hands. She denies it of course but with all the best will I can't leave her in charge of little Georgi.'

Bunch smiled to herself. It was so typical of her sister to have made up her mind about the sex of her unborn infant without anything more concrete to base it on than the midwife's assurance. 'Poor old Nanny, though it must be a mixed blessing. I love her to pieces but not sure I'd want to inflict her regime on a child of mine. And Georgi? What if it's a girl,' she said. 'Do you have another name? Just in case.'

'Georgianna.' Dodo folded her hands over her thickening belly and beamed like a golden-haired Buddha. 'My Georgi might be gone but nobody will be allowed to forget that this is his child.'

'As if they would. And yes of course we shall come up to Town with you. Everything else all right? Have you got nursery help sorted out?'

'I think so. There have been so many young women joining up already. But I have daytime help organised, at least.'

'And nights? Barty isn't going to like it of the sprog keeps him awake.'

'Barty is being an absolute brick. I'm seeing a very different side to him since— Well, since January.' Dodo glanced at Cecile as if unwilling to return to the subject of death in her presence.

'We have all suffered loss,' Cecile raised her cup to her lips.

Bunch and Dodo followed suit in the silence that followed, each consumed by their own tragedies of the past months, until Dodo rattled her cup into its saucer like a chairman tapping a gavel. 'I heard something today,' said Dodo. 'About the drapers in Pulborough. The shop burned down two nights ago.'

'I hadn't heard, no. What happened?'

'Barty was telling me all about it. He still has a few friends on the magistrates' circuit. Two people died. The Coroner has suspended the inquest. It seems it wasn't an accident.'

'How awful.' Bunch took another biscuit and nibbled gently at its edge, sensing there was more to come but puzzled at Dodo's reticence. She was not usually so reserved with local news. 'Goldmann's? I've had a few outfits altered there. Goldmann is a superb tailor.'

'Apparently Mr Goldmann was injured, according to Barty,

and a young girl who was staying with them. German, I believe. A refugee.'

'I'm assuming foul play is suspected?'

Dodo leaned back in her seat and eased her legs, sighing heavily. 'The place reeked of petrol, or so I've heard.'

'Arson. How dreadful.'

'Isn't it.' She rubbed at her belly, looking from Bunch to Cecile, a deep frown creasing her brow. 'Why would anyone do that?'

Bunch shrugged. 'It's happening all over the place. An awful lot of people are still reliving the Great War, I suspect. Anyone that sounds vaguely German is the enemy.' She pulled thoughtfully at her bottom lip and glanced at Cecile who had noticeably paled. 'Sorry old thing. Shouldn't have brought that up. I'm sure it has nothing to do with your Pa. Benoir is hardly Germanic.'

'But foreign.' Cecile replied.

The sisters stared at each other with raised brows.

'I'm certain people would know the difference between French and German,' said Dodo.

'Yet not between German and Dutch? Or Pole? It does not seem to matter much too some people,' Cecile replied. 'You have not lost friends to such things. We fled Berlin before the real violence began but I saw it begin there. It started in such small ways. A shop closed here, a colleague suddenly vanished there. You heard of *Kristallnacht*?'

Dodo was puzzled but Bunch nodded slowly. 'Night of Crystal,' she said quietly. 'It was in the papers.'

'Terrible things happened that night. Businesses destroyed. Homes abandoned by force. It had begun long before then, of course, in a smaller way. People from the university had been vanishing. Jews mainly, but others as well. Everyone knew what was happening but nobody spoke about it.'

Bunch exchanged looks with her sister. Cecile's bitterness cast a darkness over the sunlit veranda and Bunch was not sure Dodo needed to hear any more. 'Is that the time? There's a new Land Girl arriving this afternoon and I should be there to see her settled.'

'I thought you'd stepped down from the Land Army post to manage the estate?' Dodo looked a little put out at the visit being cut short.

'I have.' Bunch patted her sister's arm and got to her feet. 'I still have to be there. Parsons's health really isn't good and we still haven't been able to replace the chaps we've lost to the forces.'

'None of us have,' Dodo replied. 'Who can blame them. The army can afford to pay young chaps more than we can.'

'Very true. At least it's only the young chaps so far. Sorry it's such a flying visit. See you at church perhaps? And we shall see you on Monday, whatever.' She leaned down and planted a kiss on Dodo's head. 'Take care darling. Thank you for the tea. Let Barty do all the donkey work, won't you?'

'I shall.'

'Thank you, Daphne.' Cecile offered her hand.

'You are welcome Cecile. Good to see you again.'

~~~

'You're close,' Cecile said as they rode back toward Perringham Dower. 'You and your sister.'

'We are. Surprising really because there's quite an age gap. I suppose it comes of our parents being away so much. Not that we saw them when they were home.' Bunch looked toward the head of the valley where the top-most tiles of Perringham House could be glimpsed between the trees. She laughed sharply. 'Daddy was always happy to be at Perringham. But Mother prefers staying up at Thurloe Square. I think being at Perringham reminds her too much of my brothers.'

'I had forgotten you'd lost siblings.'

'So do I at times. I was barely old enough to remember them.' She allowed Perry to slow his walk long enough to snatch a mouthful of cow parsley bending toward him from the grass verge. Her gaze strayed southward, from habit, and took in the line of cloud drifting up from the coast. The conversation was an odd one and getting too personal for her taste even with such an old friend. 'They died a long time ago,' she said finally. 'Not much more than a vague memory for me. Different matter for Mummy. Must have been quite bloody for her. She's never recovered.'

'My mother once told me she should have liked more children, but she didn't have that option.'

It was an unexpected reply, which made Bunch curious to hear what was on her guest's mind. 'She couldn't have more?'

Cecile shrugged. 'It is not a question one asks one's parents.'

'No, I suppose it isn't.' *Wrong tack,* Bunch thought. 'You miss her still?'

'I do, yes. Mummy was not able to get out much and we couldn't afford a nurse for her, so I was at her side all through her last months.'

'Good memories though?'

Cecile stared ahead as they rounded a bend just before Perringham House would appear into view, several hundred yards further along the lane. 'Not always,' she said at last. 'I was very close to my mother.'

'Not your father? But you worked for him all these years.'

'Yes I did.'

Yet again Bunch had the certainty that Cecile was reluctant to share something. Many of Bunch's acquaintances barely knew the people they called Mama and Papa, but Cecile had lived and worked with her father since leaving Mont-Choisi. She doubtless knew him better than Bunch knew her own frequently absent father, certainly better than she or Dodo knew their mother. 'Was he difficult?' she said.

'At times he was quite impossible,' Cecile replied. 'Brilliant. A genius in fact. I would not have learned anywhere near as much working anywhere else.' She smiled shyly. 'I have never been in the same league as Emma Tinsley. Never quite managed to get all the right things done. Once Mother was gone I was expected to keep the house for Father.'

'Not his fault, surely.'

'Yes and no. We should have left far sooner than we did. On the other hand, of course, Berlin is far kinder to women in academe.' She shrugged. 'Though on the whole I'd rather be here with all of the problems than gaining my prestige under Herr Hans Kuhne.'

'Who?'

'A party member who… It doesn't matter. I am here now.'

'You don't sound sure.'

'There are others who left in secret as we did. I don't know who or how many.' Cecile turned her face away, seemingly intent on watching the hedgerows as they passed them by.

The thought crossed Bunch's mind that perhaps Cecile knew who had murdered her father. She dismissed it as rapidly. There was no rhyme or reason for her to remain silent about her father's killer when his death effectively rendered her destitute. There was every reason for her to be in shock. 'I—' the sound of an approaching vehicle made Bunch look over her shoulder. She steered the cart into the layby close to the drive entrance and waited for the military staff car to pass them. As it did the driver sounded the horn and waved and Bunch had time to recognise Colonel Ralph before it swung around the corner.

Perry started forward, tossing his head and snorting indignation, lurching the cart onto the grass verge.

'Steady. Steady old chap. Woah.' Bunch leaned back in the seat pulling the reins tight in. Perry was not a nervous creature and she knew he was more startled than afraid, but the long grass hid drainage ditches at the base of the hedge that were all too easy to fall into, as she knew from bitter experience when she backed the shooting brake into them, way back in the mists of time when she had first learned to drive. 'Stand,' she called to him. 'Stand, Perry. Steady.'

The horse made a few more token objections, stamping his outsized hooves and tossing his head as far as the tightened straps would allow, but calmed quickly now that the vehicle was out of sight.

'Idiot.' Bunch frowned in the car's general direction. 'I shall have to have more words with that damnable Ralph character. He should bloody well have known better.'

Cecile paled noticeably and Bunch reached out to offer a reassuring pat. 'I say, are you all right? Damned fool making that racket around a horse. Good job it wasn't Dodo's mare or we'd be half way to Worthing by now. That one sees tigers behind every bush at the best of times. Some Sandhurst fop blasting car horns on her heels would be the absolute end.' She was glad when Cecile joined in with a polite laugh. 'No harm done but I think we should get home and find you a stiff drink.'

'Yes please.'

'Right ho.' Bunch slackened the line and rippled the leather ribbons along Perry's back and called out 'Walk on.' She drove the cart passed Perringham's drive in time to see the rear of the car vanishing into the tunnel of trees. Cecile kept her gaze fixed on the road ahead, her whitened fingers still gripping onto the seat rail, and said nothing all the while. A reaction Bunch considered out of all proportion to the level of danger. *She's been through a lot but I thought even she had more spunk than this.*

They pulled the cart into the stable yard that was in turmoil.

All the Land Army girls were gathered there chattering as noisily as a tree full of rooks.

'Miss Courtney!' Kate Woolridge, the leading light of Perringham's Land Girls, came to hold Perry's bridle and took the reins from Bunch as she stepped down. 'It's done. Mr Chamberlain has stepped down and Mr Churchill has formed his government.'

'We expected that. What's all the excitement about?'

Kate glanced around the gathered woman who had fallen quiet. 'It was just on the wireless. Gerry has taken Belgium and Holland and they've marched into France.'

Bunch looked back at Cecile. 'Already?' she said.

'No details as yet. We can hope it's not quite so desperate but…'

Cecile stepped down behind her and nodded to Kate. 'Cecile Benoir. We shall be seeing a lot of each other, I think.'

Kate prodded her own chest. 'I'm Kate. This is Pat Quinton, Elsie Barnett, and Annie Marsden.' She pointed at each in turn. 'That—' she waved wildly toward a beanpole teen at the back of the gaggle '—is Brenda Green. Our other two new girls are Vera Mostan and Dorothy Holmes, the Welsh contingent. You'll meet them later. Are you staying here for long?'

'Kate, this is hardly the time,' said Bunch. 'I'm sorry Cissy. I'm sure you will get news of your family quite quickly.'

'No, no. It is quite all right.' She smiled around the ragged circle of women. 'Rose, Miss Courtney, has been kind enough to offer me a roof, at least until the matter with my father is settled. But I shall be working for my crust, the same as all of you. I hope we shall all be good friends whilst I am here.'

'Welcome to Perringham Farm, Miss Benoir.'

Bunch glared at Kate to stave off more questions but when she turned back Cecile was already crossing the yard and turning toward the arch that led to the estate office.

'All right you lot. There's stock to see to. Off you trot.' Kate held on to Perry's bridle, claiming the task of unbuckling the traces before walking Perry free from the shafts and allowing them to drop. She tethered the pony outside the boxes.

Bunch looked around to check the rest of the women had cleared the yard before she spoke again. 'I'd appreciate it if you'd keep the gossip about the war down to a whisper, especially in front of the Miss Benoir.'

'Yes, I am sorry.'

'You were not to know. Apology accepted. Just be kind to her. She has relatives in eastern France and no idea what has happened to them.'

'I'm sorry, that was terribly clumsy of me.' She slipped a woven collar onto Perry's head and hung the bridle near the door. 'Will your friend be rounded up?' she asked.

'Pardon?'

'Miss Benoir. Will she be interned?'

Bunch paused in rubbing Perry's legs and belly free of dust and grass seeds. The question took her by surprise and whilst she and Kate had become almost friends in the time the Land Girls had been billeted there, it seemed a little impertinent. 'Why would you ask such a thing?'

'My aunt in Richmond has two lodgers, you see. Jewish sisters from Stuttgart. Barely more than children. Auntie sponsored them about a year ago.'

'Was that on Bertie Samuel's sponsorship scheme?'

'I suppose it must have been. I know they were given a low enemy alien classification, but Auntie's neighbour is a Home Guard captain and he told her if Churchill got in he'd have all of them arrested.'

Bunch nodded. 'I am sure your aunt's lodgers will be fine. I mean, they can't lock them all up. And no it won't affect Cissy

– Miss Benoir – because she is French not German. And France is still our ally.'

'For now at least.'

'Do be careful what you say, Kate. I know you are only thinking aloud but some of the girls aren't as educated as you and Pat. Careless talk and all that.'

'Of course. If Miss Benoir is staying at the Dower she won't be needing the empty cottage? I'm assuming Frank Haynes won't be coming back. Parsons has managed to hide it from the evacuee's board so far but that won't last.'

'Hayes will not be back. If the police catch up with him he'll be serving a few years at His Majesty's pleasure.'

Kate grinned at the bite in Bunch's voice. 'I thought he might. I'm asking because with seven of us now the billet is a getting a little crowded. And as it's next door so if you could see your way to letting us spill over?'

'Have you spoken to Parsons?'

'Yes, this morning. He said to ask you.'

'Did he?' Bunch frowned. 'Any idea where he is now?'

'He went home.'

Bunch looked down at her boots. 'Parsons never went home without good cause.'

'He isn't well. Hasn't been for a couple of months,' Kate said. 'Heart, I gather. I've seen him taking those little nitrate pills.' She smiled briefly. 'My Uncle Thomas used to take them all the time.'

'I see. Thank you for telling me.'

'I doubt he will. Thank me, that is.'

'No, he wouldn't.' Bunch grimaced. 'Parson's is one of the old school, thinks he's indispensable.'

'And indestructible.'

'Exactly. I shall call on him later. Meanwhile I don't see why you shouldn't spread out a little. Best ask old Mrs Haynes if she wants to clear out her son's belongings first. I'm sure we can find some furniture in the attics to kit the place out.'

'Thank you. It will be a huge help.'

'Sorry I hadn't thought about it before. Let me know what you need. And let me know if you hear any more gossip about our new book keeper. I'd like to nip it in the bud before it gets out of hand.'

'Of course.' Kate gathered up Perry's bridle, detached the bit and threw it into the bucket of water, avoiding Bunch's direct query.

'I'm not asking you to split on your chums, Kate. Please know that. Just tell me any general gossip.'

Kate's relief was obvious in the lift of her shoulders. 'Yes of course I shall. Is that it for this old chap for today? Shall I turn him out in the small paddock for a bit?'

'Yes, thank you. Fetch him in again before the dew starts to fall. And make sure that tack is cleaned properly. The links were full of green crud this morning.'

'Yes, Miss.'

Bunch smiled grimly. 'I know that wasn't you or Pat that cleaned it.' She hid a sigh at Kate's light shrug. She understood the code of silence between compatriots but it could be irksome when that silence was waged against herself. 'I know you're all busy,' she said. 'And a lot of these Land Girls have never seen a cow before they come to us. But that is exactly why we need to keep a careful eye on them. We can't afford our best – if not our main mode of transport – to get a mouth infection from a grubby bit. God help us if this war goes on as long as the last one but if it does tack is going to be harder to replace than the horses.' She waved a hand toward the farmyard and the direction the rest of the Land Girls had taken. 'You're the senior here, along with Pat. You both come from country families so you do at least know one end of a sheep from the other.' She relaxed a little to see the Land Girl grinning at her. 'Mr Parsons is unwell and we are not going to get a new estate manager all that easily so we shall need to make a few temporary adjustments. I would like you to step up and take charge of the Land Girls. Deputise Pat if that simplifies it all. You've been doing a lot of that already. I shall oversee it all, of course, but if you could allocate work and keeping an eye on them for me… All of them.'

'All of them?' she asked.

'I am trusting you to take charge when Mr Parsons is not here. It may raise a few eyebrows with some of the old timers but most of them are as old as Parsons, so it will be you girls taking the heft.'

'Yes of course.' Kate made a point of examining the strapping carefully before hanging the bridle on a handy hook. 'A few cracks. I shall get Annie to take care of that with an extra coat of saddle soap.'

'Thank you, Kate. Don't forget to bring me a list for the cottage. I shall be in all evening.'

'Thank you, Miss. I will do my very best.'

'I know you shall. Now I must dash. I have a dozen things to do before dinner.' Bunch hurried toward the rear of the house. She paused at the entrance to calm Roger's ecstatic greeting and to swap her outdoor shoes for a pair of light pumps, and sighed at the need to go everywhere via the boot-room. Once upon a time she dreamed of a life that revolved around all things equine. Much as she loved horses and driving the cart she missed the days when she stepped out of the Crossley and through the front door. Or even the days at Perringham House when there had been enough staff not to worry about a few muddy footprints.

She trotted upstairs to the attic and her private study and rifled through the papers on her desk. Her claim to Kate, of jobs to finish, was perfectly true but if she were honest most of them revolved around the estate office and she was reluctant to go down there and deal with Cecile right at that moment. It was not that she was tiring of Cecile's company, rather that she was exasperated by the woman's complexity.

It was not a character trait Bunch had much time for. She knew herself to be obstinate and occasionally arrogant. Forthright and at the same time reserved as situations demanded, but she was fairly sure that people knew what to expect from her. Cecile's silences were doubtless a result of her grief. *And heaven knows the Courtneys know enough about that to write the book but she's keeping things bottled up and that's never a wise thing.*

~~~

A vehicle drawing up in the driveway had Roger barking from the back of the house and lured Bunch to her bedroom window. She watched Wright step onto the gravel drive. *What on earth could he want?* She went to drag a brush through her dark hair and for just a moment her hand hovered over the lipstick. *Would that,* she asked herself, *be conveying the wrong signals? It won't do for Wright to think I make a special effort for him, on any pretext.* She waited for a light tap on her door and for Shiela's tousled head peer around it.

'That Chief Inspector Wright's 'ere, Miss.' Sheila bobbed a strange kind of disembodied curtsey and vanished once again. Bunch sighed, making a mental note for Knapp to smarten the girl up a little.

Wright was staring across the gardens as she entered the drawing room, with Roger padding quietly at her heels. 'Chief Inspector Wright. To what do we owe the pleasure?'

Wright remained where he was, at ease in the military sense, his hands clasped behind his back. 'The view from here is rather different without the snow,' he said. 'Still peaceful.'

'Which you would know if you had ever paid us the odd

visit over the past five months. Tea?' She went to pull the sash hanging near the fireplace and returned to the only tall-backed chair in the room. A tactical move that she was certain would not be lost on her guest. 'Granny will be home at any moment. I'm sure she will love to see you. Do sit down.'

'I hope Mrs Courtney is well?' Wright came to perch on the small sofa that she indicated. He rubbed at his neck, an unconscious gesture of fatigue that matched the dark smudges beneath his eyes.

Bunch felt a little guilty at her sniping. 'Granny is very well, thank you. It seems a little insensitive to think it aloud, but this war seems to have given her a new lease of life.'

'I hope she doesn't over do it.'

'Oh, she will. There are no half measures with my Grandmother.'

'A family trait.'

'Not a bad one, I hope.' She smiled sweetly and waited as the maid brought in the tea. 'Thank you, Sheila. I shall pour.'

'Yes, Miss Rose.' The girl scuttled away in a flurry of starched cap and apron that dwarfed her skinny frame.

'Sugar, Inspector?'

'I gave it up. My landlady would never forgive me if I used her baking ration in my tea.' He accepted the cup she offered him and sipped gratefully. 'Always the best blend,' he said.

'Of course, though for how long is another matter. Now how may I assist the Sussex Constabulary?'

'I brought your statement to sign.' He pulled an envelope from his inside pocket. 'My apologies for taking so long. We have such a backlog.'

'Can't get the staff?'

'Exactly so.'

'Is this for the incident in the Marquis Inn?'

'You've made other statements?'

'Well, forgive me for being precise but there is the small matter of poor Cissy's father.'

'Touché.' Wright smiled grimly. 'I doubt that we need a statement from you for that. You were not there. Were you?' Bunch shook her head. 'That's something, at least. It's not often we have someone attached to so many incidents.'

'It's a knack.' She sat back in the chair, hands grasping the arms in her best imitation of Beatrice's dowager persona. 'Any information on what happened to de Wit?' she said. 'On who killed her, that is?'

Wright shifted guiltily and hid so far as he was able behind his cup.

He doesn't want to tell me. He doesn't trust me. After all we went through. 'Oh, stop it. Gauche does not suit you.'

'I can't divulge any details of that incident,' he said. 'It's a security matter.'

'You don't trust me?'

'I do. But you're a civilian.'

'For God's sake, man. I thought we were friends?' She grinned slyly. 'You never know. I may even be able to help.'

'My career barely survived your last attempt to help me. I cannot tell you how much trouble came down through channels over that.'

'I do not need protecting.'

'It's my being in the Commissioner's line of fire that concerns me.'

'What? Uncle Walter? You should have told me. He's a funny old stick but he's a darling, really. Next time just leave him to me.'

They stared at each other across the tea. The only sound to disturb the moment was an anniversary clock ticking loudly from the mantle – and then a deep sigh from Wright. 'You won't stay away whatever I do or say, will you.'

Bunch shook her head and waved at the statement papers. 'Absolutely not. Now, do you know how she died?'

'She was poisoned.'

'I could see that for myself, man. I saw the poor girl pop her clogs. Sorry, that was a tad insensitive. I watched her die. Right there in my arms. I was a nurse, remember? What kind of poison was it?

'We are still confirming that. But we suspect rat poison. Strychnine to be precise.'

'We have a killer going around poisoning people at random?'

'I sincerely hope not. Especially with strychnine. There's tubs and tins of rat poison on every farm and small holding in the county. It doesn't exactly narrow the field.'

'And Professor Benoir?'

'Killed by a massive dose of a noxious substance in his wine. Coroner has not made a full report yet, but we suspect it to be cyanide. He only needed to take a mouthful. The Dutch girl's dosage of whatever it was that killed her seems to have been slipped into her coffee by person or persons unknown. You'd think she'd've noticed the taste.'

'The coffee there is not the best.' Bunch took a taste of her own tea. 'Reminds me of that old music hall joke. Waiter, this coffee tastes of mud…'

'…it should do. It was only ground a few minutes ago.' They both laughed out of all proportion to the feeble gag. 'I'd almost forgotten how it felt to laugh.' Wright leaned back to stare at the ceiling. 'Joking aside however, the de Wit murder does seem to have been a completely random attack. As far as we can tell she knew no one in the area and nobody knew her.'

'Was she known to the police?'

'In as much as she had applied for asylum. So far as the police are concerned she was a harmless secretary, as far as we are aware.'

'Yet an unknown passer-by dropped rat poison in her coffee?' said Bunch. 'One has to imagine she drew the attention of someone for whatever specific reason.'

'Not that we have been able to ascertain. It isn't the first such case.'

'Is it not?'

He shook his head. 'We've had a number of incidents in this area since Easter that involved foreign nationals. A couple of Polish airmen were ambushed coming out of a pub over at Parham last month because the local LDV patrol thought they were enemy paratroopers.'

'I heard about that. Not very civilised.'

'People are afraid. And to some of the less worldly any European accent just might be Gerry.'

'I suppose it will only get worse,' she said. 'Can we assume the Prof was also bumped off for the sin of not being British?'

Wright nodded and shrugged in the same movement. 'That was our initial assumption.'

'I sense a *but* in the offing.'

'Most of the attacks are spontaneous. In de Wit's case we think our killer was chancing his luck. She happened to be there and she was a simple target. We had a very similar attack on a Jewish refugee in Worthing. Fortunately, in that case the girl had thought her drink smelled off and taken a very small sip to check it. She was unwell but she survived. The wine bottle for the Prof contained a massive dosage. Enough to kill half a regiment. And that bottle was delivered to him personally, if his daughter is to be believed. His was a pre-meditated assassination.'

'By a different killer?'

Wright shrugged. 'We have no idea at this stage.'

'Do you think Cecile is in danger?'

'Perhaps. But she's as safe here as anywhere. She should be especially watchful. You do know we've been told to prepare for internments?'

'Already?'

'Mr Churchill's exact words were to "collar the lot". All enemy aliens are to be rounded up starting here along the south -eastern counties. Refugees and residents included. I suspect it will rouse some patriotic fervour and people may start trying to help things along.'

'That should not affect Cecile. She's French. Half French, at that.'

'And her father was French born and bred,' he replied. 'But they both lived in Berlin for many years. The Super is happy to leave Miss Benoir in your care, but I do have to ask that we be told if she needs to leave the area.'

'We are going to London on Monday. Dodo has an appointment in Harley Street. We shall probably be staying at Thurloe Square overnight.'

'Provided she remains with you and your sister I see no reason to object.' He drained his teacup and stood to leave. 'I have six deaths on my books and now we have enemy aliens to round up.' He waited as if expecting Bunch to comment.

She reached out to pick a cigarette from the lacquered box, lit it without a word and gazed at him through the smoke.

'Drop your statement with PC Botting when you have a moment,' Wright muttered. 'Now I must go.'

'Do keep me informed about Miss de Wit. And Benoir, obviously.'

Wright scratched at the back of his head and then smoothed his hair. 'I will do my best. With luck we shall have fewer incidents of this kind once the internments have been completed. I would hate to think we have an epidemic on our hands.'

'Is this an epidemic – or a single killer?'

He looked at his feet, working his lips as if chewing on his words.

'Oh, don't be coy. This is me, Bunch Courtney the diplomat's daughter. I can be trusted not to blab all over the county you know.'

'I trust you to keep quiet,' he said, 'and to resist going off half-cocked out of some weird notion that you are responsible for anyone and everyone that you know.'

'If you mean, would I help Cissy if I had some information? Then yes. She doesn't have anyone else to fight her corner. No more than the Dutch girl.'

'You do realise you can't take up the cause of every underdog in the county.'

'No. Yes. Perhaps.' She stabbed out her cigarette with enough force to send the ashtray skittering to the table's edge. 'Janine De Wit died right there in front of my eyes. Cecile Benoir is an old friend whose father died at hers. And if there is anything I can do about any of that, then I shall do so without any apologies to you. '

'Nor should you. I admire your sense of justice.' He came close and touched her elbow. 'Nothing could have saved Professor Benoir. Not with the amount of poison he had ingested.' He sighed, dropping his hand away. 'And the same applies to Miss De Wit but she was the third alien death in as many weeks.'

'Second?'

'Third if you include a ballroom dance host who was knifed in an alleyway in Worthing. Though I suppose we shouldn't count him because we arrested the killer on the spot.'

'But he wasn't poisoned. I read about that. I just hadn't realise he was foreign.'

'He wasn't but his name was Sigmund. Apparently died

because his mother had a passion for opera.' Wright said. 'We have no idea if these three are linked. Quite possibly not. Whether it is one killer or three, they are plainly not sane and according to our MO probably not above striking out at anyone they see as a threat. Leave this to the police, Bunch. Please?' He strode out of the door, clicking it shut with typical finality.

Her nickname on his lips disarmed Bunch; not for long it was true, but long enough for her anger at Wright that had built up over the months to melt away. She went to stand at the same window and looked out on the same vista as he had. Much of it was as it had been all her life. Long lawn edged with foaming borders and a view of the South Downs that was quite breathtakingly and achingly familiar.

Sunday 12 May

The Church of St John the Baptist started out as a simple chapel which was replaced by this current building in 1425. Its tower, chancel and aisles were added over several centuries.

Bunch scanned the words without needing to read them – she had been perusing this same booklet all her life. Several stacks of them lived at the end of the Courtney box pew because, sited to the right of the chancel steps, it was one of the few places that remained undisturbed. She knew that the booklet would go on to explain how *many of the carved pews dated from the 16th century,* that *the half-screens around the altar and font were Victorian,* and that *the numerous brass plaques and memorials inlaid into the floor and walls made it a popular stopping place for ramblers and brass rubbing enthusiasts.*

It was like many such missives in similar parishes all across the country.

She glanced around the pew built for large Victorian broods, and at its six occupants, all seated in the accepted social order. Beatrice, Bunch and Dodo in the front, whilst Barty and Cecile, and Dodo's sister-in-law Emma, were relegated to the row behind. *This,* Bunch thought, *is an end of an era. This ludicrous separation from the rest of the congregation. Courtneys have a place but without Perringham House we're simply a page in history, neatly packaged in this ridiculous booklet.*

The small church organ, half-hidden behind the pulpit and choir stalls, slurred then faltered for a moment. Bunch smiled at the choirmaster turning from his singers to glare at his stand-in organist. *One has to feel for Mr Ferris. Half of the choir and his organist have joined up already.*

Bunch flicked at the edge of the booklet and stared vacantly at the chained candle sconces hanging from iron bolts driven deep into beams in the dark recesses of the roof. A wisp of spider thread trailed from one socket, vanishing and reappearing in the light pouring in from the east and south windows. She took a deep breath, inhaling the scent of the church: dust, stone and cut flowers, mixing with the warmth of beeswax and lavender polish and just a hint of sacramental wine. Her mind drifted lightly from wondering when there had last been an attack on webs and dust to what trail she would take when she rode out on Perry after luncheon.

Beatrice's disapproving glare penetrated her musings and she laid the booklet on the seat next to her and stared dutifully toward the pulpit. Sneaking her handkerchief from her bag she mopped discreetly at her neck. The heat wave that had struck in the past week or so had caught them all unaware, but without staff to assist she had yet to break out the summer clothing from the impenetrable maze of attic storage. She noted Dodo fanning herself with another of the booklets. Even Beatrice allowed herself a rapid few flips of the bookmark from her *Common Prayer*, her attention fixed on the people kneeling at the altar rail to receive communion.

Bunch looked across the congregation. There were the usual families, people she had known for years – and toward the rear, a row of unknown faces, three in uniform, one of them Colonel Ralph; the rest were civilian men and women. A scant few considering how many people had to be living at Perringham

House. She studied them intently and guessed that at least some were not English and could not help thinking of Wright's theory that, despite the disparity in poison being used, the killer of de Wit and Professor Benoir could be targeting foreigners just like them.

Is it somebody that lives here in the village? Or one of the hamlets? Cissy and her father lived in Chiltwick and that's only a mile or two west of here. The thought once percolated through her mind was not so very strange. *The man seated right behind me was married to a killer for decades – and never knew it.* She thought back to the Marquis Inn and the ill-disguised venom that the publican Maude Vernon had shown for Janine de Wit, more concerned with having to close the inn on market day than for the dead girl on the dusty carpet.

The empty pews between the strangers and the usual worshippers highlighted a distinct 'us and them' between locals and incomers. She could not help seeing them as such, if for no other reason than they had stolen her home. A glove tapped her on her knee, dragging her attention back to the service.

Beatrice was glowering at her from under the wide brim of her hat. 'Rose,' she whispered. 'I shouldn't still be telling you at your age to set an example.' She nodded toward parishioners shuffling back along the pews whilst the last half-dozen – Colonel Ralph, an airman in a uniform, and four young women – filed up to take their *wafer and sup.*

Bunch watched intently now. Leaning forward to see the last moments of the rite.

A tiny grin lifted the older woman's cheeks. 'Handsome devil isn't he,' Beatrice whispered. 'I do believe your father went up to Oxford with his uncle.'

'Didn't everyone?' Bunch sat back, arms crossing and uncrossing, mortified that her grandmother had mistaken curiosity for something far more significant and worse, chosen one of the very few places where she could not escape her teasing. *My attention can't wander but she can gossip?* 'I was wondering who the women were, as it happens,' she whispered back.

'Of course you were, my dear.'

Ralph and his people were already walking back to their places and the Reverend Day signalled them all to kneel. Bunch could sense Beatrice's inner smirk at her small victory and was never happier for the choir to end their piece, though she knew her grandmother was all too able to crow and pray at the same time. She leaned her elbows on the top of the prayer book ledge, fingers laced in a double fist against the bridge of her nose as she peeked toward the rear of the church.

'Our Father who art in heaven…' Reverend Day began, with the congregation following up in a ragged litany.

She noted three of the civilians remained seated though they mouthed along with the rest.

'Thy kingdom come, Thy will be done…'

One of the women leaned forward, hands clasped much as her own were, and Bunch noted a dark line of beads draping down from her slender hand. *Are they Catholic?* she thought.

'Forgive us our trespasses, as we forgive those who trespass against us…'

Bunch noted the woman lean further forward and the girl next to her slide a surreptitious arm around her shoulders. *Loss and comfort. The universal gesture.*

'But deliver us from evil…'

A nudge at her elbow from Beatrice pulled Bunch's attention back to the altar and she muttered the final words in unison with her fellow parishioners. 'For thine is the kingdom, the power and the glory, for ever and ever. Amen.'

'The grace of our Lord Jesus Christ, and the love of God,' the vicar intoned. 'And the fellowship of the Holy Spirit, be with us all evermore.'

'Amen.'

The organ wheezed into life with the 'Sussex Anthem' and the congregation broke into 'Father Hear the Prayer We Offer'. Bunch sang lustily to forestall her grandmother once again. She was out of the stall and down at the doors almost before the Reverend Day had arranged himself there to speak with his flock as they filed out into the sun.

'What do you think you were doing?' Beatrice demanded as they walked away from the church doors. 'Don't think your fidgeting escaped the vicar. He was giving you the evil eye, if that is possible for a clergyman. I expected it when you were twelve but really... You should know how to behave by now.' She tugged on her gloves and took a firm hold on her prayer book.

'Sorry Granny.' Bunch smiled at her. *At least she's forgotten her commentary on our Colonel Ralph.* 'I wish old Day would write some new sermons. I've heard his 'though shalt not kill' so often I swear I could deliver it for him. And it was possibly not entirely appropriate. I hadn't seen our Reverend Day as an appeaser.'

Beatrice tapped Bunch's wrist. 'Do not change the subject. Being bored is not any excuse for fidgeting through the entire service.'

'You were the one commenting on Ralph's family.'

'Quite beside the point. I realise you are not a pious person but one has to set an example.'

'Sorry Granny. Oh look, there's Emma.' Bunch waved wildly to Emma Tinsley even though she was only standing a few yards away. Tall and slender to the point of skeletal, her expensive wool suit hanging limply from bony shoulders, prematurely greying hair cropped short and crammed beneath a crumpled cloche hat, Emma was as unlike either of her parents as it was possible to be. *Every inch the scholar.* 'Nothing changes, hey Nanki?'

Emma frowned at the nickname gained in the school's disastrous *Mikado* and shook her head. 'Sadly not.'

'Home already?' said Beatrice. 'I thought the year didn't end for another month?'

'It doesn't but our college has been taken over.'

'By whom?'

'By the damned military.' Emma pulled a face. 'You of all people know how *that* can be.' She glowered at the two men deep in discussion with her father. 'Daddy's having trouble with setting up this LDV. He's been appointed local commander but there are those who think they're better qualified.'

'Ken Butcher? Or Dickie Bale?'

'Either or both. Neither one of them advanced beyond the rank of Captain, for God's sake. Damnable nerve.'

'I *do* know how that can be. But your father can look after himself.' Beatrice replied. 'Do excuse me girls. I must go and speak with Doctor Lewis.'

'Of course.' Emma smiled politely and waited for Beatrice to move out of earshot. 'Poor Lewis,' she murmured. 'I gather he's had to close one of the free clinics at the cottage hospital because he no longer has the staff, but your granny doesn't see that as a valid excuse.'

'Granny's always quite the firebrand. See here, I am sorry about your course being suspended, Em. I know how much your research means to you.'

Emma looked around the crowded pathway between church and lychgate and sighed. 'It's annoying, but I hold a Chair so I shall start up again after this war.' She glanced irritably at her watch. 'I do wish Daddy would buck up. I don't want to dawdle here all morning while that awful man Bale rants on and on.'

Bunch took a closer look at the man now talking with Barty. His stature was not small, she realised, so much as shrunken. As if he were the shell of a far larger man collapsed in on himself. Bale was a nodding acquaintance – he was not one of her parent's circle. From choice, she gathered. She had never seen him at a church service before today, however, so his presence had her curious.

'Vile man,' Emma said. 'Fancies himself quite the academic. Even claims to have a doctorate though I've no idea where from. He's never ever held a Chair to my knowledge. I wish Daddy would just tell him his fortune and be done with it. I've got a mass of things to do.' She laughed sharply. 'Not college work, sadly.'

'No way you can carry on your research without the students?'

'It's not only a lack of students. Half of our faculty has been called up or co-opted into various ministries, so I think a suspension of academic pursuits was rather inevitable until all this is done.' Emma waved toward the coast, a gesture Bunch had noted many people use of late. She smiled a quiet satisfaction. 'For now I shall be happy to have a break. I think Dodo and Father could do with my help.'

'You are home for the duration?'

'Perhaps.' Emma rubbed at the tip of her nose. 'I've had a few offers of work in various Government departments, so we shall see. I'm not the only pigeon come home to roost, I notice.' She gestured toward Cecile, just visible in the lee of the ancient yews in oldest part of the churchyard. How did young Cissy get here?'

Bunch watched their mutual friend, waving arms wildly in what seemed to be a heated discussion, though Bunch could not see with whom. A clutch of worshippers blocked her view for a moment and when they cleared away Cecile was subdued, standing with her arms now wrapped around herself, still talking to some half-hidden figure. 'A long story, Em,' she said. 'Hasn't Dodo caught you up on that?'

'I'm sure she doesn't know it all.'

'Can't upset the old thing in her condition.'

'I'm not fooled by that fragile English-rose facade.' She nudged Bunch's arm and grinned. 'Your sister is as tough as old boots. All of you Courtneys are.'

'Perhaps. It comes of long practice, you know. Look here Em, you're taller than me. Can you see who Cissy it talking to?'

'It's that chap from Perringham House. Ralph is it?' Emma craned her long neck to see over the congregation still drifting away from the church doors. 'Yes, it's him. Daddy's had him over for lunch a couple of times.'

'Colonel Ralph? Are he and Barty connected?'

'Couldn't tell you, sweetness. Something to do with the LDV, I expect. He's rather a dish, though.' She brayed amusement at Bunch's expression. 'I know people think I'm a dried-up old blue spinster but I'm not blind.'

'Looks belie the man,' Bunch replied. 'He's a nightmare but since he's here I do need to speak with him. Excuse me, will you?' Bunch wove rapidly between the gossiping parishioners in time to see Cecile wandering through the tombstones, pausing to read an inscription – and completely alone. Bunch glanced around her, puzzled. The churchyard was bounded on that side by a wall topped by an iron railing fence dividing it from the village school. *Curious,* she thought. *None of my business who Cissy talks with, of course, but she seems a tad upset.*

She spotted Colonel Ralph strolling along the gravel pathway that circled the church itself. *Nonchalant* was the word that sprang to her mind. *Cool customer.* Bunch moved toward him cutting across his path at the corner of the wall. 'Mr Ralph,' she cooed, 'how lovely to see you again. Your predecessor never managed to attend our services here so top marks"

'Miss Courtney.' He inclined his head, that fringe swinging loose from its Brylcreamed mooring. 'I don't get to a church communion often. Tend to have our own padres so no need, as a rule, but it seemed the thing to do this morning.'

'Why today in particular?'

'I've a few civvies on our books who wanted to attend a service here in the village. I think they find our padre a little – shall we call him *forthright*? Military to his eyeteeth. Not always suitable for young ladies. Thought I might as well run them across. Apart from anything else, I hoped I might run into you.' He gazed at her, rocking on his heels with hands clasped behind his back.

'Did you.'

'Yes, I rather felt we got off on a wrong foot. Thought perhaps I could take you to dinner?'

'I don't know. I…' Bunch tilted her head and returned his gaze without blinking. 'Have you cleared my woodland yet?'

'On my list, I assure you. Soon as we've seen this round of trainees off and away.'

'You train who to do what, exactly?'

'I teach eager young minds to be better,' he replied. His tone remained jovial and his smile unstinting, only his eyes gave any hint that she might have walked into military quick-sands.

She laughed. 'Understood. Not for public comment. But have no fear – I am the daughter of a diplomat.'

'You are,' he agreed. 'And the offer of dinner remains open. I am sure there must be a good hostelry in the district or we could take that jaunt up to Town.' He looked to right and left like a stage comic and leaned in to add, 'I have petrol, you know.'

'I am sure you do.' She glanced back toward Cecile, now

standing with Emma on a rapidly thinning lychgate path. 'You've asked Cissy already?'

'Beg pardon?' he looked in the direction that she was gesturing. 'Asked who what?'

'Never mind.' Bunch knew when she was being fobbed off and she was disappointed. She had assumed this Colonel Ralph might be a gentleman. He had the pedigree. She had checked him out in Debrett's. *Which told me that you are the Honourable Everett Bertram Percival Ralph,* she thought. *Colonel, Scots Guards, with a list of military honours long enough to choke a goat. And if Emma Tinsley says you were speaking with Cissy, then you, Colonel Ralph, are also a lying little toe-rag.* She glanced once more at Cecile. *But why lie at all? That is the burning question.*

~~~

Lunch was a quiet affair with Beatrice valiantly attempting polite conversation against fairly heavy odds. Cecile had barely uttered a dozen words since returning from the Sunday service. Bunch was little better, still turning over the morning's events and wondering what she should be asking, if anything. It was obvious that Cecile was deeply troubled by something the *charming* Colonel Ralph had conveyed and Bunch was furious with him for it.

He was as different from the base's previous CO's brash militarism as it was possible to be, and in theory should have been so much easier to deal with. Kravitz had been openly arrogant and totally disdainful of social nicety but she could at least put that down to cultural difference. She and Ralph shared similar backgrounds and, Bunch assumed, similar values – but therein lay the problem. The man was charming and amiable – and a consummate liar. Her father would have considered him the perfect diplomat. There was no doubt in her mind that Ralph's machinations were somehow at the centre of Cecile's current distraction.

She watched Cecile toying with the grilled trout on her plate barely aware of the morsels that managed to find their way into her mouth. 'Fancy going for a hack?' she said. 'Getting out in the fresh air will do you so much good.'

'No thank you.' Cecile placed her cutlery neatly across her plate. 'It's this heat. I have the most dreadful headache. But you're right. Some fresh air might do me good. I think I shall go and sit in the garden and read.'

'I can come with—'

'Rose dear. I think Cecile is looking for a little peace.'

'There are things I need to think over and best done alone.' Cecile came to stand by Bunch's chair to rest a hand on her shoulder. 'I hope you understand?'

'Yes of course.' Watching Cecile walk out and carefully close the door behind her, Bunch was perplexed. 'Was it an error of judgement asking her here, Granny?'

'No dear. It was all that a friend could or would do. Your error, if you made one, may be in expecting that your act of kindness was all that she required. Now, if you don't mind, I am also going to leave you. I have had a rather hectic week and I am going to sit and lose myself in a book in the quiet of my room. I know you are going riding so you won't miss me.'

'Yes, do go and rest. You must be careful Granny. You've been doing too much.'

'It will be easier now. We have the last of the evacuees moved on to new destinations. Not a moment too soon. Now you run along and have a good ride.'

'I shall.'

~~~

Changed into her riding outfit, Bunch wandered into the yard to find Pat and Kate sweeping out. 'What are you two doing here? It's Sunday, you know.'

'We're on milking today. Hello Rog.' Kate bent to scratch

the dog's back and he began wagging his entire body, from tip to of nose to tail, in that way that Labradors can, until he flopped onto his side. 'Enough now, you daft old thing.' She propped her broom against the wall and fished a pack of tobacco and papers from her breast pocket. 'Those two little Jerseys are super, you know. Though one of them seems to be a bit tetchy today. I think she may be about to drop her calf. Today or possibly tomorrow. Thought I'd tidy up here whilst I keep an eye on her. The rest of the girls are moving furniture into next door.'

'Mrs Haynes was happy to empty out her son's possessions?' Tied cottages are never left empty as a general rule, especially with evacuee families looking for billets, but it seemed poor form to add to the older Haynes's troubles. 'I don't think Mr Parsons gave them much choice,' said Kate. 'I don't think he's very charitable toward that family.'

'Is he not? That's rather sad.' Bunch nodded at the slender cigarette taking shape between Kate's fingers. 'Are you reduced to those things?' She took out her case and offered a tailor-made.

'I'm fine.' Kate licked her cigarette paper and patted it down. She handed it on to Pat and started another. 'We're *poor* Land Girls and this saves us a lot of money. I also find rolling them quite satisfying.' She struck a match and all three women, in defiance of superstition, leaned in to light-up.

'Perry is all saddled up.' Pat waved her skinny smoke toward the stable building. 'Left him inside because it got a bit warm to stand him out in the yard. Which way are you going?'

'Not far. Since we had the pony cart renovated the old chap has been worked rather hard. I was going to go up to the edge of Hascombe and along the top of the coombe but I can hear them shooting over that way.'

'I gather the Lower Nitch is still full of mines,' said Kate. 'I should avoid Chiltwick as well.'

'Why?'

'The churn lorry driver told me there was a fire at the Tea Rooms when he came through early today.'

'The poor Miss Manns. Perhaps I *should* go over that way and see what can be done for them. Besides, it's flat terrain for the old boy.' She crossed to where Pat had led Perry out and paused for a moment to offer the fell pony a quarter of apple she had filched from Cook on her way out. 'Sorry boy. No sugar.' She scrubbed her knuckles affectionately against the animal's forehead and gathered his reins in her left hand as she reached her left foot up into the stirrup. Roger whined and danced a few awkward steps toward the yard entrance as she swung herself into the saddle. Bunch snapped her fingers and pointed for him to sit. 'Not today Rog. It's a bit too far for you. Keep him here, will you Kate. I hope you are getting some rest, girls.'

'We shall,' Kate replied. 'Have a good ride, Boss.'

Bunch winced but said nothing. Since the 'girls' had been to see Bogart in *Invisible Stripes,* she had acquired this new title with mixed feelings. It was a sign of affection, she did not doubt, but wondered what Granny would say if or when she heard it

~~~

She ambled Perry across the fields. Though he had not been out the previous day he was putting in a lot of trips with the cart and she had no wish to overwork him. He seemed eager enough however, even breaking into a slow trot across the meadow that ran along the side of the brook.

Bunch noted the tang of smoke in the air some minutes before she reached Chiltwick. The fire at the Jenny Wren that Kate had spoken of was quite obvious. Black-smoke stains ran up from the front door to the eaves and one of the front windows was charred. As far as she could see the rest of the building seemed largely intact other than the flower beds to side and front, which had been trampled. *By the fire brigade,* Bunch assumed.

Bunch dismounted, tethering Perry to the railing well away from the gardens and went to inspect the damage at closer quarters. The hamlet was not a busy one though the Tea Rooms usually remained open until four. Voices drifted across to her from the Anchor Inn. Otherwise the quiet was a little ominous. When an event such as a fire occurred in such a place she would have expected to find it abuzz with people. *But then,* she realised, *if this place was ablaze in the early hours they've had ample time to talk it out.*

She looked along what passed for a high street, which on that side consisted of a small terrace of four cottages and a larger detached house set back behind an unkempt hedge; where something, or someone, moved through the shrubbage, though she could not make out who it might be. A few seconds later she heard a door slam.

The cafe claimed her attention once again and she strode down the path to knock on the door. No reply. She tried again, twice, but nobody came to answer her. She noted that the garage doors were open and saw the front of the Mann's car.

'Somebody is in,' she muttered. Venturing around the side of the shop she cupped her hands against the window and peered into the kitchen.

'Hello?' She called. 'Miss Mann? Hello? It's Miss Courtney. I've come to see if you are all right?'

The door opened a crack and dark eyes in a pale face regarded her suspiciously. 'Good afternoon, Miss Courtney.'

'I thought I'd call to see you were unharmed.'

Hilda, the younger Miss Mann, opened the door more fully. As Bunch stepped forward Hilda barred the way. Polite yet firm. 'I'm not injured' she said. 'Enid has been kept at the cottage hospital, however.'

'Nothing serious I hope?'

'Smoke on her chest, the doctor said. She has a heart condition, you know. I'm only here to fetch what she needs and then I shall be back there.'

'I am sorry.' Bunch knew she was being inadequate but the lack of invitation to enter threw her slightly. 'Can I be of any help?'

'There is very little that can be done in these circumstances but thank you, Miss Courtney. Your offer is appreciated. I shall be collecting Enid very shortly and then we're going to our cousin's house in Winchester. He has a small restaurant there and he's said he will welcome our help.' She looked around her and frowned. 'We simply cannot stay here.'

Bunch stared up at the building. 'Is the place very damaged?' she asked.

'We've no electricity,' she replied. 'And everything is either soaking wet or black with soot. Or both.'

'But repairable?'

'The shop? Perhaps. But…' She glanced at the houses next door. 'With all that has gone on we don't feel safe here.' Hilda winced at a shout from somewhere along the row. 'Murders and fires and all those comings and goings at Perringham.' She smiled apologetically. 'Not your fault, of course, but we have all kinds of vehicles coming and going at all hours along this street. And now this.'

'I suspect it will be worse before it's better. Can we talk indoors?' Bunch murmured.

'I'm sorry, where are my manners? Do come in – but mind yourself. The soot stains terribly.'

The old lady was not exaggerating. Every surface seemed to be covered in a greasy black film and the air was thick with fumes that caught at the back of Bunch's throat and stung her eyes.

Hilda covered two chair seats with newspaper and gestured Bunch to be seated. 'I can't offer you any refreshments. I'm sorry.'

'I quite understand, Miss Mann. I came to offer you help, not the other way around.'

'Thank you. That means a great deal to me and to my sister.' Her features quivered and already pink-rimmed eyes watered, fat tears dribbling unnoticed down the papery cheek. 'It has been terrible, these past few weeks. It all started to become difficult after Professor Benoir passed away. He lived just along the Green Lane, you know.' She waved vaguely toward the road that led to next village.

'Yes, I know. I invited Miss Benoir to stay with me at the Dower.'

'Did you now?' Hilda nodded. 'You were always a kind child. She's best away from here with all the goings on.'

'Do tell.'

'Somebody started leaving the most dreadful messages daubed on our door.'

'About what?'

'Mostly about our parents not born here. In England I mean, not Chiltwick. Though God alone knows that would be crime enough for some of them. It was our mother's mother. Father's side are as English as the rest of them.'

'Some of the people here can be a little … parochial.'

The old lady managed a vestigial smile. 'I think they can, Miss.' She heaved a sigh at the stinking carnage. 'This is the world we are living in now. Forty years we've lived in Chiltwick. Most of it in harmony and now this.' She fixed Bunch with a scowl. 'It was not an accident. Somebody did this to us. Some person that we know.'

'They set a fire whilst you slept?'

'After they wrote terrible things on the door. I scrubbed it off before the firemen had even left. Such an evil thing to do.' She paused, steeling her features against further tears. 'We've done nothing to them. Evil, evil souls.'

Bunch covered the old lady's rheumatic hands with one of her own. 'I saw a girl die very recently from this self-same ignorance. I am so sorry.'

'That girl over Storrington way. I heard you were there. Was she German?'

'Dutch.'

'Grandmother was Polish. My mother was born here in England, as were my sister and myself, but that doesn't matter to someone. It was pure coincidence that we had Polish pilots several times over the past weeks.'

'Why did they come here? The pilots I mean.'

Hilda frowned and then shook her head. 'No idea. We had no family connections that I could tell. Somebody spread those rumours a little further afield.'

'You don't think it was the Professor?'

Hilda looked puzzled but shook her head. 'No. He sat with them on at least one occasion but he didn't seem to know them. Things like that give idle tongues an added wag but I cannot see that it would make people do something like this.'

'People liked him?'

'I wouldn't go that far. I hate to speak ill of the dead, naturally, but he wasn't a very nice man. He did have an abrasive way with him and he did have that odd accent.'

'He was French.'

'He was?' She shrugged. 'It did not sound quite right to me but then it's a few years since Enid and I went to Paris. Father insisted we learn to cook at the very best schools.' Her brow furrowed. 'Miss Benoir doesn't sound very French either. '

'Who can say what conclusions people will draw.' Bunch

frowned. Parsons had been right after all. Guilt by association was a genuine fear. 'Do you know who it was?'

'Nothing I could say in court. There are always people who talk brave, but talk is cheap.'

'Chiltwick is not so big that you have a wide choice.' Bunch leaned forward smiling, hoping to wheedle a name from Hilda one way or another.

Hilda shook her head. 'It's only a feeling and I would rather not say anything because you know I could so easily be wrong.' She looked around her and sighed. 'We have loved it here.'

'If you have suspicions you should still tell the police. I shall have words with a few people.'

'You're very kind, Miss Courtney, but there's no need. I've told PC Botting as much as I'm willing.' She shook her head. 'No, I have to be honest with you at least. Enid and I've been thinking of retiring for some while. We have insurance for the stock and some savings put by, so perhaps this is a blessing in disguise. Given us the push we needed to retire whilst we can.' She eased herself to her feet. 'We shall settle in with our cousin and come back another day to organise the clearing of the premises.'

'At least let me send you some help with that. It won't be an easy job alone.'

'Thank you. I would appreciate that.' She went to stand in the doorway and looked toward the neighbouring house just visible through the hedge that neglect had turned into a line of trees. She smiled suddenly, a hint of mischief touching her voice. 'Chiltwick will miss us and our shop more than we shall miss Chiltwick.'

'Of that I have no doubt. Here, this is my card with my number. Call me when you need some help. Oh … just remembered I shall be out until Wednesday. I shall leave orders to give you every assistance. If you are quite sure there is nothing I can do now?'

'No thank you. We still have our car and enough fuel for the drive to Winchester.'

'Then I shall get on. Good bye, Miss Mann. My regards to your sister.' On impulse she engulfed the old lady in a bear hug, patting her back like a mother nursing a child. She held the pose for a long moment before she stepped back a pace, still holding Hilda by the shoulders. 'I shall miss your Struesel.'

'I shall send a recipe to Mrs Westgate.'

Bunch nodded. 'Cook will like that. And I do mean it when I say anything I can do you only need ask.'

'You are still a kind child.' Hilda patted her cheek and then pushed her gently toward the door. 'Goodbye. Miss Courtney.'

The old woman closed the door softly, leaving Bunch outside on the step.

~~~

Bunch rode away from the Jenny Wren feeling deeply disturbed by what Hilda Mann had inferred. The local police doubtless knew that the fire had taken place, but she wondered if the constables would ever think that this was an attack on the Manns for their distant heritage. She doubted most even realised they were not the genteel English ladies that they appeared to be – and indeed were, in Bunch's estimation.

She would have needed to be blind now not to notice how feelings against foreigners were running high. The country was at war once again and most people had cause to remember the Great War all too well. Either from personal memory or the loss of fathers, uncles, brothers and neighbours. There could hardly be a soul who had not been touched by the old conflict in some way.

The papers had not mentioned attacks on alien nationals but Bunch had no doubt that this was not a lack of news but a deliberate cap placed on such things by the government to calm the public. Still, it did not stop people talking among themselves and she could see how an obvious incomer like Janine de Wit could be targeted. She could imagine how Professor Benoir might be viewed by the uninformed if his long-standing connections with Berlin were to become generally known. But the Miss Manns. That took a very particular knowledge of who they were, and an especially rampant xenophobia to attack two old ladies who had lived here all their lives. If the children of immigrants were to be targeted then half the population was at risk.

Three crimes against people, that Bunch was aware of, who had no apparent links with each other, and in such a small area, could not be co-incidence. That two of those attacks required local knowledge made it very clear to her that the culprit was someone who lived in the vicinity.

The air was sultry with a threat of storm. Thick and heavy so that every movement brought on a sweat. She left the road and followed the headland at a slow pace, skirting a field of wheat undulating under the force of a rising breeze; ox daisies and scarlet poppies nodding at each other across the waves. The hedge that divided one field from the next was higher than usual and a little unkempt without its usual winter cut. The field's head, awash with may blossom with its sickly-sweet odour of decay made stronger in the leaden air, was like a portent of things to come. The frith beneath it was a mass of campion, buttercups and cow parsley, which added fresh green pungency beneath Perry's hooves. All things so familiar to Bunch that she barely noticed them.

She watched the storm clouds boiling in from the south turning a burnished grey of old steel in the sun, and heard the first rumble of thunder. She nudged Perry into a brisker pace. Her hat and riding jacket would ward off a light shower but the signs were for a real downpour – and there was almost a mile to go. She reined in to open a gate from one field to the next and paused to watch the landscape being visibly devoured by cloud-shadow on the stiffening south-westerly. As she closed the gate to move on she spotted a flicker of colour along the headland at a tangent from her own route.

There were many strangers wandering the land recently and her run-in with stock-thieves a few months ago made her cautious. It was a walker, a woman, who had climbed the style from the Lower Nitch. The Lower Nitch that Ralph had insisted was too dangerous to enter.

The woman looked back, seemingly shielding her eyes to gaze along the path she had taken. Bunch made out a second figure standing at the gateway where the woodland met the road. That person was waving his arms and began to climb the gate when a third figure appeared. Even at this distance Bunch could see the violence with which the man was pulled from the gate. She watched the drama in silence, ignoring fat drops of warm rain that had begun to fall.

The men still tussled by the gate and though the woman was still plainly being hailed by one of the men, it was equally certain she did not want to respond. She was running now, labouring up the slope, stumbling through the long grass and flowers. Bunch could see her red skirt and white blouse quite clearly. She had seen that same outfit just a few hours before worn by Cecile Benoir.

Over your headache, then? What have you been up to, mademoiselle? Cecile was moving fast, glancing back every few moments though the men had vanished from view.

The rain began to fall in earnest, sending up a sharp waft of ozone as parched clay and chalk drank the water in. Bunch nudged Perry across the field to intercept Cecile. 'What brings you out here?'

'I needed to walk.' Cecile waved at the fields around her. 'I wanted some air but I hadn't thought it would rain.' She gazed up at Bunch with wide eyes from under the brim of her neat straw hat, which had already begun to droop.

'I should keep out of there.' Bunch waved toward the Nitch. 'Until we get the all clear from Ralph.' She smiled without humour. 'You probably know that. Who was that calling you just then?'

Cecile had the grace to look guilty and she could not prevent a rapid double-take between Bunch and back along the way she had come. She managed to both shake and nod her head at the same time. 'No idea. He sounded angry so I did not stop.'

'He seemed to know you.'

'Rose... Bunch please, I...' A stage director could not have timed *The Tempest* more effectively as a booming of thunder vibrated around them. The two women were hit by a sudden deluge.

Cecile's hat now hung pathetically over one eye. 'All I can do is ask you to trust me. Please?'

They stared at each other, one willing the other to believe in her on trust, the other willing herself not to believe the apparent facts. *But we are friends. That has to count for something.* 'Bit of a squeeze but do you want a ride home?' Bunch said.

'Yes ... please.' Cecile looked helplessly at the hand Bunch held out, plainly unsure of what to do.

Bunch kicked free of the left stirrup for Cecile to step into and leaned down with her right hand to grasp her friend by the forearm, and Cecile slid onto Perry's withers ahead of her. The rain was falling harder and faster, stinging bare flesh and drowning out all other sound. 'Hold on tight,' Bunch called and urged the fell pony into a rapid trot home.

~~~

Perry clattered into the stable block where they dismounted, and Bunch started to unsaddle him, to lead him into his box, while Cecile lurked in the passageway, her arms wrapped around herself. 'Rose,' she began, 'I wanted to tell—'

'You should go and get dry.' Bunch avoided looking at her as she finished unsaddling the pony and began to scoop up handfuls of straw to rub the worst of the water from his coat. She felt a rush of genuine anger toward Cecile. The woman had clearly fibbed about going for a rest. What she had been doing anywhere near the wood was a mystery but given the circumspect chat with Ralph earlier, Bunch knew it had to be linked to that irritating man.

Two and two don't always add up to four but in this case? I'd lay odds on it. She grunted a wry amusement at herself and wished she was as certain on that score as she was trying to tell herself. *There could be any amount of reasons for her being there. Good ones. And what she does is none of my damned business – but she lied to me.* The argument with her own logic made her all the more annoyed.

Cecile had not moved, plainly wanting to talk. 'It will dry. I don't have too many things left to wear,' she said. 'We left so much behind, one way and another.'

'Good thing we are going up to Town tomorrow.' Bunch carried on rubbing at Perry's flank, her back turned on Cecile so that she sensed rather than heard her leave. She wasn't sure why she had not wanted to hear what her friend had to say, especially when Cecile so plainly wanted to spill the beans. But after the morning's oddness and now this sneaking around near the woods that were out of bounds, she needed to have this conversation when she felt calmer. When the aura of betrayal was tempered with a little common sense.

Bunch bent to brush out Perry's feathery legs and paused at a swelling in the hind fetlock. The joint was hot and the animal flinched as she gave the leg an experimental grasp. 'Damnation.'

'Trouble Boss?' Pat asked from the doorway. 'Is the old boy all right?'

'Slight sprain,' Bunch replied. 'At least I hope it's just that. My fault entirely. We've been working him too hard. Damn and blast.' She got to her feet and patted Perry's haunch. 'I'm sorry old chap. I should know better. Bad form.'

'Should I fetch Sam Burse?'

'Yes please. Has it stopped raining?'

'Yes, it stopped as quick as it started. Summer storms in May.'

'Okay. Get the hose out in the yard for me and tell Burse to come and take a peek when he has finished the hay turning.'

'Yes, Boss.'

Leading Perry back out into the yard, Bunch cursed under her breath at the obvious favouring of the limb. Once she had him tethered she stood playing the hose over the hoof and joints to take out the heat. She knew Burse would only recommend the same treatment. Two of the grooms that worked at Perringham had joined up months ago and Burse was the only horseman remaining, other than Parsons, and she had no intention of inviting a lecture from the old steward. She felt quite guilty enough already about the breakdown of her relationship with such a loyal man.

She was still cooling the injury when Edward Courtney sauntered into the yard, preceded by Roger.

'Daddy!' The hose fell from her hands to jump and twist on the cobbles like a beached eel and she ran forward to greet him.

'Steady Rose.' He returned her hug, embracing his eldest child with unusual affection, only standing her away to turn off the tap as the hosepipe twisted itself onto the two of them.

'We didn't know when you would be home.'

'No, it was sudden – and quiet.' He glanced around and moved her into shadows. 'We received a summons from

Winnie a fortnight ago. He knew what was coming and he wanted me back before the drawbridge went up.' A bucket clattered somewhere between them and the farm buildings and he made a small dismissive gesture with one finger 'We can talk about that later.'

'Walls have ears?' Bunch nodded understanding. 'Is Mummy here?'

'Of course. She wants to see Daphne. Her first grandchild is an unexpected pleasure. We'd both begun to think it was never going to happen.'

'Dodo always comes up with the goods.'

Edward eyed her suspiciously, sensing his daughter's mood. 'Don't spoil the occasion, Rose. This is a reason to celebrate for all of us. Your mother and I want to see both of our girls thrive. She is so excited about her grandchild. As am I. We would have been home before Easter if we could have managed it.'

'Duty first. Always the diplomats,' said Bunch.

'Now more than ever.' He sighed. 'Things are very tense all across the Far Eastern territories.'

'Japan?'

He nodded. 'Enough of that. What's happening here?' He waved at Perry steaming gently in the warm sun, which had returned as quickly as it had gone.

'Don't. I was so stupid giving Cissy a seat when the poor old boy has been working all week.'

'And now you're grounded? Simple answer is to get another horse.'

'Get rid of Perry? Never. He's just gone a little lame. You can't possibly think—'

'Calm down, daughter dear. Allow me to rephrase that. We need an additional horse. Robbo is past his best, too. He's not up to being a work horse even if he fitted into the shafts of that toy cart. But we do need something a little larger than your pony. I'm sure there must be a cob or two going for a good price. So many people are getting rid of their non-breeds.'

'Something harness broken?'

'Nothing changes with my little Rose does it. Every conversation begins and ends with a horse.' He kissed her gently on the forehead. 'We shall sort it out. Meanwhile get the old chap settled and come and change for dinner. You mother has got Cook on course for a dinner party.'

'Has she not heard about rationing?'

'Cook claims she can do it, and it's only family. Now get a wiggle on. Your mother is looking forward to seeing you, but preferably less redolent of the stable yard.'

~~~

Beatrice set down her napkin beside her plate and at the signal her family came subtly to attention. 'I had got quite used to quiet dinners when it was just Nanny and me, but it is good to have you all here, if only for a day or two.'

'Just tonight I'm afraid Mother. I have to be back in Town tomorrow.' Edward Courtney raised a hand to silence her. 'Plenty of time to go over things in the morning. For tonight we should enjoy each other's company.'

Before another kind of storm, Bunch thought. *Though no-one is going to be so uncivilised as to mention it.*

'Quite so, Edward. And in view of that perhaps we ladies should forgo withdrawing and merely adjourn *en masse?* Knapp, we shall all take coffee in the drawing room.' Beatrice led the way without allowing a reply.

'So nice to have everyone together.' Dodo sat next to her mother and slipped her hand under Theadora's arm. 'I am so glad to have you and Daddy home.'

'We go where the Foreign Office sends us.' Theadora patted her daughter's hand as she leaned forward to pick a cigarette from the box, so that the contact was broken. 'Nice to be home when the sun is shining but I shan't be here for long. I shall move back into Thurloe Square, obviously. There simply isn't room for us all here and I always have such a lot to catch up on in Town.' She simpered at her youngest daughter. 'I was hoping perhaps you would come with me?'

'To London?' Dodo stroked her bump and laughed without humour. 'I have too much to do at Banyards. I'm a farmer now.' She beamed at her mother.

'Barty, can't you deal with it?' Theadora slotted the cigarette into the holder and held it to her mouth for her husband to light.

'Don't drag poor Barty into things.' Edward glanced at him and cocked one eyebrow in unspoken exasperation. 'This is simply not the time to drag our daughter into the social treadmill.' Edward snapped the lighter and held it for her, exchanging glances along the tenuous link. 'I can't believe you even suggested it.'

'Darling, you know I must do the rounds.' Theadora's voice took on a wheedling tone. 'And don't you think it might be a good idea for Daphne to be having a little fun before the baby arrives? With things as they are.'

'It would be rather nice for us all to have some fun. But London trains are not the best place for her at this moment.'

'Edward darling. We've just come all the way from Singapore without so much as a hair out of place. It's the London line I want to take her on, not the Orient Express.'

'Hardly the same,' Edward muttered. 'But still not safe.'

'Don't be silly dear. We're going to London shopping in any case so what would a longer stay hurt?'

A look passed between the two that confused Bunch totally. It bordered on affectionate, which was outside of their natural state. She wondered what her mother might have to do that was so important. Nor that it could not be completed by whisking Dodo off to dance the nights away.

Edward appeared oblivious to the rest of the room, his whole attention focussing on his wife as he held her hand and her gaze.

'Hardly the same thing, Thea old girl,' Barty agreed. 'Edward is quite correct. Even if the route wasn't stiff with troops, which it is, a girl in Daphne's condition can't go gadding about the place. It's a hair-brain scheme and I won't hear of it.'

'I won't keep her long. A few weeks at most. I simply can't wait to take her visiting.'

'Mummy, everybody who can is leaving Town,' said Dodo.

'Then it might just be days.'

'No, my darling. London is not the place for either of you to live right now. We talked about this.'

An awkward pause hung over the assembly before Theadora smiled brightly, doing her utmost to skate over the rebuff, and turned a dazzling gaze onto Cecile. 'We are being terribly rude and leaving you out of the conversation. I was so sorry to hear about your father.'

'Thank you. It was a shock but I am getting over it.'

'You have the funeral arranged?'

Cecile shook her head. 'The Coroner will not allow it. Perhaps soon.'

'That must be distressing for you.'

'Yes. If it were not for Bunch I don't know how I would have coped.'

'Nonsense.' Bunch flushed deep pink. All of the suspicions that she had entertained over the course of the day felt like a betrayal, and for once in her life she wasn't sure what to think or say.

'Rose knows her duty.' Beatrice's face was a mask of

composure that Bunch could only envy. 'Now, Edward. You were telling us about internments?'

'Not much more to say. I haven't read all of the papers and you know there is only so much I can say, but Churchill wants enemy aliens rounded up, starting here in the south east and effective as of now.'

'Simple as that?'

'Hardly.' He exchanged glances with Barty. 'It's just the start and it will not be fair on a great many people who have already lost a great deal.'

'Can't be helped.' Barty took a gulp of whisky and frowned into the glass. 'Given the awful incidents that have occurred on our doorstep these past few days, one might say it is for their protection.'

'Wright said something of the sort,' Bunch muttered.

'Who?'

Dodo put her hand to her mouth to hide a smirk. 'Chief Inspector Wright. Bunch's policeman chappy.'

'He's not my chap.'

'Is too.'

'Is not.'

'Girls.'

'Sorry Granny.' Bunch went to fetch herself a large scotch and sat down heavily next to Cecile. 'Chief Inspector Wright was in charge of the investigation into Johnny's death. And he's cropped up again with regard to the Dutch girl that was killed last week. Bound to really, considering how few senior detectives they have left.'

'He questioned me over my father's death,' Cecile added. 'It was to be expected. A good man, I think. Most efficient.'

'Going to have even more on his plate with internments,' said Barty. 'I think the LDV should be called in.'

'Who are they?'

'Local Defence Volunteers, Thea. Finally had the okay from Whitehall last week. Silly name, sounds far too amateur, but we were outvoted on that one for now. I'm told it'll be announced officially this week and our chaps can start training soon.'

'I cannot imagine the arrest of citizens being placed in the hands of local men,' Edward replied. 'Rather open to misuse.'

'Not at all. Barty puffed his cigar thoughtfully, his free hand clasping his lapel, and Bunch glimpsed a tiny piece of the old Major. 'Got a squad of good lads ready and waiting, with a few notable exceptions.'

'Some of the old Lambs?' Bunch said.

Barty stared at her, plainly perplexed.

'I saw you talking with Dickie Bale after morning service. Emma said there were some questions about chain of command?'

'No questions,' Barty replied. 'None at all. Man's a lunatic thinking that they'd allow a captain to be in charge when they have a full major in the village. He's gone off in a huff. Just as well. Man's not fit.'

'There's a medical?' Dodo said.

'No, my dear. But there are limits, you know. The man's as mad as a hatter.'

'Well it's comforting to know that you have it under control.' Bunch said. 'Have you many men under your command?'

'Twenty so far. But we have many more expressing interest.' Barty beamed at the prospect of a full platoon. 'Most of them were trained up in the last lot so we shan't be caught napping.'

'I shall be up in Whitehall tomorrow and I shall try and find out. But I wouldn't be too eager. I rather think the police will be preferred for maintaining confidence. You were a magistrate long enough, Barty. The army are who the public expect to make arrests.'

'Hmph, you may be right.'

Dodo yawned and stretched. 'I am sorry to be a killjoy but I really must go home and sleep. We have a long trip tomorrow.'

'I can give you all a ride in,' said Edward. 'I think it would be better for Dodo, anyway. The Ministry is providing me with a car and my driver is collecting me at nine sharp.'

Theadora clasped her hands together. 'Oh yes, I can go with you to the appointment.'

'Cecile and I could take the train,' Bunch said. 'It will be too crowded with all of us in the same jalopy. We could shop for Cecile's clothes and then catch up with you at Fortnum's for tea?'

'Heaven's, my dear,' Beatrice said. 'Are you certain? Constance Frain went last Thursday and said it was absolute hell. Not a spare seat to be had. Even in first class.'

'I have it on reliable authority that there will be a lot of troop movements expected over the next few weeks,' Edward said. 'All leave has been cancelled so the trains will be packed with troops being called back to their bases. It honestly would be better to come with us in the car.'

The thought of a two-hour drive crammed in cheek by jowl no matter how large the seat was, held no appeal for Bunch, much as a trip up to Town was something she had been looking forward to. And if she were honest, there were a lot of matters at Perringham that needing her attention.

'We can take Cecile shopping if you would rather.' Theadora pouted, lowering her chin and eyeing her eldest daughter. 'I had rather been looking forward to a lovely night in with my girls before I'd left for Washington.'

'Washington?' Bunch glanced at her father, who shook his head minutely.

Theadora sighed. 'Not any more. It seems your Father can't go, so neither can I. But never mind. I can still have some time with my girls and I have a delightful soiree planned. A few select friends, nothing fast. I called the McHendrys and they have promised me that Campbell is in town. He's stationed at an airfield—' She paused. 'I suppose one shouldn't say where, should one. It's not far out so he can get in easily, and of course they have the mews house.'

'Campbell? Oh Mother. Please.' It was so like Theadora: one day home and she was arranging suitable dinner partners. *But she's scraping the barrel with Campbell McHendry. The man's a chinless wonder.*

'Don't pull faces, Rose. Campbell is a perfectly nice man.'

'He is also an idiot. Daddy, I really do think you and Mummy should stop throwing eligible bachelors under my feet. I have been fending men off ever since my coming-out season. If I wanted a husband purely for appearance sake I could have had my pick of any litter then.'

'If you girls have quite finished,' Barty muttered, 'I want to get Daphne home. Doctor Lewis said she needs her eight hours, you know. We must go.'

~~~

In the flurry of Dodo and Barty's departure, with Beatrice and Cecile also leaving the room, Bunch found herself alone with her father.

'How are things here?' he asked. 'I got your note about Parsons. As it happens, it was already on my horizon. He has a heart condition that is getting worse so perhaps we can slot him into an elder-statesman's roll.' He came to sit near her, leaning his elbows on his knees and regarding her with an air of solemn query. 'I am going to be tied up with F.O. business for the foreseeable future. And I'm thinking Thea might benefit from a few weeks fishing in the glens.'

Bunch pursed her lips. Thea's mood had been hard to ignore and the trips to Scotland had in the past been code for darker things. 'Is Mother well?' she asked.

Edward drew a noisy breath, shaking his head. 'Not at all. I had been planning to cross the pond. Foreign Sec wants to start some sort of dialogue with the Yanks. We are going to need their muscle and Congress is not keen to supply it, not in the least. But I asked for someone else to go. Thea is not up to another long trip at the moment. She was quite unwell when we left Singapore.'

The euphemism of ill health did not escape Bunch and she wished her father would be more open on the source of her mother's fragility. 'Hitting the sauce again?' she said.

'I would not put it quite that way.' Edward shook his head. 'Most of the time your mother is perfectly well, but when she's under stress then yes she may have a little more than is good for her. But you can see she had it under control tonight.'

'I though she was on rather good form,' Bunch said. 'Little excitable, perhaps.'

'The prospect of not being at Perringham House always lifts her mood. But she's been rather under the weather so I shall be taking a little run down Harley Street with her tomorrow. Rather fortunate that Dodo already has a visit planned. Saves some drama.'

'I am sorry, Daddy. I rather thought Mummy was over all of that.'

'She has been doing really rather well for the longest time but this war is getting to everybody. I'm going to get her away to the Lodge for a while. Spot of fishing and complete rest. Away from the London crowd she keeps sober most of the time. I'd go with her but Winnie needs all hands on deck in his private office.'

'Winnie's staff? Not the FO then? What does he want with you?'

'Things that I cannot talk about. And you know better than

to ask, my dear.' He looked away for a moment. 'You should come up to the town house with us tomorrow. It would mean a lot to your mother.'

'So she can have the satisfaction of getting me married off to some chinless idiot?' Bunch managed a laugh. 'Granny gave up on all that Victorian brood-mare nonsense years ago. Can't Mummy see I am not going to be auctioned off?'

'It's not like that, Rose. And you know it.'

'Then why does it feel that way?' She ground her teeth together, her lips held in a line of furious white. 'I tried so hard and I ended up crashing a bloody car – twice! Now I can't even be useful to the war effort because the bloody medics say I'm not fit.' She grabbed Edward's arm. 'All my life I have known Mother was angry with me for being alive when Edward and Benedict are not. She wanted sons and they died and all she's left with is me. I've tried to be a good son to her but you know something? It may come as something of a surprise to you both but I'm not a man.'

'Is that what you think?' Edward pulled her into a hug, his hand on the back of her neck holding her face close into his shoulder. 'My poor sweet Rosebunch, nothing is further from the truth. Your mother...' He slackened his hold and smoothed her hair. 'We grieved for our boys and then we were all so taken up with travel for the FO. You seemed happy enough, between Mother and Nanny and your wretched gee-gees. I never dreamed you thought that way.'

'Most of the time I don't.' She fought the impulse to sniffle, like some tortured damsel of the silver-screen. 'Daddy, I want to feel as if I am doing something useful.'

'You are. Running the estate is a huge responsibility.'

'Yet I still feel as if I've been handed the runners-up rosette. Good old Rose. She tries hard but never quite makes it. I had to bunk off the FANY training because Mummy had one of her turns and then I was chucked out of the ATS boat because I crashed a jalopy.'

'Invalided out,' he said. 'Not the same thing at all.'

'I never get to finish things,' she replied. 'And I need to finish something.'

'Rose, dear thing.' He cupped her face in both hands and kissed her forehead. 'I could not manage without you. Mother is too frail to run this place and I should never have called on Parsons to come out of retirement. I can't stop your mother from digging in at Thurloe Square. It's down to you – and you're doing a marvellous job. Never, ever think for one moment that I or your mother value you any less for being our eldest daughter. You are the eldest Courtney.'

He stared her straight in the eyes and she deeply regretted her outburst. True, she was angry at being kept out of the action but she did not lay blame on anything but bad luck. She also recognised a pep talk when she heard one and loved him for it. 'I know Daddy. Thank you.' She hugged him briefly in return. 'I shall do my best.'

'I know you shall. And tomorrow? You genuinely want to miss out?'

'I have a lot to do here so it will be no hardship to remain behind. Frock shopping is not my gift. Truly.'

'So busy that you can't take a day off? Now you have me a little concerned.'

'It's not only estate business. Mother will adore having Dodo to herself and shopping for Cecile will be her idea of heaven. I do have personal business to get done that I can't complete with Cecile and Dodo trailing in my wake.'

'Such as?'

'Oh … things.'

Edward sighed. 'Bunch, you are not getting involved in matters that do not concern you, I hope? Mother told me about your dead Dutch girl and then trotting off to see the Manns after the tea shop fire. You cannot involve yourself in those things. Leave it to the police'

'I'm not getting involved, I just—'

'Concentrate on estate business, Rose. Please.' He went to the tray and poured a fresh tot and sat down watching her face carefully. 'And you will tell me if it's too much for you? Your grandmother will be able to advise you, of course, if she can tear herself away from the WVS. Keep an eye on her. She likes to think she's still Lady of the Manor. But without Nanny to keep her in check she is rather inclined to forget she has a heart condition. With your mother being as she is I know you already do more than your share.'

'You make us all sound like a bunch of old crocks.'

'I dare say we are no worse than any other family. In my mother's case, it's her age. Your mother however?' He shrugged.

'I can manage Granny.' Bunch glossed over the moment with a small laugh, avoiding her father's look, picking idly instead at her fingers. 'Speaking of old crocks, I had a word with my old CO last month. I'd been rather angling to get back to the ATS. The leg is so much better now.'

He sat back, slapping at the cushion beside him and grimaced at raising a small cloud of dust. 'I do understand your need to serve. And I do understand that you feel your job out there with the BEF was left half done. But France is not the place to be right at this moment.' He stared into his glass and Bunch felt a pang of guilt at the pain in his face. He never spoke of his year-and-a-half in the trenches – few of his cohorts ever did – but it was not hard to imagine how it coloured his thinking now.

'I still have friends out there,' she said and laid her hand on his forearm. 'I have chums, Maddy and Dibs, who are still RTs with field command.'

He covered her fingers with his own without looking as her. 'I know how much you want to do your bit, my Rosebunch.' He swallowed the contents if the glass and gazed into the empty vessel for a moment. 'Thing is,' he said, 'I very much doubt they will send any girls out there now. Not even nurses and the ATS. What would they ask you to do? Drive officers and Ministry men about the place or type letters in Whitehall. Any Debutante with a half a brain can do that. Only you can take this place on. Duty, my dear. Still duty. Just of a different kind.'

She rubbed at her thigh, feeling the ripple of scar tissue under the fine silk of her dress, and said nothing.

'Does the leg pain you a great deal?' Edward murmured.

'Hardly at all.' She was not fooling him. The bones that she had broken in France, and in the car crash that had killed Barty's wife, did not hold her back but they frequently ached at the end of a long day. And she knew her father was aware of that even though she said nothing. She chuckled in a wry amusement. 'I doubt they'd ever find me fit for service, would they?'

'Probably not. And even if they did I wouldn't allow it. I really do need my daughter and heir right here. Is that understood?'

'Yes, Daddy.'

'Good. Now, I called Archie Beeston just before dinner.' The subject was ended and Edward moved on in that clipped way of his. He was used to his edicts being issued and obeyed – he expected obedience and got it.

A smallest spark of rebellion rallied deep within her for the chance to be her own person. He was right, she knew that, and yes it was her duty. That wasn't to say it didn't rankle but she was too well schooled to ignore it. 'The horse dealer over at

Dorking?' she asked.

'That's him. He has a six-year-old gelding, trained to harness. Shall I call him back?'

'Do you trust Beeston?'

'Not in the least but I happen to know who he bought the beast from, and he's a nice little thing. Oh, and I've ordered a new tractor to speed things up a bit. A latest model of Davy Brown – a little more oomph than the old Fordson. I know the Land Girls do a grand job but we are still down on labour and the War Office will be asking for a lot more acres to go under the plough.'

'Chalk land? What for? It's not good for much beyond pasture.'

'I know. Parsons won't like that either but it's not by choice. There is a wait on delivery for the machinery. Pulled a few strings to get them by the end of the month or at least before the harvest sets in properly. Certainly before ploughing.' He ran his hand over carefully barbered hair.

Bunch knew the signs. *There's a 'but' moment coming up. About to say something he knows I won't like.*

'One last thing,' he said. 'There's the small matter of the Lower Nitch.'

'What about it?' She glared at him. Anything to do with the infuriating Colonel Ralph stung her into belligerence. 'I told that man it's not his to have.'

'Normally I would agree. Except that they truly need it.'

'And we don't? We get our firewood from there, which we shall need that when coal gets as scarce as I hear it shall. Plus, we have fences and wattles.'

'Which you can get from our section of Hascombe Woods.'

'But it's simply not on. He just wandered in and took it and you let him get away with it?'

'An acre or two of coppice is neither here nor there.'

'I told Ralph he had to give it back.'

'And I have told him he can have it. Sorry Rose. I don't know why it's such a sticking point for you but his needs are greater than your pride just at the moment. I know we thought Perringham was going to be a nice genteel officer's mess – but it's been subsumed by a bunch of … well, I don't know what they are exactly. But Ralph assures me he needs that woodland to train his people a lot faster than he anticipated now that Hitler's forces have marched across the line.'

'He is ruining the place. Have you been there? Just a few months and you would think Attila's horde just went through.'

'I wasn't aware.' Edward raised an eyebrow. 'I shall drop by and see him later in the week and see what can be done. But they do have full jurisdiction. It was part of the agreement so all I can do is drop a friendly word.'

'I know. It's just that man is so bloody infuriating.'

'Is he though?' Edward chuckled. 'I have no doubt he will get better on acquaintance. You should have a lot in common.'

'Daddy! We've been through this. I'm not going to schmooze that Ralph creature to please anyone.'

'You do know his father has a superb stable down in Dorset?'

She didn't reply. Did her father truly think she could still be distracted by the mere mention of all things equine? She caught the vestige of a twinkle in his eyes and threw a cushion which he batted away.

'It sounds as if Theadora and Mother are retiring so if you will excuse me—' Edward got up and stretched and leaned forward to kiss the top of her head. 'Thea and I have been travelling for days and we need our beds. Almost forgot, I've asked Mother to clear one of the attic staff rooms for Sutton. He's taken a room over the stables for now but it not ideal. I shan't be home that often but I will need him close to hand when I am. I hadn't anticipated your house guest being here. Goodnight Rose.'

'Goodnight.'

Bunch poured herself another drink and went to the window, slipping past the blackout curtain and opening the French doors onto the veranda. The evening was still warm in the exceptional late spring. With only a quarter moon on display the stars freckled the sky in a broad swathe and she stood for a long while gazing at it, smoking and drinking. The trip to London had lost all appeal.

Her father had landed a mantle of duty on her shoulders. As the heir to the Perringham estate it would always be her future, but she had hoped to dodge it for a few years yet. All hope of returning to the ATS had slipped away after speaking with her old CO. Added to that, Dodo was in danger of being swept into the tornado of their mother's fractured psyche. And Cecile? She was not sure what to think about Cecile Benoir. She had even been thwarted in her attempts to wrestle back control of a tiny patch of scrubby woodland.

She gazed up at the quarter-moon, breathed in the scent of wisteria draped across the walkway to one side of the garden, and listened to the owls calling across the valley. The glass had mysteriously emptied of its liquid as she stood in the dark and her cigarette burned away to ash.

'Stupid', she muttered. 'You might not have a chance to get back to your posting in France, Rose Courtney, but you can do something about the rest.'

Monday 13 May

Edward's ministry car left early. After a couple of hours fruitlessly battling paperwork Bunch gave up on milk returns and set out across the estate on Robbo at an easy amble, aware of his dubious soundness but knowing he needed the exercise. She headed toward Chiltwick, avoiding the edges of Perringham's grounds by taking the road toward the hamlet. Seeing her old home, even at a distance, was depressing now that she had seen the damage that had been done.

As she walked the hunter along Chiltwick's single street she was rather gratified to see three women gathered outside of the Mann's shop and cafe. *People will miss the Miss Manns.* The whiff of burning still permeated the air though there was no longer any smoke curling from the charred window.

Bunch dismounted and tethered Robbo in the shade. 'Good morning ladies,' she called, pulling off her riding gloves as she sauntered toward them.

She was answered with a ragged chorus of 'Mornin' Miss Courtney.'

'Closed I see.' She pushed gently at the shop door, though she knew full well it would be bolted from the inside. 'The Miss Manns decided to go after all.'

'What're we going to do?' One woman asked and wafted a

booklet. 'Chiltwick it says. We can't get served nowhere else.'

Bunch took the folded card and read it before handing it back. 'I suspect you can transfer to Wyncombe stores easily enough.' From the corner of her eye she noted a figure standing in the lane toward the end of the row of cottages. 'I gather it's been hard for the Miss Manns in recent months,' she added. 'Lot of gossip being passed around?'

'Gossip's rife in this place,' a younger woman said. 'But I bain't heard nothin' bad about Hilda and Enid. Nice old maids. Not easy at their age 'avin the Tea Room and the stores to run.' She looked down at her own ration book. 'Our books are only valid for here.'

'And the Post Office,' said the other. 'We'll 'ave a long walk.'

'I suppose the Royal Mail will send someone eventually. Or perhaps not. Chiltwick is very small. If nobody buys the business from the Miss Manns I imagine it will remain closed. Which will be such a shame.' Bunch was barely listening to them, intent on a lone figure watching from the roadside. She waved briefly, recognising her now as Hettie Bale. Hettie did not respond. *It's the distance. Perhaps she doesn't see this far*, she thought.

The young woman noticed the move and grinned slyly. 'She's a piece, is old Hettie.'

'So I'm told.'

'Keeps to themselves, them Bales. Think they'm a cut above all of us,' the young woman said. 'They'll 'ave it hard. Can't see en walking to Wyncombe.'

Bunch smiled from habit as she turned back to the women. 'We all have to make changes. I spoke with Miss Mann yesterday. She and her sister were going to stay with a cousin. I understand the elder Miss Mann was quite ill after the fire.'

'Shock.' The younger of the women nodded sagely. 'And

smoke. Shockin' what smoke will do.'

'Sad,' the other added. 'Poor old dears. Somebody settin' fire to 'em like that. Shockin'.'

'It is. Who would do such a thing to them?' The women exchanged glances and Bunch could not help noticing their attention flicking toward the door of Flint House.

'Lot've yapin' been going on hereabouts. Some folks are more *foreign* than's good for 'em.' The older said.

'I can't see how anyone can be off from misagreeing with that Hettie Bale. They 'ad money once over but they've fallen on 'ard times. Some folks can't be doin' with that.' The woman shrugged. 'There's always one or two that'll listen to her.'

'What was she saying, Miss…'

'Liz. Mrs Lizzie Hurst.' Lizzie took a few steps closer and half-turned her head in the direction of the house without actually looking. 'I 'eard someone sayin' we was riffen with fifth coalmanists.'

'Is that so?' Bunch raised her eyebrows and stiffened her face against the urge to laugh as Lizzie nodded emphatically.

''Cos furrin pilots as started comin' here. Polish, my Toby reck'ned. And then that Professor as got given poison. Hettie told us that Prof was yappin on reg'lar with one of 'em.'

'With one of the pilots?'

'S'pose.' Lizzie's shoulders lifted briefly. 'From the big house, mebbe.'

'Possibly.' Bunch grinned apologetically. 'I have no idea what goes on in there anymore, believe me.'

'Aah, 'e did,' the other woman added, 'there's some odd comin's and goin's from there of late. All sorts of row in the wee hours. Bangs and guns and such.' All three nodded agreement with each other.

'Must be hard,' Bunch said. 'But do be careful. I am reliably informed the woods are not safe, so warn your kids not to play over that way.'

'Taint just the kids,' said Lizzie. 'There's a few old enough to know better as creeps about in there at night.'

'Who?'

'They pair of old codgers. Snaffling rabbits and the like I'll know. Same as they allus have.'

'The Jenners.'

'Aah. Saw the pair of 'em comin' up from there a few days back. I was lookin' out cos there was such a racket being kicked up over the Hall.'

'I shall go and talk with them now. Meanwhile do keep an eye on the shop. It would be simply awful for the Miss Manns to lose any more. And if you see them do tell them if there is anything I can do for them to call at the Dower. Thank you, ladies.'

~~~

The Jenner's cottages lay at the other side of the coombe and it took Bunch almost half-an-hour to reach the lane running past them. It was late morning, and already warm, but it was that time of day when she knew there was a reasonable chance she would find the brothers there. She guided Robbo down the twitten running alongside the cottages and came out in the yard to the sharp spicy smell that marked the Jenner's industry: cut wood, sawdust and smoke.

She dismounted and looked around. Evidence of the brothers' trade was everywhere. A battle-scarred hurdle-mould held ten hazel rods, evenly spaced, where split-and-trimmed wands were being woven between, and around it lay a detritus of stripped bark and nub ends. Through the open doors of the main workshop she could see the besoms, Sussex trugs and log baskets to be sold at market, neatly stacked against one wall, and at the far end a pair of finely crafted Windsor chairs awaited their final coat of beeswax.

A motor chattered into life in the workshop at the end of the yard, joined rapidly by the clatter and buzz of a wood lathe. Bunch headed for those signs of life. The turning-shed door was ajar and the smell of sawdust and wood shavings was stronger, with an added piquancy of paraffin and machine oil from the lathe. This was the real heart of the Jenner's empire.

Fred Jenner stood at the lathe, cutting dips and curves into a slender length of elm, his head bowed as he watched the curls of wood spinning away from the cutting edge, whilst his right foot worked the treadle. Roly was sanding the finished chair legs on the motorised lathe, and it was he who looked up as she entered the workshop.

'Good morning gentlemen.'

'Mornin' Miss Courtney. Nice mornin' too.'

'It is.' She loosened the silk scarf at her neck and slipped it though her fingers. 'Warm again.'

'Too warm.' Roly hefted the spar in his hands and sighed. 'Timber's dryin' too quick. It can crack if'n it don't get oiled.'

'I can imagine. Is that another Windsor? I saw two in the store.'

'Just chairs,' Roly replied. 'Kitchen chairs fer the Reverend Day.' He put the wood down and came forward to meet her. Fred allowed her a slow nod and a grunt that might have been 'mornin' Miss', his treadling only slowing momentarily before turning his attention back to the wood. The whine of the blade was loud in the confined space, making Bunch put her hands to her ears

''Old up, Fred,' Roly shouted. 'Can't 'ear Miss Courtney with all that racket.'

Fred scowled at him but stepped away, letting the lathe shudder to a halt.

'How is Mrs Jenner?' she asked. 'I heard she was laid up.'

'Aah, she is.' Roly shook his head. 'Poor old gal's ate up

with the rheum-attics, suffers summat chronic. If is weresn't for our Mavis comin in every day I don't know as she'd cope.'

'Has she seen Doctor Lewis?'

Roly shook his head. 'Not much 'e can do 'e said last time. Didn't get much fer our two bob. My old mam laid store on a goose-fat and chickweed poultice. Or a sting of've old dumbledore when she goos down too bad.'

Bunch had a soft spot for the Jenners but she knew better than to push the point. Doctor Lewis did his best for the older folk but most could not afford the medicines he prescribed, nor the fee for his call out. If she offered to pay it would be taken as a slight. *But maybe I'll ask Lewis myself,* she thought. *See what can be done.* 'Well give her my best and do let me know if she gets any worse,' she said.

'Aah.' He nodded but she knew he would do no such thing.

'Has Mr Parsons asked you for the hurdles?'

'Aah.' Roly waved at the half-made wattle in the yard. 'Came to see me last night. Dozen, he said.'

'Yes, but if you could make it fifteen? We've had a couple more broken. Well, crushed would be more precise. One of the land girls drove the tractor over a stack.'

'Them they machines be a bit much fer maids,' Roly murmured. 'They does they best I reck'n.'

'They do very well. Some idiot left the hurdles on the headland and the grass grew up around them.' She shrugged. 'Accidents happen. We had the Min Ag agent in, demanding we plough Leigh Corner and sow flax, would you believe. Idiots. I know they need it for uniforms and such, but flax? I would have thought it was too dry.'

'Leigh Corner, you says?'

'Yes. Along the side of Lower Nitch. I heard you were over that way a couple of nights back. You do know that copse is dangerous now?'

'Few Tommies crashin' about?' Jenner grinned. 'Don't sound so atchety.'

'Not Tommies. Ordnance,' she said. 'Land mines I've heard.' She scowled. 'I am not best pleased I can tell you, but Daddy tells me there's nothing we can do.'

''Tis a jigger,' Jenner agreed. 'Lot of things 'appening round these parts this last four day...'

'Indeed there has.' Bunch nodded sagely and leaped at the pause through which she could lead the conversation. 'I say, did you see the fire at the Jenny Wren?' She watched him carefully from the corner of her eye. 'The police say it was started deliberately. I don't suppose you saw anyone lurking around?'

Jenner thought for a moment. 'I can't 'zactly say I did,' he said at last. 'There was folks about once the flames got a hold.'

'But before that?'

He scratched at his chin and gazed at the roof beams. 'It were dark mind, but I'd warrant it weresn't a young lad I saw.'

'So an older man? Doing what?'

'Jest astanding there watchin'. From the gate. Then 'e were gone.'

'How thrilling.' She awarded the old man a bright smile. 'Would you know him again, do you think?'

Bunch was sure her feet left the ground by several inches at the voice, and all if the shed's three occupants turned to stare at Inspector Wright silhouetted in the doorway.

'Chief Inspector. What a surprise.' From the periphery of her vision she noted Fred Jenner melt away into the inner recesses of the workshop, as easily as he would vanish into a woodland dell. Roly remained reluctantly at her side though she was fairly certain he would have skipped off with his brother given half a second's warning.

Wright stepped into the shade and doffed his hat to Bunch, using the moment to wipe at his brow. 'Good to see you Miss

Courtney, Mr Jenner.'

She saw him glance over her shoulder and had a suspicion he'd noted Fred's escape though he said nothing. 'Well if you could change that order for hurdles, Mr Jenner, I'd be very grateful,' she said.

'And if you've anything to add to your recollection of Tea Room fire.' Wright replaced his hat, sliding his finger along the brim to dip the angle.

Bunch wondered idly, *Did he pick that habit up from Bulldog Drummond? He even looks a little like Ronald Colman. Just a tiny smidgen.*

'Don' rightly know if there would be anythin', sir,' Jenner mumbled. 'My recollectin's not what it were.'

'You were telling Miss Courtney you saw someone near the source of the fire. Maybe you could tell me a little more? I have a witness who saw you in the lane.'

'I don't recollect.' He was mulish, looking back into the dark corner where his brother had been. 'We saw a shadow, is all.'

Wright paced forwards until he was at arms length and Jenner was forced to look upwards into his face. 'Two elderly ladies were in that building, Mr Jenner. One of them ended up in hospital.'

'It would be such a help,' said Bunch. 'I spoke with Hilda Mann just yesterday. She told me they have been having problems for a little while.'

'Aah. Tis awful,' Roly agreed. 'Real shame. I've know'st en both fer years, an' they didn't deserve the moil and aggravation them wapsey old cats set on them but tis they cats that'll suffer the most. I heard the shop's closin' down.'

Wright nodded, his face serious, full of agreement. 'Gossips never thrive,' he said. 'Can you give me an idea what the rumours were about?'

'Just talk. Lot of daft talk about furriners.'

'Could you be more precise?'

Bunch was surprised at the exasperation in Wright's tone. It was matched only by Jenner's measured truculence. She had known the old man all her life and one thing was certain: the more Wright pushed his authority the deeper those heels would dig in. She scuffed her boot on the concrete floor and gave a discreet cough of warning, *Because a sigh would be too damned obvious*. There was a pause as both men gazed at her, seeming to realise she was sending a message but neither of them sure of what or to whom.

'Twasn't nothin', were it Miss Courtney? Folks getting wapsey, like I were sayin'. Was there anythin' else, Inspector? Only me an' Fred's got stuff to deliver.'

'If you could let me know if you remember anything else. And if you could ask your brother to do the same?' Wright handed over a card. 'Leave a message with my sergeant. May I have a word, Miss Courtney?'

'Certainly Inspector. Thank you, Mr Jenner,'

She shook Roly by the hand. 'If you can't find me at the farm talk to Kate. Mr Parsons is not there quite as much now.'

'Aah.' Jenner tipped the peak of his cap. 'Mornin' Miss.'

Wright was waiting for her in the yard and they walked Robbo out to the lane in silence and out of the Jenner's earshot.

'Wapsey?' He said finally.

'Spiteful,' she replied.

'And moil?'

'Annoyance? I think— I don't know all the local idioms. Half the time I have to work them out in context and make an educated guess.'

'You know a lot more of them than I do. And you are plainly better at getting that old curmudgeon to talk to you.'

'The Jenners are a pair of sweet old men. Rogues at times,

but terribly sweet. They don't have a very good relationship with the law, it must be said.'

'You mean they've been arrested for poaching once too often.'

'Something of the sort. I came to warn them about the woods being dangerous territory these days.'

Wright frowned and took her by the elbow. 'Look here Rose. I hope you are not getting too involved in this.'

Bunch shrugged off his hand and took a step away. 'You cannot think I would let them just wander into danger if I can prevent it? I have a responsibility to them. Just as I have to see that the Miss Manns have justice. They are tenants after a fashion. They have a long lease on the Tea Rooms from the Perringham Estate.'

'The tea shop was your property?'

'Yes. Not that it would make the slightest difference. I am affronted, Inspector. Surely you do not imagine I would be so crass as to put property before people?'

'Plenty would.' Wright held up both hands. 'But not you of course. My sincere and abject apologies. This job makes cynics of us all.'

'Apology accepted. And if it's any help, I am sure Mr Jenner knows a little more than he is saying. He and his brother.'

'Then perhaps I need to—'

Bunch grabbed his arm. 'Give them a little time to think it over. You took them by surprise and they probably would not tell what they know to the constabulary in any event. But they know what's right. I am certain they will get word to me if they hear anything.'

'There may not be time for their conscience to prick them.'

'You think this arsonist will strike again?'

'I have not the faintest idea, which is what I find so

frustrating.' He looked up and down the lane as if he might spot his perpetrator lurking in amongst the willow-herb and parsley and the waving fringes of growth from uncut hedging.

'We'll find out. And don't look at me that way. I am doing my job just as much as you are.' She pulled Robbo's head up from snaffling another swathe of cow parsley. 'Leave it alone, you greedy old sod. I shall be in trouble with the girls if they have to spend another half-hour scrubbing green crud off your tack.' She backed the hunter a few paces, fussing with his reins. 'Do you think it's the same person who killed Benoir? Or Miss de Wit? They are all attacks on foreigners and all within twelve miles of each other.'

'No, we doubt that or at least we don't believe so. The first two were poisoned. Very different to arson so probably not the same person.' He sighed. 'Probably— I hope not.'

His prevarications peaked her attention. 'There are more?' she asked.

'It's been a bad week. There have been a few incidents. Nothing so serious and hopefully internment will bring most of it to a close. Having a maniac running through these lanes killing at random with anything to hand will do very little for keeping the public calm.'

'As if they need any more hints that their lives are in some sort of danger.'

'The public need reassurance.'

'Don't be a pompous ass. Remember who you're talking to.' Robbo snorted the green frothy remnants of his snack against her shoulder. 'And you, Robbo m'lad, need to be on the move, I know.' Bunch gathered up the reins, put her left foot into the stirrup and hauled herself into the saddle. 'Come for supper and we can have a long chat. It will just be Granny and me. Everyone else has hot-footed up to Town.'

Bunch did not give him a chance to reply. She urged Robbo

past the car, nodding curtly to Glossop sitting behind the wheel flicking through a magazine. Her father's words on her returning to the ATS reverberated around her mind: *'So what would they ask you to do? Drive officers and ministry men about the place.' He's right of course. Sitting about for hours. God forbid it's me sitting there waiting for William Wright. At his beck and call twenty-four hours a day. I'd far rather have him at mine.*

~~~

The three of them sat down for supper far less formally than Beatrice would have liked.

'Pigeon again.' She looked at her brandy balloon and sighed. 'Meat rations really don't go very far do they, Chief Inspector. I wonder when coffee will follow it?'

'Let's hope it's all over before we get that far, Mrs Courtney.'

'Beatrice, please. William isn't it?'

She beamed at their guest and Bunch eyed her suspiciously. The faux cheer did not fool her for a second and she was concerned. The fatigue was clear in ever line and shadow of her grandmother's face – the ebony walking stick propped close to the table was a further worrying sign. Whilst Beatrice had seemed to take on a new lease since the turn of the year, in no small part she secretly suspected due to the absence of Nanny's autocratic presence, the fact remained that her grandmother was an octogenarian with a heart condition. 'Let's not think about that for now, Granny,' she said. 'How was your day?'

'Splendid. We have another van for our rounds so we can cover the lookout crews up near the windmill and the monument. Mobile canteens,' she explained to Wright. 'We can reach any number of small units now as well as the camps.'

Bunch leaned over and tapped her hand. 'Which can be left to your lieutenants to organise. You know Doctor Lewis said you should be resting in the afternoons.'

'What does he know? I haven't felt so well for years. Now, William. What can you tell us about the fire? I assume that is what brings you here?'

'Not entirely. I'm not dealing directly with the arson attack but I understand that so far, we have very little to go on. Somebody poured a combustible liquid through the letter box and dropped a lit paper after it.'

'Who would carry out such a horrendous act?' Bunch demanded. Wright hesitated and she snorted impatiently. 'Don't be such a stuffed shirt. You surely must have some idea. Chiltwick is hardly a seething hotbed of criminal activity. Even people in the county barely know it exists.'

'The burned paper appears to have been a propaganda poster. A small segment had become lodged under the coconut matting.' He shrugged. 'As far as we know, the residents of the property are not enemy aliens so we are at a bit of a loss as to why they should be targeted.'

'Ask the neighbours.'

'We have carried out house-to-house interviews. It doesn't take long in a place like this.'

'I would strongly suggest you ask again.' Bunch stared at the rug around her feet as she related her conversation with the women of Chiltwick. 'If the neighbours are not guilty then there is a reasonable chance they know who is.'

'We've conducted the interviews but not found any real evidence to go on. Seems the Jenners are not the only locals who are not keen to talk with the constabulary. Fear perhaps.'

'Of the police? I would doubt it.' She peered at Wright over her glass as she took another taste, rolling the spirit around her tongue before she swallowed. 'I can understand the Jenners being reluctant. Avoiding the constabulary comes as second nature to them. I'm less certain that the rest of the Chiltwick residents would be so closed mouthed. They're law abiding people and the Manns were well liked so it seems odd that the neighbours would not say anything at all. Perhaps they simply don't know? Or they don't wish to stir the ant hill.'

'You think they know who did this?'

'It would be a strange sort of village if they had no suspicions at all.'

'Why would they shelter an arsonist?'

'Now that, my dear Chief Inspector, would be genuinely perplexing.' Footsteps out in the hall made her pause. The staff had all retired for the night and none of the live-ins would use the front entrance, not even Knapp. She glanced down at Roger who was already settling back into sleep. *Not that anybody is going to wander in willy nilly, but still. Good to know the old boy knows who it is – except that everyone is in London.* 'Hello?' she called.

'Good evening.' Cecile sidled into the room. 'I'd hoped not to disturb anyone.'

Bunch thought her friend looked tired beyond mere lack of sleep or fraught travel. Her eyes were deeply shadowed and slightly sunken as if she had not slept for a week. Which she supposed was quite likely. 'You're back already? I thought you were staying in Town?'

'I decided not.' She held a hand out. 'Don't worry about Dodo. Your father said he would bring her home tomorrow. The trains are simply dreadful. Even first class was absolutely bursting at the seams. Monsieur Courtney seemed very anxious. I think he would have sent Dodo home already, but...' She pulled a face at the remembrance. Madame Courtney *war verärgert.*'

Bunch winced at the last words. Fatigue, perhaps, making Cecile forget she was no longer in Berlin. *That kind of slip up is something she should watch.* 'I'm glad Daddy will provide a car. Dodo shouldn't be pushing and shoving on the trains in her condition. Come and have a nightcap with us.'

'I…'

'You look as if you need a drink.' Bunch went to the side table, her hands wavering over the bottles. 'Scotch? Or a gin and tonic?'

'All right. Gin, please.'

'Did you buy the frocks?' Beatrice patted the sofa beside her. 'I can't imagine my daughter-in-law would allow you to choose for yourself. Even though you're French.'

'Yes, we found two evening gowns and some nice outfits for the day. Nothing special, you understand, because I am working now. I wouldn't want people to think I am swanking it.'

'Very wise,' Beatrice said. 'Well I am sure it will be tres chic. You wear clothes well. Such a change after Rose's interminable jodhpurs and tweeds.'

'Oh Granny.' Bunch handed Cecile her drink and took the empty glass Beatrice handed to her for a refill. 'Good job Nanny isn't here. She would have something to say about this. Another snifter William?'

'No thank you. I was about to leave but I'm glad Miss Benoir is here. I wanted to have a few words. We were speaking of the fire at the tea rooms and shop in Chiltwick. I understand you knew the proprietors?'

'I have met them.' Cecile looked bewildered and a little guarded. 'I would not say that I knew them.'

'I talked with Miss Mann and she told me that your father had tea there often.'

'He did?'

'According to Hilda Mann he went there for coffee at times.'

'Perhaps.' Cecile's shoulders rose in a half-hearted shrug. 'I don't know. I was not permitted to work with him and he has always kept strange hours, so maybe so.' Cecile reached out for a cigarette and smiled gratefully as Wright lit it for her. 'My father was not a very forthcoming man.' She blew smoke up to the ceiling and tapped ash that had yet to form into the ash tray.

It was a nervous gesture, though there was not a flicker of emotion in those perfect features and Bunch wondered if she had imagined their first conversation in the Jenny Wren. She was inclined to think she had. *Because Cissy has always been such a bad liar. What game are you playing, old thing?* 'Perhaps the regulars will remember,' she said. 'They may not all live along the row. I imagine the police have spoken to Mrs Bale, and Miss Lewis goes there quite often.' She turned to Cecile with a smile. 'You remember the women who were there when we met up?'

'They were not terribly pleasant. Father mentioned comments made in the past weeks. For him to notice them I imagine those comments were quite pointed. He always sounded like an Alsatian, from the Alsace region, you understand Inspector? It has an accent all of its own and to some it might sound less French. I have had my own share of confrontation since we came to England. My accent is not strong. I've always thought that I sounded as English as my mother, but the local people seem to have an instinct for any who aren't entirely their own.'

The telephone rang in the hallway.

'At this hour?' Beatrice glanced at the clock. 'Past eight. I do hope it's not bad news.

'It is late.' Cecile took a mouthful of her gin and yawned. 'I hate to be antisocial but I'm terribly tired. It has been a very long day. She stubbed her cigarette and stood up. 'If you will excuse me?'

'Of course,' said Beatrice. 'I doubt I shall be long myself.'

Knapp appeared at the door, stepping aside for Cecile to pass her. 'A telephone call for the Chief Inspector.'

'Out there?'

'Yes, Chief Inspector. This way.'

'Thank you, Mrs Knapp. Excuse me ladies.'

'And then there were two, but not for long. Do you mind if I retire, Rose? I am also somewhat tired.'

'Of course not, Granny. You should be resting more. Good night.'

She gave Beatrice a hand to her feet and watched the old lady make her way out of the room by the further door. 'And then there was one, Rog.' She bent to ruffle the dog's belly and then crossed to replenish her glass from the side table conveniently close to the hall door, but she could not make out Wright's words. She did hear the phone handset's jangle as he hung up, and dashed back to her seat making certain she was draped casually there for Wright's entrance.

'Has everyone else gone?' he said.

''Fraid so. We country mice scuttle off to our nests before it gets dark you know.'

'Mouse is the last thing I would call you, Rose Courtney.'

'More of a rat?'

'I was going to say wily fox.' He was grinning. 'That was the Brighton station. I told them to telephone me here in an emergency. I hope that is not an imposition. Sadly I am going to have to leave you.'

'Duty calls?'

'Another death.'

'Oh, good heavens. Where? I'm assuming locally. A suspicious one I imagine, or they wouldn't be calling you here. You can't be the only detective they can call in the whole county.'

'Very much local.' He drained the last of his scotch. 'A body has been found in Wyncombe.'

~~~

Wyncombe's memorial to the fallen of the Great War stood at the head of the high street, close to where the main road branched into Church Lane. It was the space that villagers referred to as The Square. At its centre, four deep stone tiers supported a bronze Tommy in puttees and battle bowler, gazing southward toward the coast, his dark-metallic face gleaming in the final rays of sunset. Bunch had passed it more times than she could count and barely noticed it except as a place of gathering on Armistice Day.

This was one of the occasions when she could not avoid noticing. Not just because a collection of villagers were gathered there watching proceedings but because of the corpse displayed for full public viewing.

The body of a young man lay across the steps with arms flung wide, palms up, legs stretched, booted feet splayed outwards. His head rested on the top-most tier and as she approached it Bunch thought he might almost have been sleeping. Except that his eyes were open, gazing into the dusk. As she came closer she could see that his head was skewed at an unnatural angle. His cheek was rested on the left boot of the bronze Tommy so that he gazed not upwards at the sky but directly at the right toe cap of the statue, his death mask fearful, as if expecting a blow.

She watched Wright mount the steps and examine the corpse from all angles before retreating to the edge of the cobbles around the base to stare at the prone body. He stood immobile for some time with his hands together, forefingers touching on his bottom lip. 'Very little blood,' he said at last. 'Meaning this chap is unlikely to have passed away from a tragic accident.'

'Or to put it another way, he didn't trip and strike his head.'

'Oh yes, he hit his head as he fell. It would have been impossible not to. But I am certain he'd breathed his last before he ever got that far. The coroner will need to confirm it, of course, but he doesn't appear to have struck his skull against the statue with anything like the force required to break his neck.'

'And he's been posed,' Bunch added, 'like a marionette. Had he stumbled the momentum would have slid him right down to the cobbles.'

'Well observed.' Wright looked around the square at the buildings that had an open view of the body. Bunch stood at his side, turning as he turned, shading her eyes against the last of the sun and trying to see the familiar landscape through his eyes.

His attention settled first on the Seven Stars. The pub's frontage did not look directly at the memorial due to the curve of the road as it circumnavigated the pond. But the benches along its front wall afforded an oblique line of sight, as demonstrated by a dozen or so patrons nursing pint pots and craning necks to see as much as they could from that spot.

The rectory sat closest to the junction but in contemplative seclusion behind tall walls and hedges. Only the wide gateway and the upper windows afforded an unobstructed outlook. The church beyond it was half-hidden behind a stand of ancient yews and, like the pub, was a little distance from the statue.

Facing those buildings stood Wyncombe's village hall and the playing field beyond. A hedge, a little under shoulder high, ran for most of its boundary. Bunch knew that the field was not usually in use on a Tuesday evening and so there was unlikely to have been any witnesses peering over it.

'It's a very public place but not in plain view to that many people,' Wright said at last.

'I agree. Unless they happened to be out in the street, but the good citizens of Wyncombe will mostly be tucked away in their houses after supper.'

'PC Botting,' he said, 'we will need to obtain information as quickly as possible. Do we have a name for the deceased?'

'Toby Hurst, sir. Lives over Chiltwick way.'

'Family?'

'He has a wife and one child.'

'You know them?'

'Yes, sir. I'll get over'n tell her.'

'No, leave that to me. Have the "special" guard the body and then you can start the enquiries. I want you to question all the residents who may have been within eye or earshot of the scene. Starting with that lot over at the pub. They may talk to you more easily than me.'

'Yes, sir.'

'Who reported the body?'

'That would be Doctor Lewis, sir. On his way out to an emergency call.'

'Is he here?'

'No, sir. He had to be off. He had an emergency, as I said,' he added as if to a small child.

'Of course. Be sure to get a statement from him as soon as possible.'

'Sir.' Botting saluted and walked across the road to the special constable to pass orders down the line.

Wright peered at the hedges surrounding most of the larger domestic properties. 'I can't see we shall be told much of any use. All this greenery will shield the memorial from the front.'

'And most people will not be looking out,' said Bunch. 'They will be in their back gardens, or else sitting in their kitchens listening to *Monday Night at Eight*.' She grinned mischievously. '*Inspector Hornleigh Investigates*, by all accounts.'

'Are you a fan?

'No, but Cook is. She never misses.'

'Pity. You'd be more familiar with police procedures if you

were.'

'I know enough.'

'Then tell me what you know about Tobias Hurst.'

'I don't know that much at all.' Bunch sidled a little closer to peer at the dead man. 'I vaguely recognise his face but I don't know all of the residents over in Chiltwick. Most of them are tenants but don't work directly for the estate. Oddly enough, I spoke to his wife Lizzie outside the Tea Room just today. She said there was some reason to think that the Mann's neighbour may know something about the fire. Do you think this death is linked to that?'

'Too much coincidence for it not to be.' He stared at the body, removing his hat and running a hand over his hair. 'It will be for the coroner to confirm, of course, but this is a very neat death. Very little blood. Minimal signs of violence.'

'Apart from the broken neck,' said Bunch. 'That may appear a tad violent to most people.'

'It is brutal, I agree, but I'd call this an efficient death rather than a violent one,' he replied. 'Sudden, and brutal, but very efficient.'

'Meaning what?'

'I shall wait for the post mortem report before drawing any firm conclusions.'

'Out with it. You obviously have a theory.'

'Preliminary thoughts based on previous experience. I can't be certain.'

'Until after the post mortem. I know. Don't be obtuse.' Bunch pinched his arm and he rubbed at it. *Out of all proportion to the touch*, she thought.

'Assaulting an officer of the law is an offence,' he murmured and shot her a private grin which she parried with a deep scowl. 'But back to the business at hand,' he said. 'Hurst had to have been taken by surprise. I doubt he knew a thing about it. But what that means?' He shook his head. 'I cannot begin to hazard a guess until we have some idea how he came to be here and why.'

'You think he died somewhere else?'

'Not necessarily.' He looked around them. 'He quite probably died on this spot. He's a sturdy chap. Hauling his dead body through the middle of the village would have been hard to accomplish without someone taking notice. I'm merely mooting all potential theories.'

'And the idea of someone planting the body there seems far-fetched?' *But then*, she thought, *someone did just that to poor Johnny Frampton, so why not here?* 'Is there anything I can do? I feel rather as if I should be mustering the troops. Home ground and all that.'

'You say you've spoken with Mrs Hurst earlier?' Wright replaced his hat, tugging the brim firmly. 'I will have to see the widow. Would you accompany me? A woman can be a help in these things and we don't have any WPCs here to call on.'

'I won't be interfering with police business?' Bunch eyed him up and down. 'That is a change of heart.'

Wright let out an amused grunt. 'You've already been tramping about asking questions. Don't bother to deny it. When you decide to interfere I doubt there is much I could ever do to stop you. In this case, however, you may actually be of some help as you've at least met the wife. You may be able to help me in questioning her.'

'Wouldn't Botting be of more use?'

'In this instance? No. He has more clout in the pub. He grew up with these lads. He'll know what to ask and from whom. You have a different kind of power over these people. I don't think she would hide anything from you if you asked her discreetly.'

'I can't imagine she had anything to do with her husband's

death.'

'Perhaps not. Perhaps even *probably* not, but I would appreciate your help on finding out what she does know.'

~~~

Visitors knocking on front doors after nine o'clock were a rarity in country cottages and almost unheard of in a hamlet such as Chiltwick. With dusk falling and her husband out for the evening, Tobias Hurst's widow opened the door by a mere fraction to peer with the deepest suspicion at Bunch and Wright standing a respectful pace from her step. As recognition dawned of who was standing at her door in the half-light she flung it wide.

'Good evening, Mrs Hurst' said Bunch. 'This is Chief Inspector Wright. May we come in?'

'Miss Courtney.' She stepped back. 'Yes, come in. Afore that cursed warden do see they lights.' Wright lifted his hat to signal that Bunch should precede him and Lizzie Hurst pulled the heavy black curtain back across the door close on their heels.

'Warden's a grummut. Fined the chapel just last week for showin' light and it were only the preacher's bicycle lamp.' She pulled a face. ''E's that hatchety even the LDV won't have 'im, so I hear. Miss Courtney.'

'Sit down, Mrs Hurst. I'm afraid we have some bad news for you.'

'Fer me?' Lizzie sat, as Bunch had ordered, clutching at the table edge with her left hand as if hoping its thick scrubbed pine solidity could stiffen her nerve. She looked toward the ledge and brace door at the foot of the stairs, as if assuring herself that her child could not have gone out unnoticed. 'Toby?' she whispered.

'Your husband was found by the Wyncombe memorial a few hours ago. Doctor Lewis and PC Botting have both identified him.' Wright sat next to her, covering her hand with his own. 'I am very sorry to tell you that he has died.'

'He's… No, bain't so.' She drew back, tugging her fingers from beneath his and hugging herself, hands tucked into her armpits. 'Weresn't him. Not my Toby.'

'I am sorry Mrs Hurst. Lizzie.' Bunch pulled her chair close and slid her arm around the young woman's shoulders and for several minutes Lizzie Hurst wept quietly yet violently, drawing deep shuddering breaths between staccato sobs that she muffled into a tea towel snatched from the table.

Bunch nodded toward the Brown Betty steaming quietly on the hearth. 'Tea,' she mouthed at Wright.

'My Toby?' Lizzie struggled to bring herself under control, taking deep breaths, her eyes closed and hands wringing the cloth like the neck of a chicken. 'How? Why?' she said.

'He was attacked,' Wright replied. 'I realise this is a difficult moment for you but we're hoping you could help us with the why. Time is always important in these events. The quicker we can assemble the facts the more likely we are to apprehend the perpetrator.'

Lizzie nodded. 'People liked our Toby,' she said. 'He's a good man. Does his work and looks after me an' the bab.'

'Has he had any recent arguments with anybody?'

'Only that Bale. He made such an oration over they blackouts. Ampery bugger. He's fined everyone on the row. Give en a uniform an' he thinks he's God.' Lizzie's eyes flashed, anger overlaying her grief for a moment. She accepted a cup of tea but only took a small sip before setting it down, struggling to assert control of herself once more. 'They 'ad a right pucker two days back'

'Bad enough for it to get violent?' Wright asked.

'Nah.' She waved a hand dismissively. 'He's half the size my Toby is …. were.' Her face crumpled once more.

'Is there anyone else in the house?' Wright asked.

A shake of the head. 'Me and the little'n is all.'

'Nobody close by who can come and sit with you?'

'My ma's over Wyncombe,' she said.

'We'll send for her. And meanwhile I think Mrs Cartwright lives next door?' Bunch said. 'I'll fetch her, shall I?'

'Don't fuss on my account, Miss Courtney.'

'No trouble, Mrs Hurst. You sit and drink your tea and I'll fetch her.'

~~~

Bunch and Wright drove back to the Dower in gathering darkness, driving slowly in the shortened beams of the shaded headlamps, and in relative quiet.

'Poor woman,' Bunch said at last. 'Her husband goes for a well-earned pint and some lunatic tries to twist his head off. And a child will be waking up tomorrow without a father.'

'She seemed adamant there was nobody who wished him ill but I shall question the Bales tomorrow.'

'Not tonight?'

'Hurst was six foot tall and strong. It would take a lot of strength or else a very dubious kind of training to overpower a man like that without a hint of a struggle. I interviewed Bale myself over the arson attack and he's not a likeable man, but frankly I don't believe him capable of inflicting any harm on a strapping lad like Hurst.' He pursed his lips and nodded slowly. 'Arson might be a different matter.'

'You think he set the tea shop alight? That would be madness – he lives right next door.'

'And was the one to raise the alarm.'

'Have you any proof?'

'Only hearsay. It would be a nice neat package all wrapped up for the Chief Super, however and he does like results.'

'But you prefer evidence?'

'Exactly.'

The car pulled up in front of the Dower House and Glossop jumped out to open the door for them.

'Would you like to come in?' Bunch asked Wright.

'I have to get back to Brighton and it takes hours without proper lights. Thank you for your help, Rose. Good night.'

It was plainly a request for her to alight and she did so reluctantly. There were so many questions that she had not even begun to ask but she had a notion she would not hear any answers at that moment. 'Goodnight.' She stepped out into the semi-dark and watched the car's white-painted rear bumper vanish into the gloom.

Night noises settled in the quiet that followed and she gazed up at the sky for a moment as a movement between the trees and a sharp sound caught her attention. She caught a glimpse of a Barn Owl. Highlighted in the paleness of a quarter moon it glided across the gardens in the direction of the farm. It was the only sign of life. Not a glimmer of lamplight to be seen in any direction, not even from the solid red-brick house casting even deeper shadows in its lee.

She wondered what London felt like at such times. It was a long while since she'd been up to stay at the Courtney's town house in Thurloe Square, and she suddenly yearned for a night at the Cafe de Paris, as she had in the old days. Clubs had never been a favourite entertainment but their appeal at that moment was strong. Music and lights and human contact as an antidote to all of this death. *Anything is preferable to this drip, drip, drip of lives leaching away.*

She straightened her shoulders and turned into the vestibule, pulling the blackouts back across the doors before stepping into the hall and the silence beyond the steady pulse of the long-case clock. The longer she listened the more it felt like a heartbeat ticking away a life. She was almost tempted to reach into the case and stop it – a contradiction to her impulse for the gaiety of a night on the town a bare minute before. *Pull yourself together, Rose Courtney. It has been a ghastly day. Tomorrow will be another and better.* 'Because I am damned sure it can't be worse,' she murmured.

Tuesday 14 May

'Mrs Parsons has just called.' Kate was in the office doorway as Bunch and Cecile went out to start their day. 'She said Mr P had a bad attack in the night and he's in the cottage hospital. She asked if you could go and see her at home.'

'Heavens! Of course I will.' Bunch frowned slightly, wondering why Mrs Parsons had not called the house phone. She waved a hand around the office. 'If you can start making sense of all this, Cissy. The Min Ag. want all of our milk-yield records for April, and also the egg quotas. I know it's a bit rum of me to drop you into it head first. I was hoping to be able to help you through it this first time.'

'Filing is just about within my capabilities.' Cecile grinned, taking Bunch's place in the ancient captains' chair and pulling it up to the desk. 'You have more urgent business. I understand that. Now off you go.'

'If you're sure?'

'Yes, now go. Shoo!'

'All right. Kate, if you could take over the rotas? Ask Burse for help if you get stuck. I shall be as quick as I can.'

'Yes, Boss.' The lanky Land Girl popped off a salute and loped away toward the yard.

Bunch hurried out past the stables and into the lane. It was a brisk ten-minute walk to Mrs Parsons and not worth saddling a horse for. The manager's cottage was a detached house a little apart from the staff terraces and semis. It was tile-hung in the usual Sussex style with the typical angled eaves – softer lines that always reminded Bunch of hand-baked loaves. She strode up the short front path and lifted the stag's head knocker.

It took Mrs Parsons a few moments to open up, partly through age but also because the bolts on the front door were stiff from little use. In ordinary times Bunch would have gone around to the kitchen door as everyone else did, but she knew how Mrs P was a stickler for 'what's right', and this felt like a special case.

'Miss Courtney.'

Belinda Parsons was a slender woman dressed in a neat cotton frock, belted at the waist and with a pristine white collar. Her grey hair was pulled back in a loose chignon exposing near-perfect skin that had refused to succumb to age and wrinkle, as it might be expected to. She had been a vicar's daughter before marrying the Courtney's estate manager and had never permitted her status to be discounted. 'Do come in.' She led the way into the parlour. 'Tea?' she asked.

Bunch only just had breakfast but to refuse would have been rude. 'Please.' She waited for only a few minutes before Mrs Parsons returned with a teapot which she stood on the table beside the waiting cups and accoutrements. 'We'll just let that steep.' She sat opposite Bunch, upright and neat and smiling at her guest expectantly.

'I so sorry to hear Mr Parsons is unwell,' Bunch said. 'What can we do? Does he need anything there?'

'Not immediately, Miss Courtney,' Belinda replied. 'It's his heart. And his lungs of course. The Doctor assures me he will recover but he'll need complete bed rest for several weeks. Perhaps even months.'

'Then he must have it. I've been concerned about him for a while. I asked only last week if he needed some time off but he was so adamant he could carry on.'

'Your father had asked him to do a job,' Belinda replied. 'He considers it his duty to carry it out, whatever the outcome.'

There was a hint of ice in her tone and Bunch winced inwardly. She knew how Parsons felt about what he saw as his duty to Perringham House and its inhabitants. *Positively feudal and totally wrong*, was her own thought. But he was of the old school. 'I don't think my father intended him to work himself into an early grave,' she said. 'You tell him from me, "duty be damned". I am grateful that he answered the call whilst Daddy was away. It allowed me to recover from my accident but he owes us nothing. Quite the reverse in fact, it is us – I – who owe him.'

'Thank you.' Belinda's voice was little more than a whisper as she fought to keep control.

'He will always be our Steward, have no fear on that score,' Bunch added, and was glad to see the women relax visibly now that the demons of tied housing had ebbed away. 'Knapp told me a little about his being gassed in the trenches. I asked him about it once but he always evaded the question. Daddy does the same thing, of course. They all do.'

'Those who served,' Belinda agreed. 'He was one of Lowther's Lambs. Most were, hereabouts. You know that, of course.' Her gaze strayed to sepia photographs on the wall. Two handsome young men in uniform and another of middle years: plainly a studio portrait of Nigel Parsons and his two sons in happier days. 'Richard was taken from us at Richebourg and James on the Somme. The same gas attack that ruined Nigel's health.'

'I'm so sorry.' Bunch knew the story but she had to let the woman ramble. There was no reply she could give. The older women faltered into silence now and gazed at the brown portrait of her two lost sons. Bunch quietly poured tea, placing a cup at Belinda's right hand. 'So many lost.'

Belinda started at her voice, dragged back to the present. 'And now it's started again.' Her voice was stronger. The brisk clipped tones that Bunch was used to hearing. 'Our district lost almost an entire generation back then. Still a few about of course.'

'You have two other sons though?'

'And two daughters.' A smile lit Belinda's face. 'Nine grandchildren. I shall have a houseful because they'll all want to come and see Nigel. I'd be baking already but we're short on flour and sugar.'

'I shall ask Cook if she has a stock she can raid.' Bunch swallowed half of her tea, which was not as hot as it could have been. 'What happened last night? Did you call for an ambulance?'

'He had been out with an old friend, Gordon Fanshaw. Gordon was a Lamb.' She paused for a moment to think. 'I don't believe Gordon was there at the Somme. Not that it matters. They were at school together you see. He lives over toward Heston.'

'Bit of a walk.'

Belinda flushed. 'Nigel took the cart. I hope that was all right?'

'Perfectly all right. Can't have a man Parson's age walking that distance. What time did he get back?'

'I'm not sure. I dozed off listening to the wireless. It was dark when he woke me. He was in a shocking state, gasping to breathe, and I called Doctor Lewis straight away.'

'Poor man.' Bunch did a quick calculation in her head and felt immediately guilty. Parsons was simply not capable of such things.

'Does he keep up with all of his Old Pals?'

'Mostly. Even has a word with Richard Bale now and then, though mostly he gets back a lot of anger and bile for his pains. Fortunately the man hardly leaves Flint house these days. His health is not a lot better than Nigel's, but they all play darts with Butcher at the Stars every week.'

'Quite a feat for a man with one eye.' Bunch smiled and got to her feet. 'I hate to be rude but I must go. It's a busy week. But do remember, Mrs Parsons, if you need anything, anything at all, you only need send me a message.' She took both Belinda's hands in hers. 'I do mean that. Don't get up, I shall see myself out.

Friday 17 May

It was a week of holding breaths, with mixed reports on the fighting across the Channel, and everyone busied themselves with their own business. Between the last of the silage and starting on the hay and filling interminable forms from the Ministry of Agriculture, Bunch barely had the time to do much more than pass other residents of the Dower House on the stairs.

Beatrice showed no sign of slowing her WVS activities and was barely home, despite all Bunch and Doctor Lewis could do. Edward stayed in Town, whilst Theadora remained on retreat in the wilds of the Scottish moorlands, making Bunch eternally grateful for Cecile's form filling and filing skills. 'Decades of practise,' Cecile told her. 'The generation and filing of interminable paperwork is something the University of Berlin excels in.' Once work was done the young woman vanished to her room or else took herself off on long solitary walks.

'Which is understandable,' Beatrice observed.

The case surrounding the Professor's death had not progressed any further, any more than that of Tobias Hurst.

It was with some relief to Bunch that market day came around, as it did every first and third Friday of the month. She drove into Storrington with Roger lolling in the passenger seat.

She was grateful that no one but the dog had been inclined to join her though she surmised, correctly, that the six o'clock start had a great deal to do with it, but an early start was essential. The gelding that her father had spoken of had not materialised and to view the animals up for sale and be ready to bid, she had no option but to be in the auction sheds from the off.

She sat patiently through most of the sales waiting for the particular animal that she desired to be led into the ring. A sturdy piebald cob just around fifteen hands and broken to both saddle and harness. The need for a second horse to haul the cart had become urgent and she knew this animal's owner, at least in passing, so she was confident that Magpie would be a doer.

The price started low which did not surprise her when piebalds were generally looked at somewhat askance, but the bids rose slowly and the hammer finally slammed down at six guineas. Bid accepted, Bunch shouldered her way through surprisingly large crowds down to the pens to examine her purchase. With all that was going on across the Channel she expected people to be selling and hoped there would be lower prices. *Yet we are waist deep in buyers bidding in an optimistic defiance. Or perhaps that should be defiant optimism? Small difference, but there.*

She scrubbed at the animal's forehead with her knuckles and blew puffs of air into its nostrils to imprint herself, as Parsons had taught her to do way back when she'd been given her first pony. Magpie responded in similar fashion, nuzzling at her new mistress's face and neck and snorting gently into her face. The scent and feel of that contact was a balm to Bunch and she lost herself in muttering nonsenses whilst smoothing the animal's ears that were twitching irritably. *God knows what Daddy will say about my bringing home a piebald vanner, or Parsons. They'll think I've gone totally bananas.*

She was still communing with her prize and had forgotten her surroundings until a low voice cut into her senses. 'I'm glad Maggie's getting a good home.' The plump man handing Bunch the lead rope allowed a final slap at the creature's neck. 'Virginia didn't want to sell her,' he explained, 'but she's gone into the WAF and we are going to stay with my sister in Gloucestershire. It would be such a shame to leave such a lively creature kicking her heels in livery for however long this goes on.'

'I shall take good care of her.'

'I'm sure you will, Miss Courtney. I won't stay – might upset the old girl more. I'll leave Mr Dudman here to see about delivery.' He reached out gave Bunch a warm double handshake. Thank you and good morning.' He walked away without a backward glance, striding rapidly out of view.

'Well, just you and me, Maggie.' She rubbed the black-and-white face and led her purchase across to Dudman's trailer.

'We'll box her in a bit, Miss. No point leavin' her to go all clam until we'm ready.' he eyed the animal warily. 'She's a lively one. Got a mind've her own, I don't wonder.'

'I think you may be right, Mr Dudman. But I wanted something with a little spunk.'

Dudman snorted, though whether from amusement or disbelief she was not certain. 'Then she'll suit,' he said and flinched slightly under her glacial glare. 'Folks say you'm got a way that gets into mischief.'

'Hardly,' she growled.

He shrugged. 'People do say, is all, Miss.'

'Say what exactly?'

He looked uneasy, his ruddy face flushing a deeper rose. 'As how you likes to get mixed up in police business. Bodies and such'

'That's taking it a little far.'

'I didn't know the furrin maid but I were in the Marquis last sale day 'an I saw how you mucked in.'

'You saw that?'

'Aah, I did.' He took the lead-rope from her and looked at Maggie as he added, 'That were a rum thing, droppin' down dead. Rat poisons they do say.'

'Apparently. What else do people say?'

He glanced each way and then leaned toward her in conspiracy. 'As it were one off of the stands. Some Frenchie make.'

'The poison?'

He nodded. 'My sister's maid's a nurse over in the Royal an' she says it's common gossip.' His nod was emphatic.

'Is that all?'

'Aah, tis enough to be goin' on with.'

'It is.' She gave Maggie a final slap on her shoulder and stepped away. 'I should be back to the farm before you, I think, but just in case—' she scribbled a note on her pocket notebook and tore the sheet off '—give this to the Land Girl in charge.'

'Yes, Miss Courtney.'

Horse trading concluded, Bunch wove her way through the market stall and made a few purchases for Cook, musing over 'Frenchie-poison'. She knew the term had little to do with geography, 'Frenchie' being a local catch-all phrase for anything continental or even vaguely foreign, but it was something to think on.

She wandered from stall to stall, listening to the chatter around her. A palpable undercurrent of fear and anticipation fizzled in every corner. Conversations seldom strayed far from the subject of war and the invasion threat, of the losses in Norway and what was happening in France, or perhaps the lack of information on that score. And there was a studied determination to be normal, if normal was ever an issue. But nowhere did she see rat poison. Not that she expected to when the Poisons Book would need to be signed, but it was worth a try.

She picked up a box of candles. Who would use something as devastating as fire against two harmless old ladies like Hilda and Enid Mann? There had been no arrests, nor any word from Wright, for that matter. *I have learned nothing new on the violent death of Hurst. Nor Benoir, or even De Wit.* The tallying up of deaths shocked her. *Three murders and a fire.* She looked down the street toward the Marquis. *Only two weeks ago? It feels like a year.*

She picked up a pack of batteries, which were also getting to be in short supply. A sign tacked to the stall declared 'One Box Only'. The batteries looked old and she was certain they would not last long but they and the candles together were worth the shilling she handed over to the stall holder. *I may as well take them as not.*

Her stomach rumbled at the sight of bread on the next stall, reminding her that she had not eaten since five o'clock. Yes, she should be getting back to Perringham Farm to see the unloading of her new beast. *But since I'm here it would be a waste of petrol not to...* Pausing only to buy the two cottage loaves that Cook had asked for, Bunch headed for the Marquis Inn.

The public houses were all open early on a market day and, unlike the street outside that was heaving with people, the saloon bar's gloomy interior was unnaturally quiet. A few farmers sat around the room eating breakfast and talking over the rise and fall of prices and bemoaning the latest restrictions from the various and ever multiplying government ministries.

'Early for a drink,' she said. 'We shall have coffee, eh Roger?'

The dog looked up, tongue lolling in the early warmth, his tail lashing at attention from his mistress. He followed close on her heel as she made her way to the bar and perched herself on the same section of bar that Janine De Wit had occupied just fourteen short days before.

'Yes, Miss?' Maude asked. 'What can I get you?'

'Coffee please and perhaps a sandwich.'

'Bacon or sausage?'

Neither would be her natural choice: she was a kippers and scrambled eggs girl. Bunch knew the lunch menu would not start for another hour, yet the alluring scent wafting through from the kitchens spoke of 'off-ration' bacon and was more temptation than she could stand. 'Bacon,' she said, 'with pickle if you have it.'

'Yes, Miss Courtney.' Maude did not look her in the eye or give any indication that she knew anything about her customer beyond a name.

Bunch wondered why the woman would be feigning ignorance. *Though she must be on nodding acquaintance with so many people without knowing anything about them.* Dawdling over breakfast, Bunch could not help staring at the carpet around her. There was a lighter patch a pace or two to her right where it had obviously been scrubbed with some vigour. The image of the Dutch girl gasping her last was vivid in her mind and Bunch had a momentary pang of guilt at taking that particular seat. She wasn't even sure why she had.

Eating at the Marquis on market day was a habit of some long standing but lounging at the bar was not. Her mother would have been appalled at such brazen habits. Sitting at a table way across the room, however, would not give her any opportunity to engage Maude in idle gossip. Chatting with Ted Vernon, she realised, was not an option. He lurked at the far end of the bar talking with a pair of Gentlemen Farmers but casting wary, even hostile, glances in her direction whenever he thought she was not looking.

Bunch sighed. Was that how it was going to be? It wasn't as if Bunch had personally staged the death here. Like most, she came here because it was the closest inn to the market, one serving food above and beyond bread and cheese. There was the Swann, she knew, with the added attraction of better food but it was a good way out from the main market square, and she had not booked in advance. Her stomach grumbled, louder this time so that a thick-set tweed-suited man of middle years seated a few feet along the bar looked towards her and grinned.

'Long day if you start early, Miss Courtney,' he said. 'And Maude does have excellent bacon.'

'She does.' Bunch eyed him suspiciously. 'I'm sorry, have we met?'

'In passing.' He held out his hand. 'Austin Digby at your service.'

'Pleased to meet you. I'm sorry but I don't think I've heard your name before.' She shook the proffered hand.

'Have you not? I am the auction vet for the day. I'm marking time waiting for my call up.'

'I should probably have had some veterinary advice from you before the sales. Just bought a nice little cob but I think she maybe a little older than claimed. We needed a second shaft-broken beast for home use. You must have seen her if you passed her fit for the sales.'

'What did you bid on?'

'Piebald mare. She was first lot in the single sales.'

'Ah, yes. That one.' He nodded and avoided her eyes by taking a tactful sip of coffee.

'You know her?'

'A good conformation for her type. Sturdy.'

'I sense a "but" coming.'

He hesitated. 'It's not really for me to say.'

'I bought her at auction, Mr Digby. Let the buyer beware.

But it would be useful to know if she does have some long-standing health problem.'

'The colouring is never very popular, of course, but nothing wrong with her physically. She just needs a very firm hand. She's a biter.'

'Is that all?' Bunch leaned her head back and laughed. 'I did wonder why no-one else was bidding for her. That can be overcome. I already have a Fell who's been known to gnaw chunks out of people if they take liberties.'

'Then if you're an experienced horsewoman she's a bargain,' he said. 'She'll be perfect for a small cart. Just don't turn your back on her in the stall.' He took another sip of coffee and looked around the bar. 'I saw you in here last market day. Someone sent for me, though God knows why. Most people would be happier to have a doctor over a vet.'

'I didn't see you. Or at least I don't recall, but it was a little frantic.'

'Nasty business.' He waved his cup at the room. 'It'll cause a lot of harm to this place. One whisper of bad food anywhere locals dine will cut it dead.'

'Especially when it is poison?'

Digby chuckled and shook his head. 'It should be perfectly obvious to anyone with an ounce of sense that the type of poison required to kill so quickly could not be administered by accident. One does not keep a packet of rat bait on a shelf next to the salt-pig. Or if one does then one reaps the inevitable results. In this case it was almost certainly a fairly common household rat poison albeit a stronger concentration than most.'

'You seem to know an awful lot about it. Is the fact that de Wit was poisoned generally known?'

'A woman falls off her chair, vomiting, and then dies? Most people who were in here and saw her die would have drawn that conclusion and taken great delight in passing that knowledge across half the county before the sun had set.'

'That explains why it's like the grave in here. It must be hard on the Vernon's livelihood.'

'If they police don't find out who done it we'll be out've business.' Maude Vernon set a cup of coffee and a plate bearing the requested sandwich on the bar at Bunch's elbow. 'Tis criminal letting murderers run about the place.'

'I am sure they are doing their best,' Bunch replied. 'I take it you've heard nothing more? Mr Digby here was saying the girl was definitely poisoned.'

'That Inspector keeps comin' back and askin' questions but what can we say? The poor woman were poisined but it weresn't anythin' we did.'

'Someone slipped her a somewhat lethal kind of Mickey,' Bunch said. 'I know it wasn't your fault, Mrs Vernon. We've eaten here for years and never had so much as indigestion.'

'Thank you, Miss.' The woman's expression relaxed. 'It be' hard, this week gone. People think we'en going to kill 'em all.'

Bunch spotted a chink in the armour and took her chance. 'I shall tell them all they are wrong. Anyone could have slipped a glob of bait in her coffee. It was so busy.'

Maude nodded self-righteously. 'It were.'

'Can you remember who was standing next to her?'

'That Inspector asked me the same question.' Maude scowled and folded her arms. 'Right aggy with me, he were. I wasn't 'avin' it. I'd done nothin'.'

'Of course not. But it would be awfully useful if you could recall anyone that came close to her.'

'There was one chap. Early on when she first sat there.'

'Someone you know?'

'He's one as comes in market days now an' then. But not one I knows by name.' She stared at the bar to Bunch's right as if imagining the scene. 'Little creature he was. Proper wind-shaken, I thought, when he ordered a half – 'e wersn't well-looking.'

'Dark hair? Light?'

'Brown,' she replied. 'Going grey under all the stuff 'e had on his hair. Plastered down and scrawny like a drownin' sheere mouse. But something vexatious about him. Liked hisself far too much, I'd say.'

'Local?'

'He were a Sussex lad,' she admitted. 'Not Storrington-bred though.'

'But you had seen him before?'

'Market days,' she said. 'Usually round at the four-ale bar.'

'Any idea what brought him in here?'

Maude thought for a moment, her eyebrows meeting with the effort of recall. 'That were odd,' she admitted.

Bunch raised a brow at Digby and picked up one half of her sandwich. 'You should tell this to the police, Mrs Vernon. They may know who he is.' She opened one end of the sandwich and viewed the smear of chutney gluing bacon to bread. She's had enough army food with the BEF not to be physically repulsed by it. *I just know I really need to find a new place to eat on Market day.* The bacon smelled good, however. She sank her teeth into it and chewed delicately. It was really very good, all evidence of her eyes aside. She felt Roger's muzzle come to rest on her knee and she slipped a piece of bacon to him.

The barmaid watched Bunch dissect the sandwich with a slight frown. 'Is that all right, Miss?' She asked. ''Tis good bacon. Off Capel Farm.'

'Yes, it's lovely.' Bunch took another mouthful and chewed enthusiastically. 'Good loaf. Did you make it?'

'Aah, I did.'

'My compliments.' She took a sip of coffee. 'This chap you

mentioned. If he came in today would you know him?'

'If he tries comin' in again I'll stop him. Bain't havin' his sort in 'ere.'

'Exactly so. The police need to find this killer. For the sake of poor Janine De Wit.'

'Mebbe.' Maude's face sagged into a stony impassivity. She took the ten-shilling note that Bunch placed on the bar and slid back the change. ''Scuse me. Customer.'

Digby watched Maude surge toward a newcomer at the far end of the bar and nodded slowly. 'That hit a sore spot,' he said. 'And you were doing so well up to then.'

'Do you think she knows who it was?'

Digby shook his head. 'No, but I think she'd genuinely tear him apart if she ever laid hands on him. Mostly because he may well have sunk her business. I suspect she has very little sympathy for the victim. Now I hate to desert you, but a vet's work is never done on auction day. Take care chasing poisoners … and good luck with that mare, Magpie.'

'Maggie.'

Digby chuckled. 'Maggie, of course. Good bye, Miss Courtney.'

~~~

Bunch's first stop on reaching home was the stables. She wandered into the block and scooped up a handful of chopped beets from the bucket as she passed. 'What do you think?'

Kate was already standing by the box, leaning against the newel post watching the cob tugging at her hay net. 'Lively,' she said. 'Kicked up a storm when we unloaded her so we thought she'd be better boxed for now. I would not like to try catching her out in the paddock until we have the measure of her.'

'Oh dear. You'd think you could trust someone from the Surrey Union Hunt.'

'I think she will be all right. Just didn't like the trip in the trailer. You know old Dudman also owns a knackers yard? They can smell the blood, I think.'

'I assumed he didn't use the same trailer for live and slaughtered beasts,' Bunch said.

'He didn't. I asked. This one has a mind of her own. Probably caught the scent of blood off Dudman himself, or his lads. She'll calm down after a night inside, I'm certain. I know it's warm but maybe we should bring the others in tonight – give her some company, get them used to each other.'

'Yes please. Everything else running smoothly? How's the silage coming along?'

'Second pit is filled, Boss. I gave the girls the afternoon off once the feeding was done. Pat and I will cover the milking. I hope that was all right. We'll finish the hay and when harvest begins they won't get a lot of time to themselves.'

'You are in charge. And yes, it's a good idea to give them some time off now.'

They fell silent, not wanting to voice the more impelling reason for giving the girls a few nights of fun. Maggie snuffled at Bunch's outstretched hand and sucked in the chopped beets that she offered. The horse's ears twitched constantly but her eyes were not rolling and her breathing seemed to be calm, though she backed up a pace when her neck was patted. Maggie crunched on the root vegetables and watched Bunch and Kate steadily.

'I think she will be fine. Perhaps we should leave her alone for a bit.'

They walked out into the late afternoon and stood gazing over the gate toward the lower meadows.

'I was going to see if Miss Benoir wanted to duck out early with the rest of us,' said Kate.

'Is that so?' There was an edge in the Land Girl's tone that made Bunch's senses twitch.

'Couldn't find her.' Kate stared straight ahead of her, shielding her eyes against the sun's glare. 'She does that. She's quite the fox. Never see her come or go.'

'Have a care, Katherine. Miss Benoir is an old friend.'

'I realise that. I just thought you should know because there have been mutterings of favouritism and you know how quickly that can get out of hand.'

Bunch looked at her curiously, somewhat guiltily, wondering what Kate was not saying. Nanny had often lectured Bunch on the benefits of listening before she spoke, and she imagined this was just the kind of thing the old dear had meant. It was perfectly obvious there was more to be said but her tart putdown had seen the back of it. *Not stymieing clues in a murder obviously, but something of the sort. Not that I could ever think Cissy was a murderer, naturally.* 'Thank you, Kate. You're quite right. I shall have a quiet word. Can't have her setting a bad example.'

Kate nodded slowly, gazing into the middle distance with lips pursed. 'Of course,' she muttered. 'Can't have that.' She managed a mechanical smile and pushed away from the gate. 'I should go and see about the evening milking. I shall get the girls organised for the morning.'

'Yes, thank you.' Bunch watched Kate walk away and resisted the impulse to call her back. The line between being on good terms with staff and friendship was a thin one. Her problem now was deciding which and where that line lay with Cecile.

Sunday 19 May

Bunch held back to watch the congregation filing out of the church's ancient doors. She noted Lizzie Hurst, with her children and her mother-in-law pausing to speak with the Reverend Day. Both women were clothed in black and their mourning acted like a magnetic force field: opposite poles deflecting the congregation which curved around them at a respectful distance.

Edward Courtney was deep in conversation with Ralph. Both men were striking in their own way. Ralph, in full uniform, his trademark unruly hair incarcerated beneath his officer's peaked cap. Against him Edward was sombre in his dark suit, his face holding only the polite interest that was his stock in trade, giving no hint of what the two men may have been discussing.

His diplomat's face, Bunch thought. She studied his profile, so like the portrait of her grandfather, which had once hung at the head of Perringham House's main staircase. Strong, masculine chin, high cheek bones and a nose which some called Roman and others in less charitable mood declared somewhat equine. She regarded it as something of a curse that she had inherited that same profile, along with the rangy limbs that were pure Beatrice. Dodo by contrast, standing with Emma and Barty in gravid serenity, was the image of Theodora, with Theodora's appearance of bone china fragility and effortless elegance.

Their indomitable grandmother was missing from the parade. She had pleaded fatigue and breakfasted in her room, which was a slight worry to them all as she rarely missed her Sunday morning service. It was times like this that Nanny would have been a blessing. In the sunset years she had been both companion and lady's maid, and a calming influence. Knapp might serve her well in many areas but without Nanny's autocratic manner Knapp lacked the means of diverting the old lady's activity.

Bunch looked around for Cecile and finally spotted her amidst Ralph's entourage, his Perringham coterie. *Familiar, chatting and laughing. She never does that with the other estate staff or even me, these days.* Bunch watched Cecile leaning in to catch something said to her, chic as always, in a red linen dress and white hat and matching shrug. The enormity of that thought struck Bunch head on. *Staff? Cissy? That's rather Presumptive of me.* She let her gaze drift across the gaggles of people around her, hoping the pink flush on her neck and face could be put down to the warmth of the morning.

People were inclined to linger, discussing the progress of war from the Continent and Scandinavia as well as the continued scooping up of enemy aliens. Wyncombe was a small place but not so small that they did not notice faces being whisked away. The German golf professional from the Ashington country club; the music teacher from the private girls' school; the elderly Doctor Ferber and his wife. The latter, Bunch knew, to be a Jewish couple who had fled Frankfurt's Vogelsberg Mountains for the gentle hills of Sussex – and who had often appeared at local event, even church services.

'Came and dragged him out've 'is surgery', so my Nance heard.' Mr Brice's Welsh tones rose exponentially with his excitement. 'Good man and a good doctor. Came in reg'lar for lint and such,'

'Still a bloody Gerry,' a scratchy local accent replied.

'They come yer for safety,' said Brice. 'Bin through a lot, they 'ave. Lockin' 'em up doesn't seem right some how.'

'Mebbe you should join them in the camp. You're a foreigner, just like them.'

'I'm Welsh and last I 'erd we're still British.'

Bunch smiled at the indignation in the little Pharmacist's tones.

'I'm just sorry for 'em. Have a little compassion, man.'

'Fuck you.'

'Duw, duw, no call for that. We're on sacred ground.'

'Bloody foreigner, like I said. We don't need Gerry lovers here.'

The voice was thick with anger and Bunch craned her head to see who would speak to the amiable pharmacist with such naked hate. All she glimpsed was a slight male figure lurching through the lych gate. She tried to catch Brice's attention but he was plainly flustered; glancing this way and that to see who might have caught the exchange before scuttling off to collect his wife Nancy from her own gossip, and hurrying homeward.

'Odd.'

Bunch glanced at Dodo and wondered that her sister could drift up behind her so quietly. 'I wasn't imagining it then, Brice leaving early and missing his chance to pass on all the juicy tattle.'

'It would be a change,' Dodo replied 'He is such an old fusspot.'

'Yet uncannily accurate. You have to allow him that. I suppose you didn't see who he was talking to just now?'

'His wife.'

'Before that.'

'Not a clue. I didn't look that closely.'

'Probably nothing. Mr Brice was feeling sorry for Doctor Ferber and his wife, and somebody had a bit of a spat with him over it.'

'Oh dear.'

'They're refugees.' Bunch shuddered. 'It leaves a nasty taste in the mouth.'

'I know, but people are afraid. Perhaps some are less so than they should be.' Dodo cast a glance toward her sister-in-law Emma, still chatting with neighbours a little distance away. 'Some people seem far too sanguine. You'd think they'd be a little more patriotic.'

Bunch followed her line of sight and shrugged. She knew Emma had many friends who, throughout the previous decade, had been openly admiring of Herr Hitler's New Order. Bunch had counted many of them her own friends in the past. They had attended the same schools and universities; married into each other's families; bought stocks in each other's companies; gone to the same events; shared the same histories; had Teutonic cousins by blood and marriage.

People of money and title who saw no reason why a little thing like war should interrupt their lives. Can't help wondering how it will ever be forgotten after this is over. 'Emma?' she said aloud.

'Not in as many words but she was telling me last night how many people at her college had been involved in research in Berlin and Munich.'

'You need to give her a little slack. Poor old thing's a bit lost'

'I know.'

'Do you want me to talk with her?'

'No. It's just me being a ninny.' Dodo hugged both arms across herself.

'Is it so very lonely?' Bunch placed both her hands on

Dodos crossed arms. 'You do know you only have to shout?'

Dodo stared at her feet.

'I mean it.'

'No, I'm not lonely. Well perhaps a little. I mean Barty is a sweetheart and Em really isn't so very bad. I can't imagine she's a fifth columnist or anything like. With a father like hers, patriotism is a given. But she and I are chalk and cheese in other ways. She's so erudite and I was never even *finished*. I miss Perringham House. I miss you.'

'And you miss Georgi.'

'Yes.' The word was breathed so quietly Bunch was not sure she had heard it at all, but the glistening of her sister's eyes was clear enough. 'Silly I know. It's been over seven months.'

'I don't think there's a time limit on grief, old thing. I miss Johnny like hell and we were only good pals. Georgi was your husband. Father of that bump. Give yourself some time. Things will be different when the baby is here.'

Dodo dipped her head in silent acknowledgement.

'Make sure you do.'

'I shall.'

'Miss Courtney, good morning. I was hoping to see you.' Ralph bounced up to them and raised his peaked cap. 'Mrs Tinsley. How nice to see you again.'

'You know Colonel Ralph, Dodo. The chap whose hooligans are laying waste to Perringham House.'

'That is a little hard on us poor soldier boys.' Ralph grinned at Bunch, rocking on his heels, both hands behind him, slapping his swagger cane into his left palm.

'And are they soldiers?' Bunch nodded toward the women still chattering with Cecile. 'They seem rather casually dressed.'

'Soldiers all,' he said. 'In their own way.' His eyes glittered, taunting her to say more.

'Rose. Are you being difficult?'

'No Daddy.

'I apologise for my daughter, Ralph.'

'No apology required, old boy. She's quite right. Some of the previous chaps had made a bit of a dog's dinner of the place. I am trying to put some of it right. And in that spirit, I'd like to ask you for both to dinner. The Mess keeps a pretty good table.'

'That is very good of you. But I shall need to travel back to Town later tonight. I did want to extend an invitation myself. Shall we say Friday week? Mother insists we dress, by the way.'

'Right ho. I shall look forward to it. Miss Courtney, Mrs Tinsley.' He tipped his fingers to his cap and loped away.

Edward watched him go. 'He reminds me of a Springer my father had before the Great War,' he said. 'All bounce, hair and enthusiasm.'

'And no brain?'

'The dog or Ralph?' Edward grinned. 'You'd have thought that dog was a little mad at first glance. How is it that you young things put it now? Goofy? Her name was Polly, Pollyanna Tennyson Laing, to give her full title. In fact she was the brightest little bitch I've ever known. Never missed a bird whatever the terrain and damn near anticipated every command. Faithful as they come. Bloody shame she was shot.'

'Good heavens. How awful. Who by?'

'Damned fool cousin of your mother's – at a weekend shoot up at the Lodge. That was before you were born. Doesn't matter now. Fetch Cecile, will you or we shall be late for luncheon and your grandmother will have apoplexy.'

'She'll have apoplexy when she finds out you've landed a dinner guest on her.'

'Not half as much as Cook.'

~~~

'We shall have to get the saddler to measure up a new rig.'

Bunch leaned down to tweak the traces. 'I thought Perry was tubby but Maggie here is a real podge.'

'She's not a pony,' Edward replied. 'Just a few inches into horse-dom. Nice animal. Good doer.' He gently slapped the piebald's neck. 'Shame about the colouring. It'll raise a few eyebrows but we can't be too choosey right now. I think she will serve us nicely.'

'I hope so. Kate thought she might be cribbing a little but that could just be the upset of moving. And we have been keeping her boxed until she's settled. She may not be used to that.' Maggie snorted and lunged half-heartedly at the arm holding her bridle. Bunch gave her a little shake and a clipped command to 'stand'. 'Let's hope so. I was warned she was a nipper. Not until after the sale, sadly.'

'Surprised the dealer owned up to it even then.'

'He didn't. It was the vet chappy. Austin Digby? We got talking in the Marquis.'

Edward stared at her. 'Digby, you say? What did he look like?'

Bunch cast her mind back. The meeting had been so commonplace she barely recalled him. 'Nothing out of the ordinary. He was sitting down but I would say a little under six foot. Thick set, but not fat. Good quality tweeds. Thinning hair, I think, or it may have just been hair oil.' She shook her head. 'I'm not sure I would know him again, I'll be honest. He was rather ordinary.'

Edward grinned and shook his head. 'He would be delighted to hear you say that. He works hard at it.'

'You know him?'

Edward grunted, a small laugh with little humour. 'I don't know a vet called Austin Digby but I do know a chap in a particular office in Whitehall by the name of the Honourable Digby Morris who sounds suspiciously like the fellow you're describing.'

'So you do know him?'

'I rather think I do. What else did you talk about?'

'Nothing much. He mentioned that young Dutch woman, de Wit. I gather he was in the bar at the time.'

'And you told him what?'

'Nothing of any great import springs to mind. Does it matter?'

'If it was Morris asking then it may.' Edward peered intently at the rein strap, passing it back and fore between his fingers. 'It rather depends on what you told him. Does explain a few things.'

'Daddy. I'm a grown woman and you can't control every man I talk to.'

'I would not dream of it, my darling Rose. But you might try to control what you say to every man who talks to you.'

'Who is he? Not a vet, then?'

'He is a vet, yes. Now war has broken out he's a few other things besides.'

'Such as?'

'Sorry my dear, I can't tell you any more than that. Be glad it was Morris and not a few others I can think of. The whole intelligence service is in chaos since Winnie put...' He smiled to himself and gave an almost imperceptible shake of his head. 'Never mind. What I will tell you is be more careful of what you say and to whom in future. The fact that someone informs you they like horses does not automatically make them a jolly good egg.'

'I don't understand. What does my talking to this Morris fellow mean to anybody?'

'Not a great deal, it would seem. Had it done so we'd have heard a lot more.'

'We?' Bunch scowled at him. 'You knew already, didn't you?

This… This person has already told you about all of this.' Her scowl deepened. 'I say, am I being watched? I mean was he following me?'

'Do not flatter yourself. Yes, he was doubtless there making enquiries about the de Wit case so stumbling across you was sheer luck. Good for him and bad for you. He saw you at the auction and recognised your name from the files on the case when you bid for this nag here.'

He gave Maggie a friendly slap and the horse muttered peevishly. Bunch had some sympathy for her. Being patronised was never to be taken lying down. 'And thought he'd find out if I was some sort of sympathiser?' she snapped. 'Well, that makes me feel so much better.'

'There are arrests being made. Others are imminent – no, don't ask. You know better than to ask though I think you can guess some of them. Be careful. I mean it. Being the Honourable Rose Courtney will not help you a great deal if you really are deemed a security risk.' He handed her the rein and patted her on the forearm. 'Don't get mixed up in things you don't have any real conception of. Leave the unfortunate death of this Dutch girl to the police. And I have had that direct from Gladys.'

'Gladwyn Jebb? What business is it of his?'

'Nothing I can talk about, even to you. He informed me that he finds your antics amusing but getting in too deeply would be ill advised. Don't rely on his being a family friend to act as some sort of magic pass.'

'Hardly my fault. I just happened to be there at the time.'

'But you went back to ask questions.'

'It seemed to be the right thing to do.'

'You were on the scene when the police were investigating the man who was strangled.'

'I understand that his neck was broken, Daddy. Quite

different – and yes I was there.'

'Which is exactly why I want you to stay away from it all. Look after your sister and leave the derring-do to your friend Chief Inspector Wright and his chaps.'

She stared down at the crease in her jodhpurs, struggling to control a rising temper, as angry with herself for the tears lurking behind her eyes as with her father's admonishment. She loved her father dearly but hated the way he could reduce her from sophisticated woman to gauche school girl in a sentence. Small wonder he was the FO's first choice in tricky situations. She wondered if he would have said the same things to her brothers, had they survived the flu epidemic and grown up to be the men that she felt Edward plainly wished she was.

'Rose. Bunch, it's not your job.' He stroked her head. 'There is a man out there who kills in cold blood and catching him is a job for the police. Promise me you will not get involved any further?'

She shrugged and looked up with a lopsided smile.

'And I should save my breath to cool the porridge.' Edward shook his head. 'You never could resist sniffing out secrets. Always been the same. Hiding your birthday presents was a nightmare from the moment you could walk.' He smiled grimly 'I repeat, leave it to the authorities. And in future be very careful what you say to strange men in public houses. *Careless Talk.*'

'I…'

He smoothed a strand of hair from her face and kissed her forehead. 'New poster campaign. You may have seen the beginnings of it already and you'll be hearing a lot more of in the coming months. Rather relevant to our conversation, don't you think?'

'Excuse me, sir?'

Edward spun on his heel to glare at the housemaid, lurking

nervously at the entrance to the yard. 'Yes?' he barked, sharper than expected so that the girl flinched.

'Sorry sir. If you'll excuse me, but there's a telephone call for you. Mrs Knapp says it's urgent. From Whitehall.'

'Thank you, Sheila. Tell them I shall be there directly.' He gave Maggie a knuckle-rub to her forelock. 'Damn it,' he muttered and then to Bunch, 'It seems I shan't be able to come out for a spin after all. Duty calls.'

'I know, Daddy.'

'I have a feeling I won't be here when you get back.' He gave Maggie a strong pat to her neck, avoiding any glance at his daughter. 'Take care, won't you. And please, stop meddling. You have enough to do with running this place. I'm only sorry your mother can't be a great deal of help. She is not at all well. Nerves are all over the place.'

'I do understand. Really I do.'

'I know. You're a good girl. Now, are you quite happy to take this one out for a spin alone?'

'Yes, Daddy.'

He nodded curtly and she watched him stride away, staring after him long after he was out of sight. The idea that she was under surveillance shocked her to the core. The fact that she had been so easily identified and questioned frightened her. That her father had come to hear of it so quickly did not surprise her – any more than his still thinking of her as a child.

Maggie snorted, jerked her head and backed the cart a few feet, dragging Bunch's attention to the present. 'Come on then, Maggie. Let's put you through your paces, shall we?' She stepped up into the seat of the cart and slapped the reins lightly along the horse's back. 'Walk on.'

The piebald leaned into the harness and started toward gate, her hooves scraping slightly on the cobbles as she started to move. Bunch guided her toward the lane that passed

Perringham and on to Banyards. The ride was smooth, with her new acquisition walking briskly along the back lane making light work of the unladen vehicle. Maggie was stronger and quicker than the smaller and ageing Perry, though Bunch was loathe to admit it.

Bunch guided them into a gateway as a van rattled past, and smiled at the animal's response. Maggie had crunched at the bit, laying her ears back against her head. Not nervous, it appeared, only irritated, and that attitude amused Bunch. Like Perry, this horse was shaping up to be a handful, which suited her own personality, though she had a suspicion that others who needed to drive the cart may not be quite so happy. The deal was done, however, and schooling the animal into better manners would at least be an interesting challenge. After being talked down to by Edward she felt a little guilty at her sense of triumph. 'You're a feisty little madam, Maggie. But you'll do. Walk on.'

She slapped the reins lightly along the animal's back and they were soon rattling toward Banyard Manor at a clipped pace that ate up the distance in short order. When she arrived it was a little too early for afternoon tea but Dodo made allowances and ordered tea in any case.

'Come out onto the terrace. Such a lovely afternoon. I can't believe this weather is going on for so long.'

'I am praying it holds off for another week,' Bunch replied. 'We took a chance and made an early cut of hay. If we can get that stacked before the rain we might get a decent second cut.'

'Do take care, Bunch, you are starting to sound like a regular Farmer Giles with all this farming malarkey.'

'I would far rather be doing something a little more exciting. I was turned down yet again for a posting, you know.' She rubbed at her aching leg. *Crocked in France last autumn and crocked again courtesy of Emma's sainted mother. I'll never pass that ATS medical in a million years.*

'Quite right too. I should hate for you to go away again.'

'If it is any consolation they turned me down as well.' Emma leaned across to pass Bunch her tea. 'I applied for the Wrens but failed muster. Eyesight.' She pushed her glasses more firmly onto the bridge of her nose as if to prove the point. 'Damned shame, but there you are. We're a pair of old crocks together.'

'What will you do instead?' Bunch asked.

'I shall be helping out here. At least until Dodo's sprog arrives.' Emma sat at the table, adjusting her hat against the sun as she settled between the sisters. 'I was offered a job as a researcher for one of the Ministries quite recently. That's something I can do with eyes closed.'

'Very patriotic.' Bunch watched over the rim of her teacup for any hint of dissembling, but the woman seemed perfectly sanguine. She felt a trill of relief. *Emma's an odd sort but I'd hate to think she is a bad sort.* 'Are you going to Plumpton next Saturday? Might not be any more racing there for a bit so it could be our last chance.'

'You know I'm not really the racing type.' Emma paused. 'I am sorry, that sounds ungracious. It would be good to get out somewhere and meet different people. One can get so tired of the same folks, day after day.'

A frisson of antipathy was almost visible between the resident sisters-in-law and Bunch could quite see why. Emma, rather like Cecile, was a dyed-in-the-wool intellectual and always had been – a swot by any standard but, as with Cecile, Bunch had always got on well with her. Dodo was not stupid, but her interests had seldom strayed beyond the social round and allied pressing matters captured between the pages of *The Lady*. Bunch could quite see how, without the buffer that Georgi had provided when he was alive, the two would find very little in common. Weeks thrown into each others company through necessity was taking its toll and she had a fleeting sympathy for Barty, caught between them. 'I shall check to see how we are for fuel,' she said. 'And see if we can round up a few of the crowd that aren't signed up. It could be jolly good fun.'

'Of course.' The tone was polite but disinterested and an abrupt change of subject. 'Did you hear they were scooped up for internment?'

'Such a shame after all they went through to get out of Germany,' Bunch agreed. Gossip ran at all levels it seemed. Internment was the big news across the village. She supposed it was hardly surprising with so little news from across the Channel. She told herself it was tiresome having to go over the same conversations, but she knew the real reason for her irritation was her father's put-downs, which she felt were too raw to talk over with her sisters. She grunted surprise at her seeing Emma as a sister, if only by marriage. 'Poor old sausage,' she said, to cover the sound. 'And his wife is so frail.'

'Perhaps for the best,' Emma replied. 'Don't look at me like that, Bunch. I mean that they will probably be safer, at least for now. We know from the evidence of our own eyes how the press is making it rather hard for anyone with a foreign name and a funny accent.'

'True.'

'Speaking of the devil, where is Cissy today?'

'God knows,' Bunch replied. 'She has been something of a recluse of late. Sneaking off for hours at a time, according to the girls at the farm. She was a bit of an odd duck at school. Growing up into a swan doesn't seem to have done much for her confidence.'

Emma shook her head. 'Play fair. She lost her father less than a month ago and the poor creature hasn't been allowed to give him a decent burial. It has to be a hard time for her.'

'Perhaps.'

'Bunch.' Dodo stared at her sister, aghast. 'You are dreadful. We both know what it's like to lose someone.'

'Yes, we all do. But there is something else going on. I don't think grief is the half of it. Between the three of us, Cissy was not over-fond of her dearly departed Papa. She told me as much herself.'

'I don't see what you are driving at.' Emma sat back, her right elbow resting on the chair arm and right forefinger resting against her lips as she gazed at her friend. 'What are you not telling us?'

Until that moment Bunch realised she had not been thinking anything at all, but asked the question quite so boldly she knew what was bothering her. 'Who else had the opportunity to bump the old man off? Cissy may not be taken seriously here but I'm told she was quite the bee's knees at the University of Berlin.'

'You can't possibly think she killed her own father?' Dodo's carefully manicured brows rose in shock

Emma's merely tweaked into a sardonic quirk. 'Positively Medean,' she growled. 'Not sure Cissy would be capable of patricide. Far too nice. Always has been.'

'She's capable,' Bunch replied. 'We all are, given sufficient provocation.'

'And you think Cecile Benoir had reached her limit?'

The three of them exchanged looks and then Bunch shook her head. 'Wright seems to think the same person who killed the Prof also did for that chap Hurst.'

'Snapping a man's neck does seem unlikely for a little thing like her.'

Bunch nodded. 'Very true.'

'Must you?' Dodo whispered. 'I don't want to talk about it all.'

'Sorry, that was rather mean of me, wasn't it? Not something you need to worry about, old thing, and definitely not a subject for afternoon tea.' She patted Dodo's hand and then glanced at her watch. 'I should be getting back. I can't see this new horse of mine standing in harness for long without kicking out. She's a bit of a madam.'

Dodo and Emma exchanged a knowing look. 'Good conformation, I'll be bound,' Dodo said.

'For the job at hand? Excellent. She could pull a lot more than our little cart. She a Vanner of some kind. Slightly heavier in the leg and hoof than the average, but that's a good thing because the cart isn't built for anything much taller than—'

Emma held both hands up to stem Bunch's lecture mid-flow. 'Enough. We submit. She's a nice pony, so well done.'

'Sorry. Nobody at the Dower is very excited about her.' Bunch beamed at them as she stood to leave. 'Not that either of you are, but captive audience and all that.'

'You are an equine lunatic, Rose Courtney. Just go home.'

Bunch leaned down to kiss her sister on the cheek. 'Take care won't you, and you know I'm always here.'

~~~

It was a sultry afternoon, airless and still. Off to the south, toward the coast, a line of grey hinted at rain or mist out to sea but the sky overhead sported little more than the odd puff of high cloud. Bunch took a longer route home, putting the new horse through its paces along the wider Worthing road before cutting back along Ash Lane to the south of Perringham estate. She chose that road because it wound its way up an incline that crested the side of the coombe. Not a steep incline, as inclines went, but a longish haul. She allowed Maggie to set her own pace and was pleased to see her take the rise with only a slight lessening of pace.

At the summit she pulled the cart into a field entrance and

allowed Maggie to catch her wind. There was no water but the horse pulled mouthfuls of grass and herbage that in May were green and lush despite the warm spell. As Maggie rested, Bunch took in the sweep of the land. Hedgerows bordered a quilt of fields and meadows in the valley bottom and surrounded the familiar bulk of Perringham and its woodlands, with open grassland dotted with clumps of bramble and gorse on the southern rise. Being a Sunday, there was nobody in the fields and the only movement came from newly shorn sheep crossing between patches of scrubby growth, until she spotted a familiar flash of red and white. A small figure moving toward the farm. Bunch rose in the seat, shading her eyes against the brightness of the afternoon. *I can't be sure at this distance, and it really is none of my business when it comes to it, but this seems familiar because that looks awfully like Cecile Benoir.*

Thursday 23 May

Edward may have instilled some level of caution with regard to Janine De Wit but Bunch's curiosity over the late Tobias Hurst only grew as the week progressed. Rumours about the circumstances surrounding the young man's death were running wild. He had, depending on whom Bunch spoke with: been hit by a speeding troop lorry; killed during a botched robbery of the church plate – doubtlessly by Barty Tinsley's dubious in-law, Percy Guest; silenced before he could reveal the identity of a fifth columnist; murdered by one of those 'Frenchies' in Perringham House; died attempting to capture a Nazi paratrooper; or even that he had met his tragic end during a training exercise of the newly formed LDV.

By Thursday she had tired of the endless speculation and decided that since she was in the high street delivering leaflets to the church hall for Beatrice's WVR meeting, she may as well take a jolly good look at the memorial where Hurst's neck had been brutally snapped.

The rope barriers erected by the police had already been removed and to Bunch it all seemed to have reverted to the desperately mundane very rapidly. She found it hard to recall exactly how that lean and muscular corpse had lain across the steps.

Put yourself in their shoes, she thought. She stood with her back against the statue, looking southward, along with the bronze figure, and then sidled around it to view the village and continued round, seeing it all as a contiguous panorama. The surrounding scenes at all points of the compass were too familiar and as far as she could tell devoid of anything remotely out of the ordinary. She wasn't sure why she felt disappointed by that. She'd hardly expected to spot a hooded stranger lurking in the bushes but something, anything, would have lessened her frustration at not knowing.

She turned her attention to the granite blocks on which she stood. Not only had they been swept clean but the small amount of staining from bodily fluids, which had leaked at the time of the crime, had been scrubbed away. She knew this had been done on the request of the vicar so that the widow would not see evidence of her husband's slaughter every time she passed the spot, and Bunch quite understood that. *But it does not help the investigation in the slightest.*

Bunch stepped down to the next level and paced slowly in a circle around the monument, her gaze fixed on each smooth stone surface as it passed beneath her, and saw nothing. She moved down to the next tier to repeat the process. A glint caught her eye and she dropped to one knee to pounce on it, digging into a crack between the blocks and fishing out a small metallic sliver. It crumpled under the pressure of her fingers. Silver on one side and purple on the other: the faded and grubby remains of a chocolate wrapper. She smiled and was about to throw it away. It was clearly not new debris, but the memorial was so thoroughly scrubbed she felt it hard to imagine finding litter of any kind on its sterile space – especially when chocolate bars were becoming a precious commodity. *An adult had to have dropped this,* she reasoned. *Children prefer spending their ration on loose sweets. It gives them more for their pennies.*

The final step down to ground level was deeper than the rest, allowing room for the roll call of the fallen to be chiselled into its upright faces. She walked the monument's perimeter, her neck bent forward as she extended her search away from the base, spiralling outwards, hands clasped behind her back, with all her attention fixed on the patch of ground directly in front of her.

The dusty slabs of dressed stone were tightly laid and there was not a scrap of anything green or growing in any of those precise lines. Even lichen was assiduously cleaned from the stones and slabs on a regular basis. Bunch was not sure by whom. The parish committee she assumed. Beatrice would know, it being her particular arena of good works. Chairing committees was something Bunch had not given a great deal of thought to before, but she supposed it was an activity she needed to learn and be involved with now. She made a mental note to ask Beatrice and continued her search. She had no real idea what it was that she was searching for. *Some infantile memory from childhood reading. When one is investigating one searched for clues. Not that I am a detective, and God forbid I am investigating. Daddy was quite insistent on that point.*

Bunch bent to look at a small grey circle on the pavement and grunted amusement. *The Parish worthies will have a fit when they see that. Not a clue, however, unless one has a way of knowing who had chewed and spat a specific piece of gum, but that is impossible.* She was fairly confident the flattened disc had been there for too long to have anything to do with Hurst's death.

She passed beyond the paving that marked the monument's boundaries and had almost reached the hedge surrounding the village hall before she ran into Chief Inspector Wright leaning against the front fender of the police car.

'Hello. Having fun?' he asked. 'Looking for anything in particular?'

She straightened up and sneaked a glance at her watch. *Damn. Just coming up for six o'clock. I do need to talk with him but I shall need to get a wiggle on for dinner.* 'William, good evening.' She grinned sheepishly. 'I was just looking.'

'If it's any consolation I did almost the exact same search not half any hour ago.' Wright pushed away from the Wolesley and sauntered toward the statue, stopping an arm's length away. 'Macabre,' he said. 'Death at the feet of a monument to the dead.'

'Was that intentional?' Bunch came to stand beside him and followed his gaze. 'Are you saying we're being sent some sort of message?'

'It may well mean something to the killer but I doubt it will tell the two of us anything significant right at this moment.' He lifted his hat and ran his left hand across his hair. 'It's a damnable case. Not a single witness nor solitary motive.' He settled his fedora back in place with a firm tweak and gave Bunch a tired glance. 'Are these people here likely to mislead us?'

'Are you asking if the local people would lie? Good God, no. Well, most of them wouldn't at least. If they knew something I am reasonably sure they'd tell you, if only because Hurst was well liked. People here want to know who killed him every bit as much as you or I. Nobody wants to think there is a maniac on the loose in the villages. Especially one strong enough to overpower a man like Hurst without any apparent struggle.'

Wright looked across to the Seven Stars. 'Sounds quiet over there but it is one of those pubs,' he said. 'Silence the moment a stranger walks through the door.'

'I think I can help there. I am a local.' *I shall be in it up to my neck with Beatrice for being late for dinner but the chance to crank Wright for information? Too good to miss.* 'I need a pint,' she added.

'Examining a crime scene is thirsty work.'

'Beer?' he asked.

'You think I don't drink beer?'

'I won't deny I'm surprised. I though sherry was more your style. Or perhaps a little champagne? All those hunt balls and dinner parties.'

'Dodo is far more the socialite than I am. Apart from the hunt ball perhaps. And the races.' Even to her own ears it made her life sound somewhat limited. Yet horses had always been her refuge through the darkness that her parent's frequent absences had wrought on the Perringham household. 'I like beer. I got a taste for it in the ATS.' She linked her arm with Wrights, feeling inexplicably glad that he was a tall man and not shorter than her, as many were. 'Come along.'

'After you.' Wright signalled to Glossop to sit tight and followed Bunch into the coolness of the pub.

They sat at a window table with a pint before each of them. The bar was quiet. One young couple sat two tables away deep in quiet conversation and an older man stood at the bar perusing the paper. There were fewer early drinkers at that time of day, and fewer still because so many had joined up. 'You may have to wait a while for some more people to question.' Bunch supped the foam from her glass and worked the excess from her lips. 'Are you any closer to finding the killer? Or is that killers? You have quite a body count to deal with.'

'The de Wit file?' Wright stared at his glass. 'That one has been taken out of our hands.'

'Given to Scotland Yard?'

'Nothing so simple. Seems both Benoir and our little Dutch girl have become topics of interest to some of the more clandestine departments springing up around Whitehall. Well, skulking might be more accurate. Half of them don't have a name they will own up to. And when none of them communicate, even with each other, we mere policemen don't have the slightest chance of finding out what's going on.'

'I suppose both were poisoned so it would be a logical conclusion to put them together.'

'Except there seems to be no common link.' He grunted, an explosive huff, and Bunch could not decide if came from amusement or exasperation. 'I have been thinking about this. Leaving aside the guards at the gatehouse, has anyone other than civilians been seen going in or out of Perringham House?'

'I can't say I've had the time or the inclination to watch.'

'It's a question I have put to many people and none of them seem to have an answer. They all start by classifying a place military. But if you push further they'll usually admit there have been fewer soldiers around in recent months. Now that could be down to the manoeuvres over the Channel. But then again?' he shrugged.

Bunch could empathise with his point. She remembered all too clearly how the classroom she had glimpsed when she had visited her old home had been peopled with civilian-looking students, and very few of the people who accompanied Colonel Ralph to church were ever in uniform. 'You may have a point. But what would that have to do with the death of the Professor? Or de Wit. Or young Hurst?'

'Maybe nothing. Perhaps everything.' He took a long pull from the tankard, staring out the windows for a moment and then carefully returning his glass to the stained beer mat, taking time to adjust the dimpled glass tankard to the precise centre. 'I am inclined to think Hurst's murder was collateral,' he said finally. 'He was killed to keep him quiet about something—'

'Are they all linked?' Bunch interrupted.

'Given the method of his execution it would fit. It's certainly the theory higher up the chain.'

'But you don't believe it?'

He shrugged. 'It doesn't matter a great deal what I think. There are too many fingers getting stuck into this pie. I don't think anybody really knows but they're all doing their best to shut down enquiries.'

'Because they all think it's their jurisdiction?' She laughed. 'That's the way these things are run. I've watched Daddy play their games all my life. War has just given them a chance to grab a little more power.' She laid a forefinger on his wrist. 'This new Emergency Powers act will only make it easier. Take Perringhams. I honestly thought it was going to be an Officer's billet. But Daddy was packed off to the Far East to sort out some mess and it was all changed by the time he returned.' She took another gulp of her beer, her brows furrowing as she thought of how her home was being used. 'I gather it was a deal struck with his old Eton pal, Gladwyn Jebb. Nice of them to tell me.'

'Careless talk?'

'Rot.' She glared, aware that it was the second time in a day that people had said that to her. 'I do know how to be discreet.'

'I know it and so does your father, I suspect. But the bods in Whitehall don't know you beyond your pedigree in Debretts. To them you are just some horse-mad debutant spinster who can't stay away from things that don't concern her. Take care. Your father may not be able to help if you fall foul of them.'

For a moment Bunch felt a hint of that legendary temper of her childhood rising and then she spotted the glint in Wright's eye. *Is he honestly sending me a warning?* She flicked his forearm and was gratified to see him wince – just a little. 'You're an idiot,' she growled.

'Yet here we are, drinking beer like old pals.' He was solemn in the next second. 'I've been looking into the background of various Chiltwick residents and I can't see why any of them would kill a man like Hurst. He seems to have been well liked.

In point of fact, there are only two adult male residents at this moment who have an entry in official records of any kind and those are purely military.' He dragged out his notebook. 'There is a shepherd by the name of Ken Butcher. And the private tutor, Richard Bale. I gather they were both in the local Pals Battalion. There are a few others from that unit in the district. Your manager Nigel Parsons is one, and another chap called Gordon Fanshaw. Tattered remnants. You probably know all about them of course?'

'I know Parsons, obviously. I've heard of Butcher and Fanshaw by name, but neither are people I have had much to do with. I know Dickie Bale and we've talked in a general fashion at various functions, though he's doesn't mix very much. Interestingly, I did come across his mother in Chiltwick when I went to see the Mann sisters after the fire. Not a terribly pleasant sort. Both the Bales are somewhat reclusive.' She looked toward the memorial that she had been circling a few minutes before. 'You know about The South Downers? Lowther's Lambs? Ten of the names out there on that monument were men lost in a single day on the Somme. Most of the rest fell at Passchendaele. Parsons's two sons among them. The men who came back tend not to talk about it, which I quite understand.'

'I've read the records,' said Wright. 'Butcher lost an eye. Fanshaw was injured in a mortar attack. Nigel Parsons and Richard Bale were both gassed. Bale lost a lung and spent a time in a rest home for his nerves, though he's hardly alone in that because half the young officers who came off the front line were treated for shell shock at some point. There are a dozen more old hands still living but most are too old to carry out a crime of this nature, or else they've moved on. We can't place any one of them in the area in the past few weeks and I think it maybe a red herring, in any event.'

'Is any of this relevant, do you think?'

'Not a clue. The coroner was quite clear on cause of death. A very cleanly snapped neck, which he claims could only have been accomplished after expert training. That does rather point toward a military man. Assuming we discount the possibility of a Nazis parachutist, the Old Contemptibles has to be our starting point.'

'Would either Bale or Parsons are well men. Would they have the strength? Given sufficient motive I suppose it's possible.'

'That was my thought. Butcher claims to have been out on the Downs checking his flock until seven and then went home. He admits that he was alone but claims that a neighbour spoke to him at around ten when he was putting his hens away for the night. Botting is still trying to verify that. Parsons and Bale both have solid alibis, at first glance. Parsons was at the cottage hospital having been taken ill and his old comrade Bale was at the LDV meeting.'

'I would double check that. I'm told Bale had a public falling out with Tinsley at that meeting. He may well have left early. And even if he didn't, the village hall is right there on the spot.' Bunch frowned. 'If it's a military link we're searching for then there are the Canadians over at Fryern House, and any number of small military depots within easy reach.'

Wright shook his head. 'There'd been a general call back to barracks, so unless they were AWOL it's unlikely. We still have who knows how many candidates just down the road at Perringham House but I can't get access to question them. I've applied twice now and had it kicked into the long grass. It would appear that whatever Colonel Ralph and his pals are up to in there puts them beyond the bounds of justice.'

'How terribly frustrating.'

'To put it mildly.'

They fell quiet as two men ambled through the open door. 'What did you want to know from the local worthies?' she said. 'Supposing we can get them chatting.'

'Simply whether they saw anything. Strangers or locals. I would welcome any snippet.' He stared out at the deserted street. 'A man was brutally murdered in the very centre of this village and nobody saw a thing. I find that hard to believe.'

'Once the shops are closed there are never many people around to see anything. Unless there is something going on in the hall.'

'Or else the drinkers in here.' Wright craned his neck, face almost against the window to get the monument in full view. 'The scene of crime is only partially in sight,' he said. 'And you would have to be close to this window to see anything in detail.'

'Plus the blackout curtains would have been drawn by then. It wasn't dark but I know the publican gets them closed in good time. The same thing would apply with the village hall, and probably most of the houses if we're honest.' She spread her hands. 'Frankly the chances of finding a witness are not good. Unless they happened to be walking by at that precise moment, which at that time in the evening would not be usual.'

'So you think I am wasting my time in here?'

'I wouldn't say that.' Bunch took a pull of her drink and set it down again with a smile. 'For one thing you would have missed my scintillating company. But seriously, if PC Botting drew a blank on the night of the murder I doubt you will turn up much more now'

'Which brings us back full circle.'

'Then at the risk of teaching granny to suck eggs – yours that is, I wouldn't dare try it with mine – perhaps you should stop asking who and concentrate on why,' said Bunch. 'Why would anyone wish Hurst dead?'

'And there we've drawn a complete blank. As you said

already, he was well liked.'

'A plaster saint, in fact. Somehow I doubt that.'

'His wife was adamant he hadn't an enemy in the world. Though I gather he did report an altercation with a car from Perringham House. They passed him on the road in a hurry and his wagon was bumped onto the verge. It shed half its load when he pulled over to avoid them, and he wanted payment for the loss.'

'She was sure they were from Perringham?'

'Mrs Hurst was certain that was the story as related to her and we've no reason to doubt it.'

'Hence wanting to go in to ask questions.'

'Precisely.'

'Bit thin as motives go,' said Bunch. 'Half a load of hay is hardly worth killing a man over.'

Wright laughed quietly. 'I agree. In Ralph's shoes I would ignore any request from local bobbies to go through channels to question them over such a small matter. Excuse me, Minister, may this flat-footed copper come and question the residents of a highly secure military base about a few wisps of hay? I'd tell me no – in no uncertain terms.'

'Makes you think though. Some of them would be well-trained in unarmed combat.'

'Is that any better? Excuse me Chief Constable, could you possibly see your way to obtaining me a warrant to question these people on the off chance that one of your highly trained staff might be a killer?' He sighed, running his hand over his head, as she noted him doing when deep in thought. 'Without some genuinely convincing suspicions I have no real chance of success.'

'I may.' Her smile was more than a little smug. 'Everett Ralph fondly imagines he's a charmer. I think I could get in without any tiresome application for a warrant – if I go about it the right way.' She laced her fingers beneath her chin and fluttered her eyes. 'I can be quite irresistible you know.'

A short silence as Wright stared at her was ended by a loud guffaw.

'And just what is so funny?' Bunch demanded.

'I'm sorry. I cannot imagine you as Mata Hari.' He wiped at his eye and chortled a little more. 'It simply isn't a part I can see you playing.'

Whatever reaction she might have expected from Wright, this was not it. His amusement cut deep. *How dare he? I'm offering to help and he thinks it's so very funny.* 'I may not be a femme fatale,' she snapped, 'but I'll have you know I am seen as quite a catch by a lot of people.'

Wright's face crumpled and he collapsed back into laughter. 'I am sorry. Put it down to the beer. You are a very attractive woman and you have great charm, but Ralph is a hard-boiled old soldier. A genuine man of the world because if his service record is to be believed. He's visited most of it at one time or another. It's simply not going to work.'

'Oh really?' She got to her feet. 'In the absence of any other plan, good luck finding your way into Perringham House.'

'Bunch, I didn't mean—'

She allowed the door to slam on his apology.

Saturday 25 May

The promised race meeting at Plumpton had been postponed, as had many similar events in recent months. Questions had been asked in high places about the fuel needed for horseboxes and punters alike, and the fuel of another kind required to keep thoroughbreds in tip-top condition, was a waste of resources in many eyes. The racing world was holding its breath on whether the Sport of Kings was about to end, at least whilst war was poised on the doorstep.

In the absence of any official meets, a point-to-point, however, was almost as good in Bunch's eyes. She had set off with Emma and Dodo all in good spirits, though disappointed that Cecile had chosen not to join them. 'I have an appointment,' was all the explanation she offered.

Bunch had been unwilling to let it pass. 'We don't have a lot of fun, Cissy, and we'll be back before sunset so we shan't be driving through the blackout.'

'Racing has never interested me,' Cecile shrugged. 'But I know you love it and I wouldn't want to be a wet hen. You have a good time.'

'What will you do with your day?'

'I have things to do,' she replied.

'Nothing that can't wait, I'm sure. Come with us, Cissy. It

will be like old times. The picnic may not be up to much but we can take some champers and I know the gardener has some early strawberries.' She glanced at Beatrice. 'We shall leave some for you, Granny.'

'No need, my dear. Have you forgotten?' Beatrice replied. 'I am going up to Town for a WVS dinner to attend and it will give me the added pleasure of seeing my son.'

'Lady Reading's shindig? Sorry Granny, I'd forgotten. Is Mummy still in Scotland?'

Beatrice raised one brow and paused for a count of three. 'I think your mother will be in the glens for a while. I believe a few friends have gone to visit.'

'That will be nice for her.' Bunch did not enquire further. She had no liking for those extended house parties that Theodora so adored and she was only glad that the Dower was too small to host them. 'But I thought she was meant to be resting?'

'Your mother cannot rest in solitude.'

Bunch had known better than to ask any more. Beatrice would not discuss intimate secrets in Cecile's presence because it was simply not done. She glanced at Cecile, delicately cutting her toast into tiny bite-sized pieces, and wondered what it was that her friend could not talk about and why. Cecile was playing a great deal close to her immaculately presented chest. Bunch had a suspicion it was more than the Professor's demise that occupied her thoughts. Part of the reason for this jaunt to the races had been to talk to her away from the estate. They barely had a chance to chat outside of working or during meal times, and Bunch convinced that was by design. Cecile's apparent need for secrecy was bothering her more and more as the days passed. The woman was efficient with her work in the estate's office and pulled order from chaos in a short time, but once work was over she became a wraith, appearing for meals and then seemingly vanishing into the ether. *Something is not right but God knows what.*

She tore her attention back to Beatrice, who was folding her napkin and preparing to leave the table. 'Do you need any help, Granny?'

'To do what? I'm old but I think I can still catch a train on my own. I shall get a cab to Thurloe Square.'

'If you're sure.' Bunch tapped her fingers on the edge of the table. 'Well, there you are, Cissy. Come with us, do. I hate to think you will be on your own.'

'I will not be without company.'

'Oh?' Bunch waited for more but Cecile just carried on with breakfast. Secrecy seemed a natural state for the young Frenchwoman and Bunch could not help feeling that it was not all due to the regime that she had lived under and ultimately fled from.

'I was not sorry to leave Berlin,' Cecile had once told her, and gone on to talk about how she had adored Paris until they had been obliged to flee once again. Her father, however, was a subject that Cecile would not permit to be raised.

With all she's been through she has every excuse, Bunch decided. *It's only natural.* 'Emma was looking forward to a chat,' she said. 'Can't you just—'

'I am meeting a friend,' Cecile replied.

~~~

The three women arrived late at the ancient earthworks of Cissbury Ring where the meet was being held. It was a demanding course with few hurdles but taking the riders across slopes too steep to be included, as yet, in the drive for the planting of more crops.

Ranks of horse boxes were congregated near the start of the course. Estate cars, with their rear doors open and tail-gates loaded with baskets and bottles, took up position so spectators could view the five races on the card in comfort. It was a noisy gathering as friends who had not met for weeks gathered to catch up on the gossip. Few were taking any real interest in the races themselves.

Dodo and Emma seemed too intent on enjoying the day to allow the heat to dampen their mood.

A heavy humidity along with the noise made Bunch's head ache and by the time the last run was due she was feeling unusually anti-social and close to regretting that they had come at all. Several nights of poor sleep and hectic activity around the estate had her out of sorts. The crowd gathered around the finish line was almost feverish in its intensity. *Bravado*, Bunch realised. Rumours and gossip brought across the Channel by Britons fleeing home indicated that fighting was heavier and casualties higher, contradicting both the Pathé newsreels and BBC radio bulletins.

She left the picnic and headed for the hill top where she could gather her thoughts, which were plagued by the thoughts of death far closer to home. Despite all her best efforts she had not been able to gain access to Perringham House and she was no closer to discovering who had murdered the unfortunate Tobias Hurst. The wager with Wright was just an added factor, ratcheting up the pressure. Everyone was urging her to stay out of the investigations, giving her more than enough excuses. But it was not in her nature to leave anything half done. She had promised some answers for Lizzie Hurst. When it came down to it she also wanted answers for the family of Janine De Wit. *Because the woman died in my arms.* Most of all she wanted answers for Cecile Benoir. *They are all linked somehow. They have to be.*

She was out of breath by the time she crested the rise. Breathing slowly, she turned in a slow circle to view the landscape all around, a vista that never failed to inspire. She loved this place and was thankful that the race did not cross the hillfort itself to spoil its tranquillity. She always sensed an atmosphere that went beyond mere history whenever she visited this spot.

To the south lay the town of Worthing and beyond that the Channel where a solitary naval vessel steaming eastwards. No sign of the fishing fleet - she would not expect to see other vessels, given what was happening on the other side of the water. Bunch stared toward the horizon though there was no hope of seeing the coast of France, even on a clear day.

The sun shone but a line of darkness was creeping in from the south. Above the noise of the crowd she was sure she had heard the odd rumble of thunder. The sea sparked on wave tops like shards of crystal, forcing her to shade her eyes despite sunglasses.

Bunch selected a spot close the course and settled ready for the last race to pass her by. She was surprised at her sudden need to escape the noise and bustle and the smells of dusty earth and bruised grass overlaid by the sweet sharp scent of horses. She adored these meetings yet the need to think outweighed her love of all things equine. Point-to-points were smaller and more intimate affairs than a standard race meet, and because almost every owner and horse was known to her, coming as they did from the immediate vicinity, she did not feel the need to view the runners before the race. She had ridden with Perry or Robbo alongside many of the hunters taking part. She knew less of the thoroughbreds that had sneaked into the mix, against usual Hunt rules, and who was she to begrudge a local stable the chance to pit their animals against more than their stablemates.

Her chosen vantage point, a little back from the marked-out track, had an astounding view of the South Downs. With her binoculars at hand she would miss little of the race itself. Even at a distance she could recognise most of the beasts lined up at the start line a half mile further on. She sat up a little straighter as the field were off and she traced their progress with a punter's fervour. She had a small wager on Big Ben, a strapping roan she had known since he was a colt, and his rider and owner was an old friend. They had little chance of winning but it was in her nature to go against the field. Cecile herself was just such a point. Bunch had been warned against involving herself in the woman's affairs. *But what the hell.*

Occasionally, riders and mounts would dive out of view into gullies or vanish into stands of trees as she tracked progress through her binoculars. Mostly the course followed unmade tracks to avoid trampling crops but now and then the horses burst out into open country, following the contours of the ridge. Flashes of bright silks ballooned on the backs of the jockeys as the herd thundered toward and past her. Clumps of chalk and grass were kicked up around her and then the field of riders were past and careering toward the finish line, with Big Ben trailing amongst the stragglers.

She lowered the glasses, smiling at her folly of betting on the old hunter. She raised her face to the sun, revelling in the luxury of being alone with nothing but the larks and the distant tannoy to disturb her. A distant rumble to the south attracted her attention and she raised the binoculars once again. The sea glittered in the sun but she could still see several tiny shapes. Large ships had come into view, belching smoke as they steamed eastward. Given the news from France she guessed they were also naval ships. Though whose navy she could not tell from this distance. *Chilling thought. No sign of gunfire, however. Which has to be good.*

She lowered the glasses at the noise of scuffing of boots on hard earth and recognised Ralph's lanky figure ambling toward her, with mixed feelings. *Sod's law,* she thought. *Just the man I wanted to talk with – but not here and not now.*

'Ho there, Miss Courtney. Your sister told me you would be up here.' He threw himself onto the grass beside her. 'Lovely day, what?'

'So far.' Bunch gestured toward the bank of clouds moving almost imperceptibly inland. 'Odd rumble of thunder now and then.'

'Let's hope it is only thunder.' Ralph looked toward the distant water and Bunch tilted her head at him, waiting for the second part of that statement, which never came. He snapped a stem of wild thyme and held it to his nose, twirling it slowly, absently. For almost a minute they sat without moving in total silence. To Bunch, his face seen at rest was younger still, the sun and laughter lines smoothed by his apparent calm. 'You called yesterday and asked to see me. Again.'

She glared at him, suddenly aware that Wright may possibly be correct and she could not do any more than the police in penetrating Ralph's wall of secrecy. 'Yes, I did.' She brushed her hand across the sheep-cropped turf, breathing in the apricot scent of cowslips crushed beneath them. 'I'd assumed you hadn't got the message,' she added. 'You seem terribly busy right now.'

'I am. There are dark things cooking across *la Manche.*'

'War. It doesn't come much darker.'

'It does when it becomes invasion.'

She glanced at him sharply, wondering if he would say more. 'Is that imminent?' she whispered.

'I can't let slip a single bean, old girl, even if I knew what they were.' He gestured toward the ships. 'All of that is Admiralty territory. Rather outside of my remit, don't you know.'

'I understand. But until and if the war arrives on this side of the Channel I need to know a few things about what happened in Whitehall, which is rather more my field of operations.'

'Ho! Straight to the point, hey? Can't we enjoy this glorious day whilst it lasts?' He gestured at the distant clouds. 'We all need a little breather. Before the storm arrives.'

The double entendre was not lost on her and she had a certain knowledge that she was not going to break into his armour-plated bon homie. 'Are we down to discussing the weather now?'

'Polite chit-chat before we get down to business.'

'Which is?'

He turned toward her, squinting against the sun and still managing to keep his gaze steady as he met hers over a distance of inches. 'I thought I'd pop along and see if perhaps you wanted to join me for dinner? Our cook can offer up a reasonable turbot.'

'That sounds lovely, but aren't you coming to the Dower next Friday?'

'All being well, but there's no reason why we can't have a quiet dinner before then.'

'Not tonight.' Bunch looked away, cross with herself for blushing, not at refusing the invitation but the recalling of Wright's Mata Hari quip. 'I need to see my sister and Miss Tinsley home,' she said.

'I can arrange for a staff car to take them both.' He regarded her blandly. 'As you don't have Miss Benoir with you either.'

It was a simple statement and Bunch could not bring herself to be surprised by it. *This man has eyes everywhere I go and a highly disconcerting way of knowing every small doing. Is he just showing off? Or has he scattered his minions here?* 'Cissy had errands to run. I can't imagine what. She knows hardly anybody in these parts.' Bunch canted her head in the opposite direction to his. 'You seem to know her better than anyone – you were thick as thieves at church. And I am sure I've seen her walking back from Perringham House on several occasions. Which is odd considering how hard it is to gain admittance.'

Ralph was almost smiling as he gave a measured response. 'Nothing wrong in having a pleasant chat. Miss Benoir is a delight and we've discovered that we have several mutual acquaintances. One of whom is working for me at the House.' His smile widened. 'Though it pains me to admit it, she does not visit Perringham solely for my company. Now, since I have obliged you in solving that burning question, what about returning the favour and letting me spot you that dinner? I can promise you a rather good wine to follow.'

'If you have found your way into Daddy's cellar then I am sure you can. As irresistible as you think you might be I won't simply abandon my pregnant sister without so much as a song. Daddy would never forgive me.'

'She has her sister-in-law with her.'

'Would you believe Emma doesn't drive at all? Brain the size of the moon and she refuses to even contemplate getting behind the wheel of a car.'

'Everyone has their talents.'

'Yours seems to be appearing from nowhere. How did you know I'd be here today?'

Ralph laughed, studying the ground, plucking another choice stem of thyme. His fringe flopped forward in a blonde swathe. He looked toward the race meeting. 'I follow the horses,' he replied. 'It wasn't a difficult guess. And of course—' he looked back at her '—I did happen to ask that rather jolly Land Girl of yours. The tall one. Kate.'

'Kate?' Bunch wanted to be surprised that he knew the names of her Land Army staff but she wasn't. *He is the kind of chap who never forgets. Photographic memory, I wouldn't be surprised. But Kate is away with her parents this weekend so he's lying to me right from the off.* 'Did she now?'

Ralph's lips pulled back into a sly grin that was confined to his mouth. 'What was it you wanted to see me about? You do know that your request to have the woodland returned has been reviewed.'

'My father has spoken to you about that?'

'He has.'

'And I'm not going to get it back?'

'Sorry.' He finger-combed his hair back, turning on that gleaming smile. 'What will it take to get me out of your dog house?'

'Let me think— Anything?'

'Within reason.'

'How about letting me ask your people if any of them were out and about when Hurst was murdered. There is always the off chance that one of them saw something and just forgot because it seemed not to matter at the time.'

'I should have expected that. You've been pestering the life out of my adjutant for a visitor's pass for days.' He blew out his cheeks. 'And here was I thinking you had an overwhelming urge to see little me. Would this have anything to do with the death of that horny-handed son of the soil?'

'Tobias Hurst. He had a name. And a family,' she snapped. 'I told his wife I would look into this.'

'Sorry, no offence. His death is very sad naturally. I'm sorry if you think I'm totally without feeling. Your Tobias Hurst, however, had no links with my operations, I can assure you of that. Until his death he was a total unknown to me.'

Another lie. He must know about Hurst's grievance over the hay load. 'Your 'people'?' she said. 'One of them knows Cissy quite well. You told me that yourself, so how can you make the assumption they all saw nothing?'

'Because I've already asked them.'

'And that is all the investigation there is going to be? I promised I would do everything I could to bring her some peace of mind.'

'Admirable. If your enquiry was about bringing comfort to a widow I would applaud it. I'd also heard you enjoy a little sleuthing.' He pursed his lips. 'I'm told you're also schlepping for your chum Chief Inspector Wright?'

'Who told you that.'

'Wright has been digging around for the very same information about Hurst, and you were seen having a jolly little tete-a-tete with him in the Stars a few days ago. It wasn't hard to work out. I gather you made a deal, Miss Courtney. Or should I call you Miss Hari?'

She had joked to herself that this man had an uncanny way of knowing the smallest detail. But knowing that private joke bordered on the psychic. Bunch stiffened her muscles against the shiver that ran through her. Whatever attraction she might have had for Ralph evaporated like damp on a hotplate. 'How did you know...' she began and realised she had nothing more she could say aloud though the unsaid hung between them like a medium's ectoplasm: there but not there.

Ralph's trademark smile faded and he was regarding her now with needle-sharp intensity. 'I make a point of knowing everything that goes on around me,' he replied. 'Especially those who are so keen to know my business. My people are trained to see and hear all and come scuttling back to base with the tastiest birds. Rather like a pack of good gun dogs'

'You had me followed? How dare you!'

'No, I have not had you followed. Nor your policeman friend. In his case it would also be against the law.' The smile returned. 'I should hate to lose your good opinion, because it is so rarely bestowed and therefore more worth the earning.'

That sounds vaguely familiar. Did he just paraphrase Austen? she thought. *The man is a total enigma.* 'You don't help yourself in that department,' she growled. 'Spying on people, eavesdropping … it's not what friends do.'

'I have not had you followed despite all of the amateur sleuthing into my business.' Ralph spread his hands. 'You have the kind of voice that carries and you happened to be overheard.'

'Oh.' Her mind went back to the Seven Stars and the young couple who had been seated near them, and she cringed inwardly. Both she and Wright should have known better. 'What would a few questions hurt?' she asked. 'A man was killed. His neck was snapped. Inspector Wright has been assured by the coroner that it was at the hands of somebody with very specific combat training. 'Just a few questions. If you answered Wright's concerns you would not need to avoid him. Nor would you need to have us followed.'

'It could hurt a great deal. I have told you twice now, I was not having anyone follow the worthy Chief Inspector Wright. And I would not dare have them follow you.'

'But you know something. Don't deny it. What or who?'

'That is for me to know and you to never find out.'

'Do you honestly think you are above the law? I find that thoroughly reprehensible.' She heard her voice rise, a touch of shrillness creeping in. 'You think you have my father at your beck and call but believe me, Colonel Ralph, he would not condone an innocent man's murder.'

She raised her hand as if to slap him and Ralph's mood changed. In a blink he grabbed her by the wrist and pulled her off balance, his body leaning against hers so that she was unable to move. Bunch was too shocked to do very much beyond stare into his eyes, which were far closer to hers than she was comfortable with. She could feel her heart racing and told herself to *Stay calm, it's a public place. He can hardly do me any harm.* 'I could scream,' she hissed at him. 'Or I can kick your shins into next week. How dare you manhandle me.'

'I don't see you as the screaming type.' His face was close to hers, their noses almost touching. His slow minty breath with a hint of scotch caressed her cheeks. 'You started the violence, old thing. This is merely by way of a demonstration.'

'Assaulting young women?'

'I think you know me better than that. I do not deserve that attempted slap, Miss Courtney. You have my word, on my honour, that none of my people were involved in any act of murder in or around Wyncombe. I suspect those executions were all carried out by somebody far closer to home.'

'Executions?'

'Assassinations. Murders. They all mean the same thing in the end. I have seen these same things happen wherever I've been in the world. Your father will tell you the same thing. When – if – the perpetrator is identified they will be local. Take my word for it.'

'Closer to Hurst's home?' she said. 'Do you mean Chiltwick?'

He gazed at her, unblinking.

'Your word? Coming from a man who is currently holding me prisoner I have no idea how much that means.'

'No more and no less than your own,' he replied. 'If I could tell you more I would. Are you calm now? Can I let you go without risk of further violence?'

She didn't reply. *He has a real knack for flipping my switches. Much like Wright. Or is it me?* Edward had always said she was too volatile, too ready to march out on crusades. Too quick to draw conclusions.

Bunch was no fool. She knew that whatever Ralph was up to, it had the highest clearance and logic told her that he would not be in that position if he had not the trust of some pretty important people. *And yet…* She was looking into those soft puppy eyes and saw nothing but sadness and regret. 'I'm calm,' she whispered.

'Good.' Ralph leaned in to brush her forehead with his lips and was on his feet before she caught her breath. He held out his hand to pull her up. 'Please accept my apologies. I didn't mean to be quite such a brute. Am I forgiven?'

'Perhaps.' Bunch dusted the chalky soil from her dress, not wanting to look at him as she sorted out a suitable reply. She was unspeakably angry with him and also with herself for trying to impress Wright by putting herself in a tricky position with this impossible man in the first place. She looked up finally and saw an empty space. She whirled around and fancied maybe she caught a glimpse of him slipping into the cover of gorse and bramble, but though she stared at the spot for several minutes it was clear that Colonel Ralph had carried out one of his infamous vanishing acts.

Bunch was not sure of how angry she should be and barely aware now of the view that she had climbed to see. She wished she'd had Roger with her. The dog would not have allowed anyone to lay hands on her in that way. Yet it was in defending her that the ancient Labrador had sustained damage that aged him several years in a few months. Once again she questioned whether she should be embroiling herself in all of this. *Come on old girl, don't beat your gums over it. The trouble came looking for you when the de Wit girl was killed. Not the other way round.* Ralph had been adamant that his people had not played any part in the deaths. She was sure he had provided her with information that he deemed important, dropping clues as openly as his covert activities would allow. *Is it about Hurst? Or De Wit? Or Benoir? Are they linked after all? Despite the information Wright had bee given by his superiors? Which governmental high-ups were telling the truth? Military or Constabulary? Perhaps they both were in their own way, or both lying. Or obfuscating at the very least.* She made her way down to the make-shift car park and searched out the shooting brake where the girls were finishing off the picnic.

'Feeling a little better?' Dodo poured her sister a glass of champagne and handed her a slice of pie. 'Cook swore it was pheasant but we all know it's pigeon.'

'Very good pie, as always.' Bunch forked a small portion into her mouth and looked around. Gaps were already appearing in the ranks of parked vehicles where those with further to drive were eager to be home before nightfall. Others had noted the same grey line of rolling cumulus still out on the distant horizon and were heading home before the risk of a deluge on baked soil turned the field into a pond. 'We should leave soon,' she said.

'Agreed.' Emma begun packing away the remains of their luncheon.

Far more eagerly than is warranted, Bunch thought but said nothing aloud. She knew this kind of event was not of any more interest to her than it was to Cecile. She washed another mouthful of Champagne around her teeth, enjoying the bubbles and the tang of fermented grape, and wondering how long such imported luxuries would remain available.

'Did your Colonel find you?' Dodo asked her.

'Yes, he did.' *And forgot to mention that he'd asked for directions.*

'What did he want?'

'Would you believe he asked me to dinner?'

Dodo eyed her sister up and down. 'I can well believe it. He obviously has the motor running for you. What I don't believe is that asking you for a date is the reason he followed you halfway across the county. However smitten he might be.'

The last of the wine slid past her gums and Bunch slotted the glass carefully into its place in the basket lid. There was never a time when she had been able to fool her sister.

Emma was no less able to read her. 'He told us you had been asking to see him. Seems to me that there's a little mutual smiting in progress.'

'Everett Ralph is a monster,' Bunch snarled. 'An ever so charming and well-bred monster.'

Dodo and Emma exchanged wide-eyed glances. 'I see a story here. Do tell,' Emma purred.

Bunch opened her mouth, ready to allow the floodtide of anger to spew forth, and then exhaled slowly. 'He is doing his duty,' she replied. 'Much as it burns me to admit it, he is doing exactly as expected. But oh how another small lump of me is infuriated by his charm, his manners and...'

'And the rest of you? How does the most of Rose Courtney feel?'

'A boiling pot of absolute frustration. He plainly thinks I am poking around where I don't belong.'

'He's not alone there,' said Dodo. 'Daddy thinks you should stay out of it. So does Barty. And your Chief Inspector.'

'Oh fiddlesticks. None of them seem terribly keen to find the answers. Well, Wright is but he'd still rather I was not on the case.'

'Has it occurred to you that they may all be correct?' said Emma.

'I know you don't think that, Em.' Bunch replied. 'You know how hard it is for any woman to be listened to. Would you have a chair at your college if you'd done what was expected of you?'

'Touché.'

'Then don't expect me to pay any attention to Everett Ralph merely because he's a man.' She stuffed her last forkful of pie into her mouth and chewed slowly. 'He knows far more than he is ever going to tell me and seems to find it all terribly amusing.'

'He asked you to dinner,' Emma observed. 'He can't be too worried you'd take offence. Did he tell you anything more about the murder of your Mr Hurst?'

'Not really, except that it was a local matter.'

'Local man dies on local street? Of course it's local. Question is, did any of his people have a hand?'

'No, he was quite emphatic on that point. And oddly enough, I believe him. He told me in as many words that the answers will be found in Chiltwick.'

'And you believe that? Do you think he is hiding something?'

'I'm sure he is but not about this.' Bunch slid her dirty plate into the basket and wiped her mouth on her napkin before adding it to the load. 'I'm certain he wouldn't shield a murderer. Especially if that killer was not one of his ménage. I need to think about it.'

'If there are secrets in Chiltwick it could be hard to winkle them out. It's one of those places,' said Emma. 'A rabbit couldn't pass wind without it being noted and judged. But the moment an outsider such as your Inspector asks a question…?' Emma spread her hands.

A horsebox trundled past them, big and noisy yet unobtrusive among so many of its kind, leaving just a waft of diesel and chalky tyre tracks in its wake. 'You'd think so wouldn't you,' Bunch followed the trailer's progress out through the gate and watched it moving swiftly along the roadway in secluded anonymity, only its rooftop visible above the hedge tops. As it passed a second gateway the whole vehicle came briefly into view and she allowed herself a slow smile. 'Every place has a weak spot. Come along, ladies. Time to go.'

Monday 27 May

'I am grateful for your help. I truly am. I'm never going to be able to repay you for all the troubles I've brought to you.'

'Nonsense, Cissy. What problems could you possibly bring us? Tea?' Bunch poured from the pot that Cook had brought out to the office and pushed the cup toward Cecile. A rumble of thunder punctuated the silence growing between them and both looked toward the dust-misted window. Late-afternoon sunshine added extra heat to a sultry afternoon despite the storm of the previous night. 'Going to rain again. With any luck it will cool things down a little. God above knows the crops need rain.' She took a sip of tea, allowing Cecile the space to tell whatever it was she had been holding in all day.

'Bunch, I was not intending to show you this.' Cecile took a letter from her pocket and placed it on the table. 'I think the meaning is pretty obvious.'

'Delivered by hand.' Bunch observed, noting the lack of stamp. 'Who brought it?'

'Not a clue. It was shoved under the office door. You know how big the gap is.'

'You could limbo-dance under it.' Bunch held the envelope between her fingertips, reluctant to look inside when the contents plainly disturbed Cecile so deeply. She recognised the envelopes as the same kind that Cecile had used to write to her just a few weeks before. The same brand that the Mann's had sold in their shop. *Though to be fair I suspect Jean Crisp sells the same in Wyncombe Village Stores – common-or-garden stuff.*

She extracted the single sheet of paper and unfolded it – and stifled a small gasp. Pinned to the sheet was a clipping detailing the death of Tobias Hurst. On the paper itself was a badly drawn swastika. 'Hardly subtle,' she said at last. Bunch glanced up at Cecile for her reaction but her friend only stared out of the window. 'And utterly vile. What kind of person would do this? And why didn't you say something? Straight away?'

'What could you have done?' Cecile ran a hand over her face and slumped a little in her seat. 'In Berlin, and in Paris, I was used to being self-sufficient. You didn't let your private doings be known outside of the front door because you never quite knew what others might think or do with such information.' She put her hand to her mouth, regarding Bunch cautiously. 'I did not mean that to sound the way it did. It becomes ingrained you see, secrecy. It's a very hard one to break. I have told you now, haven't I?' Her eyes were pleading for forgiveness.

'I understand, honestly.' Bunch stared at the paper, still not quite believing what she saw. 'We must tell William. Chief Inspector Wright, that is.'

'No!'

'But—'

'No, please.'

'I don't understand why not.'

'Because it's made my mind up and it won't matter soon.' Cecile grasped Bunch's wrist. 'Your friend Chief Inspector Wright would only make life more difficult for me. I do appreciate all you have done and I've done nothing but bring problems to your door in return. I've been offered a place at

Perringham House and taking it seems the right thing to do all round.'

'What place is this?'

'I can't go into details, but its something I have to do, Bunch.'

'No. You don't have to do anything. Especially not on my account.'

'I have made the decision.'

'So you're going to plunge yourself into the middle of Everett Ralph's crowd? Why on earth would you do that? I thought you had problems with jobs because of your papers? I mean to say— Isn't his setup all terribly hush-hush?'

'Isn't everything these days?'

'Not between friends. Or it shouldn't be.' Bunch stared at the letter, unsure if she should be curious or angry. *Perhaps both.* The tone of the letter rather depth-charged any real antipathy. She could only feel fear and pity for her friend. 'Why would somebody send this?' she said. 'Is it meant to be a threat? An accusation? A warning?'

'I honestly can't tell you. I can promise you that I had nothing to do with that man's death. And I have no idea why anybody would think that. I was here that night. You know that.'

'I'd never think you'd murdered him in a million years. You simply aren't the sort of person who could take a life.'

'We've both shot deer and pheasants.'

'Well yes, but that is hardly the same thing.'

Cecile took back the letter and shoved it into her pocket, giving Bunch a twitchy smile. 'That is something we might all find out rather soon. The milk collector told me there was a lot of activity down on the coast last night.'

'Troops on the move?'

'Ships. Well, boats.'

'There was nothing on the Home service.' There was a reticence about Cecile, still, that told Bunch she had yet to deliver all her news. The young woman was shuffling papers without purpose, moving them from one tray to another and back again. Thunder cracked and rolled, closer and deeper than before. The sky beyond the open door had turned a steel grey, solid in the reflected sun and dulling as the last rays were shut off. A blackbird singing from the top of the elm tree at the far side of the lane appeared louder than usual, its voice magnified by the heaviness of the late afternoon. All this she had the time to note and reflect on as she waited for Cecile to broach whatever it was that bothered her.

'Bunch.'

'Yes?'

'I truly do appreciate all you've done for me this past month.'

'You've already said that and I will reply again in the same vein. You are not any trouble to me, so what's given you the bile pills? Spill the beans, old thing.'

'There are things…' A pained expression flitted across Cecile's face. 'Better that I go away, I think.'

'Have you had any trouble from staff? Because if you have—'

'No, not from any people here. The Land Girls have been absolutely top-hole and the others around the estate are perfectly charming. Mr Parsons is such a gentleman.'

'He is.' *And why single him out?* Bunch wondered. 'There is a but,' she said. 'Please, Cissy, tell me what is going on. I know you've made your mind up to go and I can't stop you, but you can't drop vague hints and not tell me why.'

'People,' she replied. 'There is a man who has been, well, I can't say following but watching me, yes. When I go to church or to the village he always happens to be there. He's not the only one to stare, but there is something about him.' She spread her hands, at a loss for words. 'One time he did follow me. I was walking back from Chiltwick and he was behind me for some while. Fortunately he was not a strong walker and I outpaced him. I cut across the top meadow to come here more quickly. When I looked back he had started to climb the style. He was shouting to me. He seemed angry though I don't know what he said. Then a farm worker came along the lane and spoke with him and I just ran.' She laughed, a nervous giggle that owed little to humour, in Bunch's opinion. 'I expect it was nothing to be afraid of. My wild imagination … but since Papa died I have been on edge, to say the least.'

'To be expected, old thing. Losing a parent must be ghastly.' Bunch took Cecile's hand and squeezed it. 'You should have told me. I hate to think you've been afraid all this time. When did it happen?'

'Sunday before last. The day we were both caught out in the rain.'

'And I was perfectly beastly to you.' She let Cecile's hand go and engulfed her in a bear hug. 'No wonder you didn't say anything. I…' Bunch pulled back. 'No excuses, I was a total horror. Forgive me?'

'But of course. I've been acting very oddly myself, I know that. Such a poor guest.'

'All forgotten.' Bunch thought back to that incident and realised how jittery Cecile had been and felt so very guilty. 'Did you recognise the man?'

'Which one?'

'The one who followed you, you silly goose.'

'Not by name. He is one of those people you see here and there. Older man but nothing special about him. You would pass him in the street without a glance.'

'And the other man?' Bunch said.

Cecile shook her head. 'Not one who works here on the estate, so far as I could tell, though he was some distance away so I may be wrong.' She let out a small derisive sigh and shook her head again. 'I can't be more specific, I am afraid. And what could I have said? Two men that I could not identify had a conversation in a lane.'

'Very true. Nevertheless I should have liked to think you could have told me in spite of that. All in the past now, Cissy. When will you be moving to Perringham House?'

'As soon as possible.' Cecile took Bunch's hand. 'This is all very sudden, I realise, and I hope it does not leave you in too much of a jam. Everett … Colonel Ralph needs a language instructor quite urgently. I gather cramming sessions in German and French are terribly important for some of his people, given the situation across the Channel. I can't say more. I signed papers, you see.'

There was little doubt of what those papers would be. Bunch had seen reference to them often enough through her father's work even before the war had raised its reptilian head. A beefed-up Official Secrets Act, coupled with the newly announced Emergency Powers Act, had inveigled a murky and potentially deadly undercurrent into those light-hearted poster campaigns such as 'Walls Have Ears' and 'Careless Talk Costs Lives'. Bunch wondered where it left her own investigations. Were her father's warnings to stay out if of it more than parental caution? 'I quite understand, Cissy. If you have been conscripted for a post of course you must go. We shall cope. Just don't forget to drop in for tea now and then.'

'I won't.

'The tension between them did not allow for another hug. Somewhere in the previous few seconds the habitual adherence to the code of 'thou shalt not betray your emotions' re-asserted control and the two women confined themselves to a nod and smile. Cecile rose to leave.

There was more to all of this than Cecile was telling, Bunch was absolutely certain of that. She had an idea that Cecile would not tell all, even if protocol permitted her to say more. There were things that had occurred the past few days that were connected, yet not imperative to relay, in the French girl's eyes at least. Not sufficiently connected to break the Official Secrets Act in the name of friendship.

Cecile's revelations about the troubles she'd had with local people was something that did not come under such secrecy and Bunch was a little hurt that she had not been told of them. She grudgingly admitted that perhaps she had not been as open and honest herself. *Does DCI Wright have this curse?* she wondered. *Does he suspect everyone and everything as a matter of course? I hope to God not because I've given him enough reason to arrest me if he were that way.* She wished she had paid more attention that day and seen who had followed Cecile, and who had intervened. There were several candidates for both players in that scenario but she would only be making educated guesses and what she needed were irrefutable facts.

'It all hails from Chiltwick. I think I might give Wright a call.'

Wednesday 29 May

'Chiltwick is small, so it isn't a monumental task.' Bunch sat in the Wolesley with Wright and examined the list pinned to a clipboard. 'Though it depends on how far out we go, and whether we take Ralph's comment literally or metaphorically. There are perhaps twenty houses, thirty at most between here and Wyncombe. We should cover them all in an afternoon.'

'I should not be indulging you in this at all,' he grumbled.

'I won our wager. Ralph was bearded and questioned.'

'Not entirely true. The deal was that you inveigled your way into the grounds, using your infamous female wiles, and talked with him there. So all bets are off.'

'Don't split hairs. I spoke with Ralph, who I may add came to the races just so that he could ask me to dinner. So I've won, fair and square.'

'Did he now?'

'Yes.' Bunch studied the clipboard and its list more carefully than it deserved, avoiding his eye. 'I think we can discount Hurst's widow, and probably the Manns.' She tapped her pencil on the board and gazed down Chiltwick's short street. 'There are a few cottages a little way out. Most are further from Hurst's cottage than Perringham House.'

'You don't think you are taking Ralph a little literally?'

'Most likely I am, but it's a start. I think he may be correct: Benoir's poisoning, the arson attack on the Jenny Wren and then Hurst's murder can't be coincidence.'

'I agree. But we haven't found any links between the three other than Chiltwick. If you will excuse me stating the obvious, we have already taken statements from everyone.'

'It never hurts to double check. Shall we?' She led the way to Flint House, a solid two-storey building of stone blocks and flint facings, and a Sussex-stone roof, much of it obscured by a blanket of creeping plants. *Solidly built but poorly maintained*, Bunch noticed. The window frames were not just peeling but showing distinct signs of rot, as did the pitted planking of the oak door. The garden was overgrown, the paving cracked, and it took a second to spot the metal bell-pull half-buried in a tangle of Virginia creeper. Bunch gave it a couple of hard tugs and was pleased to hear a corresponding peel from within, and stood back to wait.

Wright pointed at a brass plaque below the Flint House nameplate, which declared *Richard Bale M.Litt.* 'He takes in students for private tutoring,' she replied at Wright's raised eyebrow. 'Getting reluctant small boys through high school and equally reluctant young men through university entrances. Rather poorly I'm told by a few who were treated to his charms.'

'You don't sound convinced?'

'Something Emma Tinsley hinted at. He came from good roots so I don't doubt he has the education, though I pity the poor wretches that have to come here. He's not the easiest of men.'

They were waited for some time before Bunch lost patience and gave the bell-pull another yank. Somewhere in the recesses they heard a responding jangle. A few seconds later the sound of bolts being shot was almost shocking. Even in times such as these few people in the villages locked or bolted doors during daylight hours.

The door half-opened and Henrietta Bale peered around it. 'Oh, it's you Miss Courtney.' She glowered at Wright. 'And you again.'

'Mrs Bale, just a few final questions concerning the murder of Tobias Hurst. All routine. We're talking with all the householders. May we come in?'

'It really is not convenient,' she replied, 'but if you must…' She stepped back into the shadows and allowed Bunch and Wright to follow into a hallway panelled in Victorian oak, made darker by blackouts pinned over the coloured leaded windows. The floor was paved in Minton tiles in dour shades of brown and black and blood-red; assuming that the blood in question was darkened with age. From the graded depth of colour evident in worn patches, Bunch had the impression they would have been lighter had a mop been applied in recent months, or possibly years. It was hard to ignore the dust in every corner; hard to ignore the odour of dry rot and damp despite the driest May in years; hard to ignore that this sprawling house had just two occupants. Yet she knew why the Bales were the way they were – distressed gentlefolk, as Beatrice would have had it, and she felt a little sorry for them.

Mrs Bale glided ahead of them, her head high. *Oblivious, or,* Bunch thought, *putting on as good a face as she can.*

The old woman opened a door at the end of the corridor, still without a word, and ushered the two into an untidy study where Richard Bale sat at the desk by surrounded books and papers. He placed his pen neatly in its holder and sat back in his seat. 'Excuse me for not getting up, Miss Courtney. And Inspector Wright, isn't it? To what do I owe this visit?'

Bunch caught an odd frown crease Wright's features. *Exasperation? Anger? No,* she thought, *animosity.* Wright had been there, she knew, in the trenches, and had his own legacy of permanent damage.

'A few routine questions, Mr Bale,' Wright said. 'We are trying to work out the final movements of Tobias Hurst.'

'He was sneaking off to the pub, I should imagine.' Bale pulled a handkerchief from his pocket and coughed, the slow measured cough of the gassed. 'My apologies, Miss Courtney. Shredded lungs,' He tapped his chest and stifled another cough. 'A gift from Kaiser Bill. I don't get about as much as I might wish.'

'You were not out and about the night your neighbour was murdered?'

'Hardly.' Bale's eyes flicked toward his mother, an arctic glance, and Bunch wondered what he thought she might say.

'Only that you might have seen somebody leaving Chiltwick at around the same time as Mr Hurst.'

'Why would you think that?'

'We are asking all of the people living between here and Wyncombe.'

Bale regarded Wright thoughtfully and then shook his head. 'I believe PC Botting took note of my movements, or lack of them, at the time. Mother and I were here, at home. And as we spend much of our time at the back of the house we would never have seen any comings or goings in the street – even if we had the inclination. Hurst and his family are of no great interest to us. We are not in the habit of watching them.'

'In a small place like Chiltwick it's only natural to look when you hear something outside. The click of a gate catch. A raised voice.' Wright looked from son to mother and back. 'Neither of you saw or heard anything?'

'Nothing,' Hettie snapped.

'Do you know of any disagreements Hurst may had had with neighbours?'

'None at all.'

'Mr Bale, I was told you had an altercation with him just a day before he died.'

Bunch scrutinised both of the Bales to gauge their reactions. Hettie appeared confused and a little annoyed. Her son's face gave nothing at all.

'And who told you that?' His reply was quiet, measured.

'I think you know whom.'

'Where? When?'

'In the lane close to Perringham House.'

'Balderdash. I had a pupil that afternoon. How could I be wandering around the lanes at the same time?'

'Perhaps you could supply us with the pupil's address?'

'I shall need to look it up.'

'You don't know?'

Bale shrugged. 'If I have to send a note home I send it via the boys. I don't have need to remember the address of every brat that mutilates literature under my roof.'

'But you do keep and appointment book?'

Bale nodded, a reluctant dip of the head. 'Of course ... but I have very few students now.' Bale spat an emphasis on the final word that left Bunch in any doubt of his feelings on the subject.

'Perhaps you could provide Constable Botting with that information?'

'Of course.' Bale's gaze was unblinking before he asked, 'May I be permitted to know why you are so interested in me.'

'Since you're innocent it hardly matters,' Wright replied. 'We have to follow up on these things. Routine.'

'Obviously. Now if that is all? Much as I would like to help you further, Chief Inspector, I am expecting one of my few paying pupils in a few minutes and I have a living to earn.'

'Thank you for talking to us. We shall see ourselves out.'

Wright nodded to the Bales and gestured Bunch to leave ahead of him.

She complied, mostly because she could not think of a reason not to. They were back in the car before she said anything sensible. 'They were very prickly about it all. There must have been other things we needed to ask.'

'I shall need to make a few more enquiries first. His alibi for one thing.'

'Well, that was patently a lie. How can he have an alibi when he doesn't know what time of day we are covering?'

'Once we have that snippet we shall know how to proceed.' He frowned, looking toward the unkempt house. A boy of ten or so years lean his bicycle against the fence and scuffed his way up to the front door, the yellow piping of his school blazer bright in the sunshine. 'He does have pupils, it would seem. Though how many must be the question. He is a little out of the way. Do buses run here?'

'We're not completely uncivilised, you know.'

'I am not so sure. Did you notice the memorabilia in his study?'

'No, I was not looking that closely. It was all a bit dingy.'

'There was a corner dedicated to his military days.'

'That's not unusual. Barty Tinsley has an entire wall of his den plastered in pictures of his battalion. Daddy also has a few in his study. It's what people do.'

'Pictures yes, a gun perhaps, uniforms maybe or even a bayonet. But a trench club?'

'A what?'

'A handmade weapon for defence against enemy soldiers entering the trench, or more often for the silent despatch of sentries during scouting trips by our own lads. There were units who specialised in night-time sorties on the enemy's trenches. Either for reconnaissance or to eliminate machinegun posts or sometimes simply to lob a few grenades in whilst the Germans were sleeping.' Wright stared at his fingers laced together until they whitened with the pressure of his grip. 'Those trench weapons were manufactured from whatever was to hand. Hatchets, bayonets, shell casings,' he went on, his voice low and flat. 'Regular raiders made quite substantial clubs. Bale had one. A wooden club with a grenade casing fixed over the end. In experienced hands it's the sort of thing that could crack a skull open with a single tap.'

'How horrible.'

'It's not something most men would bring home. I don't think we need to conduct any further interviews, do you?' He leaned forward and tapped Glossop on the shoulder. 'Drop Miss Courtney at her home and then get back to the Station.'

'Sir.'

Wright closed the glass divide and sat back. 'I need to dig up some more information on this chap.'

'And his pupils?'

'Perhaps. Meanwhile keep out of his way.'

'It was Hurst's neck that was broken, not his skull.'

'Raiders didn't just rely on their hand-made cudgels. They killed with trench knives, garrottes or even with their bare hands. Any method that was quick and silent.'

'But even so, Bale is such a frail man.'

'I hope I am wrong … but if not? Be careful, please Rose.' He held his hand before her lips to forestall an argument. 'I'll keep you informed. If I'm correct I hope to be back tomorrow.'

The car pulled up in the Dower House driveway and Bunch got out. 'I shall ask Cecile if she recalls anything else. We can exchange notes tomorrow.'

~~~

Beatrice was alone when Bunch rattled into the drawing room for afternoon tea a few hours later. Her grandmother was quite literally on the edge of her seat, an upright chair close to the wireless set, as she listened intently to the Home Service. She seemed oblivious to all else except that her left hand stroked absently at Roger's head. The Labrador was leaning against Beatrice's leg, his greying muzzle resting against a tweed-clad thigh.

Bunch stood in the doorway for a moment watching them and realised that the two frailest members of the household were more comfortable with each other's company these days than with hers. She didn't begrudge Beatrice her dog's loyalty. 'Granny.'

A manicured hand silenced Bunch as the news reader repeated an appeal for men with boating skills. The broadcast moved on to sport and Beatrice reached out to turn the wireless off. 'The news is not good,' she declared. 'It appears that the remnants of the BEF have been trapped on the French shores near Dunkirk.'

'All of them?' The faces of people she knew flashed through her memory and for a second she struggled to keep control. 'I thought they were regrouping along the line. Is it certain?'

'Churchill spoke to the House today and told them the whole of our forces are trapped and are in need of evacuation. The Admiralty is appealing for boats and crews to help them home.'

'Civilians? Isn't something like that down to the Navy?

'No longer, it would seem.'

Bunch looked out of the window at the rapidly darkening afternoon. The trees showed the pale undersides of their leaves in a fresh wind as the first spots of rain tapped against the glass like a thousand tiny fingers. 'Poor bastards crossing the drink in a bathtub. In this weather.'

'It will be as bad for the enemy. Ring for tea, will you, Rose dear?' Beatrice got to her feet, pausing to catch her breath, before moving to one of the sofas. Roger padded along behind her and collapsed at her feet.

'Rog seems to be glued to your knee these days.' Bunch bent to ruffle the dog's neck as she took a seat close to her grandmother.

'He and I are suited to each other. Pair of old crocks.' She glanced at the mantle clock. 'Two minutes past five. Where is Cecile, do you know?'

'Isn't she here?'

'Why would she be? I had the impression from what she told us at luncheon that she would be putting up the milk yield figures all afternoon.'

'I've been in the office and I've not seen so much as a hair of her. God, but that girl can be infuriating. She told me she was leaving, Granny. Going to work for that awful creature, Everett Ralph.'

'I'm not in the least bit surprised. I rather think she feels uncomfortable here.'

'I don't see why she should.'

'Rose, my darling. Your heart is in the right place but you really can be the most insensitive creature. She is finding it hard to work for somebody she views as a friend.'

'But she came to me and asked for a job.'

'And found the reality somewhat different than she expected.'

'I'm not sure how to feel about that. Have I been a pill, Granny?'

'Not at all. You're a good friend. There is something else troubling that young woman – perhaps we shall never know what it is. This job with Ralph might be just the thing, something more challenging than making up the accounts.'

'It's all academic now because she's moving out. She's probably at Perringham House already. It's not as if she had that many belongings to pack. I'm just a little hurt that she took off without saying goodbye.'

'We don't know that she has, but I am not holding up tea for her.'

Knapp rattled in with a trolley set with crockery and comestibles.

'Isn't Sheila serving tea?' Beatrice said.

'I sent her home, Madam. Cook had the wireless on in the kitchen and the poor girl heard about our troops in France. Her uncle is there I gather – the girl is very upset. Understandable of course. In her state the chinaware seemed rather at risk.'

'Quite right.' Beatrice glanced at the trolley with only two settings on it. 'Did Miss Benoir happen to tell you if she would be here for dinner?'

'Yes, madam, she did. A lad came with a message for her and Miss Benoir left in something of a hurry. She said that she hoped to be back in time for dinner but not to wait.'

Knapp being in the know did not surprise Bunch in the slightest. Knapp had ruled the sprawling halls of Perringham House and its small army of staff, and she knew every last detail of what went on above and below stairs. Keeping track of the Dower House was child's play by comparison. 'A small boy? Did Miss Benoir happen to say who the message was from? Can't have been Colonel Ralph.'

'She only said that she was going out and that she would be gone a few hours.'

'Did she take a bicycle?'

'I believe she walked.'

'Then we can assume she was not going far.'

'Doubtless we shall find out at dinner.' Beatrice lifted the silver pot. 'I shall pour, thank you, Knapp.'

'Yes, Madam.'

Beatrice poured the tea, adding a splash of milk before

handing a cup to her granddaughter with a small huff of irritation. 'Cecile is a dear sweet girl, but she does need to be a little more aware. Bad enough she misses tea but cook struggles to maintain a decent dinner table. Wandering off at a moment's notice really is too bad of her.'

'It won't be for much longer.'

'True. And from the way things are looking we shall have no staff left by the winter.'

'Yes, Granny.' It was not a point to argue. Bunch sipped at her beverage and looked out of the large windows into a warm and heavy late afternoon. The rain had been slight and done little to dispel the closeness of the heatwave. She knew that Beatrice had spent the afternoon dozing in her room because she did not cope with such weather all that well. It made her tetchy and mulish.

Bunch also had to agree just a little with the criticism that her friend was not being a terribly accommodating house guest. But she was more willing to make allowances than Beatrice. The old woman was not so hide-bound as many of her peers but she had lived for too many years under a ritual laid down by years of habit, that strict meter beaten out by the gong standing in the hallway. Those rituals, such as mealtimes, had become sacrosanct and such flagrant flaunting of the rules was hard for her to accept. Bunch knew Cecile's going would make life simpler but she hated the idea that her friend may be leaving because she felt her presence in the Dower was a burden. Solving the riddle of the Professor's death might go someway towards it, and whatever Wright's superiors might try to say she was fairly convinced the deaths were linked. Two poisonings in a hamlet the size of Chiltwick in under a week was *definitely* not a coincidence.

Thursday 30 May

Urgent tapping on her bedroom door entered her dreams like a spurt of gunfire and for a moment Bunch gazed at the ceiling in confusion. Gradually she realised she was not actually on a French shoreline with her old ATS compatriots sheltering from a barrage of Gerry mortars. She sat up and turned on the lamp to look at her bedside clock. A little past one a.m.

'Miss Rose?' The door opened quietly and Knapp sidled in. Her hair was pinned up in papers and crammed beneath a fine net and she clutched her plaid dressing gown protectively at her throat despite the warm night. 'There's a telephone call for you, Miss.'

'At this time of night? Who is it?'

'Somebody from Perringham House. I believe it's quite urgent.'

'Tell them I shall be down in a moment.'

Bunch pulled on her dressing gown and made her way down to the hall to pick up the receiver. 'Hello? Rose Courtney speaking. Who is this?'

'Miss Courtney? Good evening, or rather good morning. Everett Ralph here. I'm most awfully sorry to disturb you at this ungodly hour but I have to know if Miss Benoir is at home?'

'Cecile? Not that I'm aware of. She went out this afternoon and we haven't seen her since. She told Granny and me that she might be staying over there at Perringham House.'

'She was supposed to be here last evening but she never arrived. Missed a rather important meeting with Captain Arnott, as a matter of fact. Not like her.'

Knowing Everett Ralph's legendary calm, his obvious concern made Bunch shiver, raising hair on her arms. 'Cissy's usually such a stickler for timekeeping,' she said. 'I can imagine a few very good reasons for her not being there but none of them good.' She listened to the silence at the other end with increasing anger. 'You thought she was missing but waited all of this time before you called me?' she demanded.

'She's an adult.'

'But now at—' she looked toward the hall clock '—at one o'clock, now you think there is something amiss?'

'I got back from London just an hour ago,' he said. 'That's when I learned of her absence. I would not be calling so late otherwise. When did you last see her?'

'I suppose it was around lunch time.'

'Did she give any indication of where she was going?'

The tension was clear in his tone. She could imagine him pulling faces at the phone. 'Knapp told me that Cecile rushed off sometime in the mid-afternoon saying that she would not be back until late and not to wait for her.'

'Her meeting with Arnott was for 2100 hours. It would have been earlier but she made it very clear she wanted to have dinner with you both.'

'She did?'

'One last dinner together, apparently.'

'She was moving away? She told me she was going to work with you as a language tutor or some such.' Bunch heard the antipathy in her own voice and winced. The man had such a talent for exasperating her. 'Her father died just a month ago and the police won't even let her bury him. Please don't take advantage of her state.'

'Miss Benoir knows exactly what she is doing. It was she who approached me.'

'I didn't know. Why would she do that?'

'Her father had lectured here on two occasions. Perhaps it's her way of honouring his memory.'

'That may have occurred to her ... though she was not missing him unduly, if we are being honest.'

'I got the impression she felt there was some kind of debt to be paid. Another reason why her absence is disturbing: she was terribly keen. For that and other reasons it truly is imperative that you find her.'

'That "I" find her?' Another silence was punctuated by the odd ticking and clicking from the village telephone exchange. *Not only the walls that have ears*, she thought. 'One moment, Colonel.' She placed her hand over the mouthpiece. 'Knapp?'

'Yes, Miss?' The housekeeper appeared almost instantly from the service door.

'When Miss Benoir left did she give you any indication of whom she was going to meet?'

'No, Miss,'

'You say a lad brought her the message. Was he a local boy?'

'Not one that I knew. He was small, dark haired.' Knapp touched her fingers to her chin as she recollected. 'He was wearing a Windlesham School uniform. I noticed that especially because I remember thinking they'd all been evacuated to Somerset. His parents must live locally. And he probably came on a bicycle because he wore his satchel on his back. Other than that he was just a small boy. '

'Thank you, Knapp. That is most helpful. I should run along back to bed now. I can deal with this.'

'If you are sure, Miss?'

'Quite sure, thank you.' She smiled at the older woman and waited to hear the door into the kitchen quarters close before she lifted the receiver to her lips. 'Ralph? Seems she had a message and hared off to places unknown. I shall ask around and keep you posted.'

'If you could. Rather important we don't lose track of her right at this moment.'

'Why? She's not working for you just yet.'

'True, but her disappearance could have consequences, nevertheless.'

'For a language tutor?'

'Languages? Yes, amongst her many unique talents.'

'Then why haven't you sent anyone out to look for her?' The silence that followed told her a great deal. *How typical. Here I'm thinking he's concerned for her and all the time...* 'All right, Colonel. In your game all secrets are secrets and I shall do what I can to help track her down. I will call you if I find anything. Obviously, I shall expect the same courtesy from you.'

'Miss Courtney, I would gladly flood the streets with search parties but we have a ... a particularly delicate operation under way. I came back from Town with the specific order not to deploy any personnel off base on any pretext. I'm speaking completely off the record, you understand. If the brass knew I'd even thought of talking to you they'd have my guts.'

'Oh.' For once Bunch had no quick-fire answer. 'Won't they want to know Cecile is missing?'

'Officially she's not one of our people. Not until she's physically signed the Act, if you get my meaning. I still feel responsible – she is one of mine, bar the shouting.'

'I understand completely. You'll tell me straight away if she does turn up?'

'Of course.'

A click, and the dial tone purred at her from the earpiece. She set the telephone back on the table and stood for a moment considering her options. *What to do? Ralph is perfectly correct. Cecile is a grown woman and she hasn't been missing for very long. I can recall a few times when I've tottered home well after midnight but that was usually in a big city. London or Paris, that one night in Rome.* She smiled as she recalled those circumstances. *But this is Wyncombe, dammit. Nowhere to go at this time of night, so where on earth could she be? Think, woman!* She opened the cigarette box next to the telephone and lit a cigarette. The smoke made her throat dry and she stifled a cough, but the familiarity of that action calmed her racing thoughts. *Okay, first thing is to find that messenger. Knapp knows just about everyone in the vicinity so if she can't place the lad then who could?*

She drummed her fingers on the hall table. The school was well enough known for there to be people well placed enough to identify him but that would take time, and Bunch did not relish visiting Flint House alone in the wee small hours. Especially when the message could well have originated from them.

The obvious course of action was to telephone for PC Botting at the Wyncombe Police House, except that she had no proof of complicity. He would only wait for orders from headquarters. To go and ask Bale questions at this hour would be of little use. If innocent, the Bales would have every reason to drag her name through the mud; if guilty of a crime they would be forewarned before anything concrete could be proven.

She paced the hallway, chain smoking her way through two more cigarettes before she finally stopped by the telephone. She picked it up, took a deep breath, dialled for the operator and asked for Brighton Police Station.

~~~

The black Wolseley pulled up outside of the Dower House a little over an hour later and Bunch was waiting on the step to hurry Wright inside.

'Thank you for coming up at this hour. I wasn't sure calling PC Botting would achieve a great deal with this one.'

'You were lucky to catch me. I was about to go off duty.' He removed his hat and followed her into the drawing room and sank into a chair.

He looked exhausted and, but for Cecile, Bunch felt guilty at dragging him on a twenty-mile drive in the blackout. 'Drink?' she asked.

'I'm officially off duty so yes please. Should have been done hours ago but the whole system is in chaos with everything going on out at sea.'

'Surely you're not part of that?'

'No, but the LDV patrol found another three bodies washed up under the West Pier and it's difficult to retrieve them when the beach is out of bounds. It's the only reason I was at the station when you called.' He swallowed half of the scotch that Bunch had handed him. 'Now, what is it that can't wait for a few hours?'

'I couldn't say much on the telephone. Operators so love to listen and all I have is a theory.'

Which is?'

'Where to start?' She replenished his drink and sat down opposite him. 'Cecile Benoir has gone AWOL.'

'For how long?'

'Nobody has seen her for almost twelve hours.'

Wright stroked the top of his head and sighed deeply. 'She's over twenty-one and has no husband or parent.'

'What difference does that make?'

'That she is responsible for her own actions in the eyes of the law. Until she's been absent for at least twenty-four hours we can't take any official action.'

'Is that why Ralph passed the buck to me?'

'Did he now?'

'She hadn't turned up for a meeting. He assumed she'd ducked out and wanted to check with me that she was safe.'

'I rest my case.' Wright spread his arms. 'To be fair to your Colonel, I gather most military personnel have been confined to bases.'

'I think Ralph had more than basic orders to deal with. Never mind him. Cissy is missing. I know her too well to think she would simply vanish.'

'She didn't tell you about her visits to Ralph.'

'Well ... yes, that's true, but I have this ghastly suspicion she might have answered a call from Dickie Bale. Bearing in mind your comments about his past we both know that is not going to be a good thing. Did you find out any new information on him?'

'That he was mentioned in despatches many times. He has a fistful of medals.'

'Quite the war hero.'

'Some might say so.'

'But?'

'Invalided home.'

'He was gassed. Hardly surprising.'

'Gassed in a German trench.' He looked up at the ceiling as he paraphrased the front-line reports. 'Without direct orders from Command he single-handedly raided an enemy machine-gun post that had been devastating the regiment in every wave. He killed the entire machine-gun crew and staggered back across the lines suffering the effects of a gas attack – with twelve human ears in his pocket.'

'Ears?'

'Trophies, I gather. He was cast as a hero for the

propaganda and was sent back to Blighty because of the mustard gas, but according to the records he should have been quietly shipped home as mentally unfit. Even the Army Medical Corp had realised he'd reached breaking point but they had a problem. His "bravery" had already been mentioned in despatches that had reached London news desks via the trench newspapers. The generals could never lose face so his shell-shock was very quietly papered over.'

Bunch felt a trickle of bile rise in her throat. She swallowed half of her scotch and let it sink back down again. 'How ghastly.' She knew how inadequate that sounded. *Yet what can one say? I know I should feel sorry for him. Damaged war hero and all that. But ears. Human ears.* She shuddered and reached for her cigarettes, lighting one with shaking fingers. 'But why?' she asked.

'He was being asked to do things no man should do, even in war. As I said, I saw his medical records and it seems he'd begun to class enemy soldiers as – as game animals. Wild boar, wolves, stags, anything rather than human. It was how he coped. Sad to say, I can quite see the why and the how.' Wright took another pull from his glass and they both avoided each other's glances as Bunch refilled. 'You believe he may have asked Miss Benoir to meet him?' Wright asked at last. 'I can't imagine she would go, much less still be there.'

'We have no other leads so it seems as good a place to start looking as any.'

'Then I shall have to look.'

'Not alone.'

'I cannot take a civilian with me to question a potentially dangerous suspect.'

'You can't go alone.'

'I'll roust Botting from his bed.'

'Do that. I'm still coming with you. Cissy would want me to

be there.'

She had expected more of an argument but Wright only sighed. 'You will come along whatever I say, so yes, but you stay in the car.'

~~~

Glossop parked at the junction leading into Chiltwick, out of the sight of Flint House, where the Jenny Wren rose from the backdrop of trees, only visible from the first in the line of cottages.

Bunch looked toward the east where a barely pink stain ran along the horizon. It was, in her opinion, quite disgustingly early. Even the dawn chorus had barely gone beyond chirping experimental bars. She got out of the car and took in the sweet scent of grass that had been mown the previous day. It merged with the heady perfume from a white jasmine clambering up the side of the shop. A clean scent of the early hours that was soporific, despite the tension she felt. She stretched and yawned as she stood next to Wright as he gazed into the gloom. She waited with increasing impatience. They had been through the plan of action in the car but still she could see he was mulling it over with himself. She understood Wright was wary of going in single-handed yet calling in the big guns seemed overkill when there was little real proof. *But we've come this far, dammit.* 'What are we going to ask?' Bunch said. 'We can hardly call it routine enquiries at this hour.'

'I shall start out with the truth and see if we get any reaction,' Wright replied. 'Short of charging in and arresting him it's the only option I have. As it stands, these are still routine enquiries for a missing person.'

'And tip them off?'

'You are assuming they're guilty of something.' He placed his hands on her shoulders and looked into her face. 'You must stay here. Your presence is not going to help matters and will quite probably lead to some unpleasantness.'

'I want—'

'Not this time. Wait here with Glossop. I need to make basic enquiries first and with all due respect that's best done without you. I doubt it will take long.'

If he imagines he's leaving me out of this he's can think again. She watched him walk away until he was no more than a silhouette in the faintest of crow-light. 'You stay here,' she said to Glossop and darted along the path that ran down the side of the deserted Jenny Wren before the ATS girl could reply.

She hopped over the fence at the bottom end into a hay field. From there she jumped Flint House's crumbling wall into a garden jungle. Old fruit trees and brambles and rampant stands of perennial plants and shrubs were all that remained of a sweeping vista once seen from the rear of the house. She pushed her way through toward the paved area at the back of the kitchens and paused. There did not appear to be anyone outdoors and the blackout curtains precluded any risk of being seen by a casual glance from a window.

Stepping lightly across the expanse of blue pavers, she laid a hand on the round Bakelite handle and gently tried the back door. *Locked or bolted. Perhaps both.*

She glanced down the twitten running between the old coach-house and the side wall and heard the distant jangle of the door bell. It was a long impatient ring that was undoubtedly louder here in the servant's domain than the rest of the house, yet the delay in answering seemed overlong, even for an elderly woman and her son both in equally dubious health.

Bunch crept to the very end of the passageway where peered cautiously around the corner to see Wright standing on the front step.

He leaned forward, ignoring the bell pull this time in favour of a black iron doorknocker in the form of a stag's head. The crash started a blackbird tuck-tucking from its nest somewhere in the tangle of Wisteria on the coach-house wall.

The alarm call made Bunch duck from instinct, hunkering down close to a blacked out semi-circular fanlight set low in the wall. It looked like a cart wheel had been sunk into the ground and glazed into place. Its sill and the mid spars of the arched window were level with the flagstones. *A cellar*, she thought. *Sculleries? Storerooms?*

The rattle of bolts and the dragging noise of the door being opened reclaimed her attention and she scurried to the end of the wall to peek around to the front of the house.

'Mrs Bale.' She saw Wright doff his hat politely, his voice carrying crisply in the quiet of the early morning. 'I am very sorry to disturb you so early in the day, but we've a missing-person enquiry and witnesses have placed the last sighting of her in Chiltwick.'

'There is nobody here.' Hettie Bale's voice was loud and carried clearly on the morning air to where Bunch crouched at the mouth of the passageway. 'Except for myself and my son.'

'I'm sure that's the case. But we've several witnesses who feel you might know a little about the woman in question. The young lady recently lost her father. Miss Cecile Benoir? She and her father had a cottage a little way out of the village. Professor Benoir was a visitor to the tea shop here in Chiltwick, so you may have seen him around?'

'I can assure you that I have never spoken with this Miss Benoir, or her father.'

'We understand that a message was delivered to her at Perringham Dower House by a young lad yesterday afternoon, and she left there shortly afterwards.'

'Why would you think it has anything to do with us?' Her voice rose in pitch, clearly angry at being challenged.

Bunch's attention was dragged from the doorstep to the

fanlight a few feet behind her. A clattering of something metallic had been dropped onto a stone floor. She edged back a few paces and leaned close to the glass. There was nothing more to be heard. She tried to peer around the edges of the blackout. There was nothing to be seen, not even the tiniest vestige of light creeping around the edges. No amount of dodging up and down gave her any hint of what lay beyond. *I'm assuming there is a light on in there. But if Dickie Bale really is fast asleep in his bedroom as his mother claims, and she is at the front door... Unless they have the world's clumsiest cat or some damnably muscular mice, I am convinced there's somebody in that cellar.*

Wright was still talking and she scrabbled back to the corner to catch it all.

'Our witness insists the messenger was a boy wearing a very exclusive school uniform. The same uniform worn by the boy spotted arriving for tutorials from your son. One has to assume there are not two such lads in Chiltwick attending that particular school. He's one of Mr Bale's regular pupils, I imagine?'

Bunch leaned forward to peer around the side of the house, wondering what it was that had made Wright enter Bale's pupil into the conversation so quickly. *I must've missed something when I checked the cellar window.*

'Your witness was mistaken. Was it that young woman next door? I'm sorry that she lost her husband of course, but one must be truthful. Elizabeth Hurst has been nothing but trouble ever since she moved here. She likes nothing more than to make life difficult for the people around her.'

'It was not Mrs Hurst.'

'Then who?'

'Mrs Bale, you should know that I saw a boy answering that description myself. He came into this garden yesterday just as I was leaving.'

'Which proves nothing. Always getting brats round here of late. Collecting for this and begging for that. He probably went to every house. And what gives you the authority to question us at all?' Hettie's voice rose in another pitch as she rounded on her questioner.

'The Sussex Constabulary gives me all the authority I need. A young woman's life may be in danger and we believe you may be able to give us your assistance.'

'This is outrageous. What right have you to drag people out of their beds and question them on their own doorsteps for all to see?' A pheasant rose noisily somewhere off across the road and she looked toward it, using the moment to drive home her point with a few seconds of righteous silence. 'I have a standing in this community,' she said. 'Have no doubt, I shall be writing to your superiors. I do not appreciate being interrogated on my doorstep.'

'I can come in if you are concerned about people seeing me here.'

Hettie closed the door a little further and raised her voice. 'You most certainly will not. Come back at a more civilised hour, Mr Wright.'

Close to where Bunch crouched, a feral noise, high and urgent, rose to answer Hettie's angry outburst, and was abruptly cut off by a dull thud. *The kind of sound that a soft netball makes when it bounces off the court*, Bunch thought. She crawled back to the filthy wedges of glass and hunched as close as she was able, on hands and knees, ear pressed against the panes. She was positive that something or someone was inside, yet the only sounds she heard as she held her breath and listened were a swelling dawn chorus and the circular conversation still being waged on the doorstep.

Bunch scrambled back to the end of the wall, thinking, *This is what Roger must feel like fetching birds*.

Wright was losing patience. 'Mrs Bale. I repeat, a young woman's life may be at risk and the boy may have some vital information. Would you please tell me who he is?'

'I have little or no dealings with my son's pupils. It would be ridiculous of you to expect me to know what they look like and certainly not their names. I can't be of assistance. Now if that is all—'

'Perhaps Mr Bale could help?'

'Perhaps he might but he's asleep. Please come back later.'

'It is very urgent. If you could wake him?'

'You might think it that simple but my son is in constant pain. Doctor Lewis has prescribed a very strong sleeping powder for Richard to take every evening,' she replied. 'Without it he cannot sleep. So no, I am very much afraid waking him will not be possible. Please come back later, Inspector, when it is more convenient. After ten o'clock. I'm sure he'll be pleased to talk to you then. If that is all? I am not a young woman and I'm getting chilled. I do not want to catch a cold because you insist on keeping me here on the step. Good morning.'

Bunch scrabbled backwards and ran the way she had come, weaving her way through the tangled garden and sprinting around the field.

~~~

'I told you to stay.'

Bunch looked Wright up and down and huffed. 'I'm not a damned dog. And be glad I didn't because that old battle axe was lying. Something, or more likely someone, was in the cellar. Perhaps more than one.'

'You saw them?'

'I heard them.'

Wright gazed back toward Flint House, the stone and flint of its eastern wall glowing pink in the early sunlight. 'Are you certain? No chance it may have been a cat?'

'Positive. There was somebody in that cellar, and as Hettie Bale was at the front door talking to you it could only have been her son. The son she claimed had taken a powder and was out cold in his bed.'

'I can't see Hettie Bale letting us in again.' Wright took off his hat and rubbed his hand across his hair, staring now at his dust covered shoes. 'Perhaps I should send for reinforcements.'

'By the time they've arrived what or whoever is in that cellar will have been moved on,' said Bunch.

'You're making assumptions. We have no reason to suspect that there's anyone in there at all. The noises might be something quite legitimate.'

'At this hour?

'Rats? Who knows.' He shook his head. 'It's quite a leap and if you're wrong all hell will be let loose.'

Does he not trust me? 'I am right. I'm sure of it,' she said. 'We have to do something.'

'There is no connection between Benoir and the Bales other than two sightings of a small boy.'

'And Cissy's assertion that Bale had been following her on several occasions.'

'You know that?'

'From the horse's mouth, dear boy. The man seemed to be obsessed with her. I've no idea why.'

'Her father died not far from here.'

'Yes, they had a cottage a little way along Green Lane.'

'Is it possible Bale and the Professor had some kind of disagreement?'

'Cissy never said anything. Though I've rather gained the impression there was not a great deal of affection there from either side. She may well not have known.' She narrowed her eyes and peered at him. 'Do you think Bale may have poisoned

Professor Benoir?'

'Anything is possible.'

'Then it's all the more reason why we have to look inside that cellar. Right now. For God's sake, Wright, you were as keen as me back at the Dower. We can't afford to wait.'

Wright nodded. 'You may be right. But this time you'll stay here.'

'Rot. I am coming with you.'

'I cannot allow you to put yourself in danger.'

'I'm putting myself in danger,' Bunch replied. 'On my own head be it.'

'It's my head the Superintendent will have on a plate. If you only knew the paperwork you caused me the last time you tagged yourself onto police matters. And I am wasting my breath, aren't I?'

'You are.'

'Then at least promise me that if Miss Benoir is in that cellar you will get her out of the building and leave Bale to me.'

'Agreed.'

'Now, do you know the layout of the house?'

'Not at all. The Bales don't socialise a great deal. Cellars are usually accessed from the kitchens, if that is any help.'

'Not likely to be another entrance?'

'Perringham House had quite a warren of service tunnels. Even the Dower has a wine cellar, cold room and a scullery down there.' She shrugged. 'But here? Not likely to be much in a house this size. Two or three rooms, I imagine. There's a coal chute,' she said. I noticed it when I was listening to you and Hettie Bale battling wits. I don't suppose the hatch cover is more than fourteen inches across but we used to get through a fanlight window smaller than that at the FANY hostel. It will be a tight squeeze, and a bit of a drop inside but I can nip along to the stairs and let you in. '

'I can't let you enter the premises alone.'

'You can and you must. I'm fitter and slimmer than you are.' She took a step toward the house. 'If Cissy is in there then she needs help. If she isn't then I'm going to look rather foolish. But I'm going. You can follow if you wish.' She frowned at him. 'Do you have a gun?'

'Only special duties warrant the issue of firearms.'

'Pity. I can't help feeling it might have been useful.'

'It would.' Wright pursed his lips, staring toward Flint House and then back the way they had come. 'Could you go and rouse your Colonel?'

'I am not leaving here.'

'You are the most infuriating woman.' Wright slapped his hand on the Wolseley's dusty bonnet. 'Glossop? Perringham House is closest. Go there and ask for Colonel Ralph. Tell him we need assistance.'

'Ralph is under direct MoD orders to keep his people on base,' Bunch muttered. 'It's why he called me in the first place.'

'Damn. Well stop anyway and leave a message at the guard post. Then go to the Police House in Wyncombe and dig out PC Botting.'

Glossop hesitated. 'Sir, you can't go in there alone.'

'Hopefully you will be back with some armed assistance before I need to confront the Bales.'

'Yes, sir.'

'Now, Miss Courtney. Let's be clear. This is pure reconnaissance.'

'Of course, Chief Inspector.'

Wright snorted impatiently and turned away. They did not speak as she led him to the rear of Flint House. Crouched in the lee of a sprawling rhododendron, they watched the house for signs of life. A drift of white dog-daisies wafting above the uncut grass were almost luminous in the soft dawn so that

Bunch almost felt they were lighting up her position, and she had to stop herself crouching a little lower.

'Blackouts are still drawn,' Wright whispered. 'But it's early. No sign of smoke from chimneys so no obvious activity in the kitchen. Do they have any staff at all?'

'No idea,' said Bunch. 'I doubt it. Proverbial church mice.' She half-rose, gauging the distance between herself and the wall. She could feel her heart rate rising with anticipation and, yes, fear. She shot her companion a cheesy grin, humour that she did not feel. 'Tally ho,' she hissed and launched herself toward the side of the house, scurrying over the herringboned pattern of blue bricks in a half-crouch. At the turn of the house she glanced back to check that Wright was following.

The cast-iron cover set into the stone flags was well worn. The makers name, 'J Every, Lewes', could just be made out. Wright pulled on the handle flap and heaved it upwards. It creaked out of its niche, scattering dirt onto the path, and slid to one side of the chute. Bunch went to move it further away but Wright shook his head. 'Noisy,' he whispered.

'All right.' She got down onto her knees and peered into the hole. It smelled of damp and coal and stale air.

'Are you sure about this?' Wright muttered. 'Let me—'

'Positive.' She sat at the edge of the manhole and inserted one foot and then the other. Bracing her hands against the rim she began to descend into the dark. Wright grabbed her by the hands, ready to lower her down. The space was tight and she wriggled to get her hips through, slithered a few feet further down, and was stopped as Wright reasserted his grip on her hands. A moment of panic took hold and she kicked her legs searching for a solid surface with the tips of her shoes, ignoring a grunt and muffled expletive from above her. The hands grasping her own were their losing grip, fingers sliding against fingers. She scrabbled for a foothold and found none. The darkness beyond the light that filtered around her from the manhole seemed absolute. The air stank of coal dust was acrid at the back of her nose and throat. She wondered whose great idea it had been and swallowed the thought down with another ball of panic.

Wright shifted his stance astride the manhole, bent double now and sinking onto one knee as he lowered her another few inches. Bunch could hear muted grunts from the effort he exerted and felt the tremors running down his arms to her own, and was suddenly struck by the thought that if he let go now she had no idea how far she would fall, or what she might fall on. For another half-second she dangled in mid-air before her weight was too much for either her finger tips or his to maintain a grip and she dropped the last few feet onto the remains of the coal heap.

The impact scrunched as dully and loudly as any sweet wrapper in a cinema and continued like rolling thunder as she slithered to the floor in a small avalanche of anthracite. She scrabbled to her feet and waited for a moment, listening intently. Muffled and distant noises did not sound like any alarm had been raised. She looked up to the circle of light. Wright's head was silhouetted against the brightness, his features unreadable.

'Are you all right?' Wrights whisper echoed around her, bouncing off bare brick walls to come at her from all sides.

'Yes – give me a moment.' She got to her feet, testing her ankles for stresses. 'All tickety boo. I'm going for the door now. Be ready.'

As her eyes grew accustomed to the dark the door became obvious and she headed toward it, her heart sinking when her fingers located a Suffolk latch. *Damn and blast it. These things are impossible to open quietly.*

She eased the thumb pad down and opened the door,

releasing the latch at a snail pace. She edged out into a passageway, a surprisingly short stretch that was no less chilled than the coal store. The walls here had been lime washed in some distant decade and what remained was cracked and flaked. The floor was flagged in stone that was slightly uneven under her feet. She looked to her left where a naked bulb lit the bottom of the stair. Opposite her was a dark archway from which emanated the smell of damp and mould.

To her right a half-closed door spilled a little light into the passage, along with Bale's rasping tones, loud in the confines of the brick passageway. 'This is not the time for sleep. Talk to me.' He was answered by a low murmur, so low that Bunch could not recognise the speaker nor pick out individual words. The flow was cut off by a sharp blow.

Bunch looked towards the stairs. Wright would be waiting for her to open the door. *If that's Cissy then surely—*

A loud bang echoed along the corridor, wood on stone, making her jump.

'Tell me!' Another cracking blow. 'You will tell me eventually, damn you.'

A shadow passed through the shaft of light. Bunch ran on tiptoes toward the staircase and up to the locked door to the kitchen. She turned the key and hurried to the rear door, also locked but with the key obligingly present.

'There's no sign of Hettie,' she whispered as Wright slipped inside. 'Probably gone back to bed. Dickie's down in the cellar and we should hurry. It was not idle chit-chat being swapped down there.'

Wright drew a leather cosh from his pocket. 'Ready?'

'I am,' she turned toward the stairwell and they both crept as lightly as they were able down to the corridor level.

'Lies!' A single word burst out of the darkness and for a heartbeat there was only the distant dawn chorus trickling faintly into the void, and then an answering thud from somewhere above.

'Door,' Wright hissed. He gestured toward the stairs.

Bunch raced back to the top and closed the door, creeping down again in time to see Wright paused near the far cellar. She scurried to join him. Their view from that door was limited because the first part of the room was a store full of shelves of dusty jars and tins. The far section was obscured by wine racks jutting out from the left wall. They were mostly empty so that light filtered through them in crenelated stripes. Bunch and Wright ducked into the room and crept up to the rack to peek at the space beyond.

It was a wide area lit by two bare bulbs hanging from the ceiling. Boxes and assorted junk were heaped to the right and left while a workbench took up the far wall beneath the boarded-over window. There were spaces in a rack of tools.

Richard Bale stood in the centre of the room, sideways on to them, a length of wood in one hand and an old Webley service revolver in the other. In front of him, tied to a chair, a woman was slumped with head forward, her features hidden in shadow.

Unconscious. Or worse Bunch thought. But she had no doubt at all that it was Cecile Benoir.

Wright signalled Bunch to stay and stepped around the end of the wine rack into the dim light.

'Inspector. Do come in.' Bale cocked his head and regarded Wright steadily, a sly smile tweaking his cheek muscles. He seemed unsurprised by Wright's appearance, almost as if he had been waiting for him.

Wright took a tentative step forward.

'Move to your left, Chief Inspector.' Bale took a few paces to his own left, circling Cecile's chair to keep her between them.

Cecile raised her head and even viewed through the racks the blood and bruising on her face clearly visible in the harsh light. Bunch breathed a sigh of relief that she was still alive.

'Bloody spy.' Bale's face twisted into utter contempt as he pointed at his prisoner. 'Straight from Berlin. Damned Hun. Just like her father.'

'My father was French,' Cecile mumbled through swollen lips.

'Liar.' He swung the club at Cecile and caught her shoulder with the very tip.

Bunch heard Cecile's swift intake of breath and she tensed up, ready to leap forward.

Wright stepped further out into the open space. 'She's not a spy, Bale, I promise you. The secret services have checked her background quite carefully.'

Bale trained his gun on Wright. 'That's the thing, isn't it? Spies need to be clever people or they would never succeed.' He waved the weapon at Cecile. 'Says she's English but she spent all her time in foreign parts.'

'Neutral,' Wright said as he took another pace forward.

'Stay right where you are, Chief Inspector.'

The sound of Bale's revolver being primed was a great incentive for obedience, but Wright took another half-step. 'War needs soldiers,' he said. 'Men like us. The ones who went through it all before. We're the ones who know what war is about, don't you think?' Wright tapped at his leg. 'I copped a round at Amiens. You?'

Bale's arm lowered a fraction, a momentary confusion apparent in his face. 'Me? Injured at Richebourg,' he said. 'Then the gas at Passchendaele.'

'We lost a lot of pals,' said Wright.

Bale eyed him up and down. 'You could only have been a lad.'

'I was.' Wright risked another step and the Webley snapped up once more. Wright raised his hands in surrender. 'I was only there for a few months but it never leaves you,' he said. 'It made no sense, all that blood and mire. It's why I became a copper. For the justice. For order.'

Bunch listened and waited and wondered how much was truth, and how much a salve for Bale's obvious insanity.

Wright was edging around the room as he talked, dragging Bale's attention with him and away from the racking that obscured the exit – and Bunch. 'Did you poison the Professor? For the gassing?'

Bale was matching Wright's progress, side stepping one pace at a time, the Webley still trained on the detective's chest. His wheezing cackle took Bunch by surprise. *Is Bale really laughing?*

'I thought about it. He was a bloody Gerry. I don't care what she says.' Wright jerked the revolver toward Cecile. 'He lived there long enough to be one. And this whole bloody village was full of them. Those Miss Manns claimed they were English, but they weren't.'

'You set fire to them?'

Bale shrugged. 'The chance presented itself. It was like that, wasn't it? You remember. Back in the trenches – we sneaked out across the lines and took out what we could. You remember? No plans. Only opportunities to be taken or lost. Like that girl in the Marquis.'

'You admit that you poisoned Janine de Wit?' said Wright. 'Why? She was an innocent girl.'

'She was German.'

'She was Dutch.'

'So they claim.' Bale raised the gun and extended his arm as he took aim.

Bunch could sense the intensity of his gaze along those

sights, those eyes focussed on the detective's heart. 'It wasn't planned,' said Bale. 'I'd bought the poison that afternoon from a second-hand trader. Opened tin so no poisons book. I wanted it for the rats. This place is rife with them.' He smiled as he took a step backward. He was close to the racking by now. Had they not been bolted down Bunch could have pushed them on top of Bale. 'I heard the fraulein ordering coffee. She could barely speak English and she was demanding Aquavit to go in it. Aquavit, I ask you. The barmaid may not have had what she wanted but I gave her what she needed.'

Bunch drew a slow breath, forcing the image of the girl's last moments from her mind. Her fingers opened and closed, gripping the racking tightly. A bottle chinked and Bale glanced toward where she was concealed, bringing her back to the present. She froze, glad that the light was not behind her.

Wright was level with Cecile now but still two long strides away from her. 'And Hurst?' he said. 'Why him?'

'Can't stop minding my business, can you. Just like Hurst. He stopped me going after this girl and then he claimed he saw me leave the Jenny Wren when it was on fire. Said he was going to Botting. I couldn't allow that.'

'He was going to the police house?' said Wright. 'Not the Seven Stars?'

'Yes.

'Hurst was British,' Wright said. 'No reason to kill him, other than for saving your own neck.'

'I do regret that it was necessary.' Bale sighed. 'A young man, young family. But he would have stopped me, and I had to finish off the raid.'

'Raid?'

'This one and her foreign pals.' He waved at Cecile again. 'Who knows how many in that nest. She'd have told me in time. We were trained you know. Interrogation techniques.

Trench raiding was not just about the killing. We gathered information.'

'Is that why you killed her father?' said Wright.

'I did not kill that bloody Gerry!' Bale shook his head, taking a sidestep to keep Wright in his sights. 'I was tempted. He was a filthy Hun. I'm not wrong about that. Ask his daughter. She knew.'

'You can't wriggle out of it that way.'

Bale shook his head. His gun hand was beginning to tremble from the effort of holding it up. 'I. Did. Not. Kill. Him. I will not be accused of deeds I did not commit.'

'Yet you're happy enough to confess to the rest. Admit to it, man, then we can let the poor chap rest in peace.'

'Justice. Isn't that what you said? Justice and the rule of law. I did not poison Herr Benoir.'

'Monsieur Benoir,' Cecile croaked. 'Professor to you.'

'Shut your mouth.' Bale leaped back and took a swipe at her with the club and shouted as Wright caught it by its tip, twisting it out of his grasp. Bale backed out of Wright's reach, another step, and another until he stood at the entrance to the larger room, near the end of the racking. He was gripping the revolver in both hands now, the muzzle pointed straight at Wright's head.

Bunch flattened back against the empty frame praying he would not take the final step that would bring him nearer to her.

'I am sorry for this. I don't want to kill an old comrade,' he said. 'But what choice?'

'You'd shoot a police officer? Not a patriotic act.'

Bunch eased a bottle from the rack, her fingers tightening around the neck.

'We are at war,' said Bale.

'Yes, but this is not the way' Wright replied. 'My driver has gone for reinforcements. If you shoot me you will be hung.'

'I would expect no less, but—'

The bottle came down on the back of Bale's head with all the force Bunch could muster. He slid to the floor, firing a single wild shot that went wide, piercing a hole in the board covering the window, slicing a beam of light across Cecile's dark head and onto Bale's unconscious figure. Bunch stared at him. She was shaking and numb and suddenly afraid she may have ended a man's life.

'Are you all right?' Wright shouted. 'Bunch.' He leapt across to grab the Webley and felt Bale's neck for a pulse. 'Bunch.' He looked up at her. 'Rose! *Are you all right?*'

'What? Yes, I suppose I am.

'See to your friend.'

Bunch stared at the still body and then to Wright. Her nurse training wanted her to run forward and save Bale despite what he had done to Cecile. The rest of her shuddered at the very thought of touching that pale skin. She stumbled across the room and knelt beside Cecile, fumbling at the knots securing her arms behind the chair's back. Her fingers were clumsy, trembling. 'Damn and blast.' She ran to the bench and came back with a knife to hack at the ropes.

The slamming of a door from somewhere above them made her freeze.

'Bunch,' Cecile mumbled through swollen lips. 'Keep cutting.'

Bunch began hacking at the hemp strands and finally the bonds slipped to the floor.

'Thank you.' Cecile rubbed at her wrists and arms, her eyes closed as she breathed long and deep.

Bunch stared toward the body crumpled by the wall. 'Did I kill him? Is he breathing?'

'He's alive,' Wright said. 'He must have a concrete head. A

blow like that should have cracked his skull at the least. But yes, he's breathing.'

'Right. Okay.' Still dazed Bunch stood, picking up the discarded bottle instinctively, and resting her free hand on her friend's shoulder. Cecile responded by placing her own bleeding fingers on top of it.

They looked at each other in unspoken communication before Cecile nodded curtly and struggled to her feet, clinging to Bunch's arm to steady herself. They hugged briefly, still without speaking, aware that Wright was watching them from beside Bale's prone body.

The house above them was silent now, but from outside came the roar and crunch of a car coming to a rapid halt.

'Sounds like the cavalry has arrived.' Wright got to his feet and strode through the doorway.

'Thank God.' Bunch put a supporting arm around Cecile. 'Come on, old girl, let's get you out for some air.' As she passed the naked light bulb hanging from the ceiling she lifted her other hand and angled the unbroken bottle toward the light. She peered at its label. 'Thank heavens it didn't break, chaps. It would have been a shocking waste of a 1920 *Latour*.'

Epilogue
Wednesday 12 June

Sunlight streamed through the stained-glass windows and reflected off the coffin on its bier at the centre of the chancel. It gave the white lilies resting on the lid an almost cheery glow.

'It seems so wrong for a funeral,' Bunch muttered to Wright as they took their seats. 'One always expects wind and rain. Silly, I know.' She looked around at the meagre scattering of mourners. 'More than I expected, considering.' Ralph and three of what she assumed were Perringham personnel, were seated half-way down the church. The usual handful of parish stalwarts, who made it their business to attend every wedding and funeral on principle, had taken up their habitual seats near to the font. She was a little surprised to see Lizzy Hurst sitting at the very rear of the building, close to the doors, with her child hugged tightly against her. The infant was grizzling, the sound echoing around them all with a note of pathos that denied the sun. Lizzy smiled apologetically in her direction.

'I'm surprised to see Mrs Hurst,' Wright whispered. 'I didn't think she had any connection to Benoir.'

Bunch leaned closer, confining her reply to his ears alone. 'She didn't. She's here out of respect because most people are convinced her husband and Benoir met their ends by the same hand. I assume Bale will hang?'

'He's unlikely to go to trial,' Wright replied. 'His brief has put in a plea of diminished responsibility on both counts of murder, as well as the attempted murders of Hilda and Enid Mann. I'd be very surprised if it was not accepted. Nevertheless it will see him locked away for the rest of his days.'

'Will Hettie Bale be charged as an accomplice?'

'Bale insists she had no idea what was going on and we have no evidence either way.' He shrugged. 'I doubt the Crown will pursue it. They want it all to go away.'

'I wonder how Lizzie Hurst will take that. She's lost her husband, with a young child to bring up alone, and Hettie Bale is still living just a stone's throw away.' Bunch flicked an imaginary speck from her dark suit. 'I've offered Hurst a job at the Dower. Not sure if she will accept it. She needs some time to adjust.'

'Mrs Bale is moving to Yorkshire. She has family there.'

'I hadn't heard. Our jungle telegraph must not be working at full stretch.'

'Not an easy woman to deal with but you have to feel a little sorry for her. Her son made life quite difficult behind their closed doors.' He smiled at Bunch's sour expression. 'She has a long history of unexplained *falls*. People will cover up for their family for many reasons.'

'I wasn't aware of that. It does explain why she kept out of the social round.' She watched the vicar drone through his paces as she mulled over Wright's comments. 'Only two counts of murder?' she said at last.

'De Wit and Hurst.'

'What about Benoir?'

'Bale is adamant that Benoir's death was not down to him.'

'Do you believe that?'

Wright shrugged. 'People like Bale invariably have a motive

in their own twisted fashion, and since Benoir lived so close by, Bale didn't lack the opportunity.'

'But?'

'He shows little or no remorse over the deaths he has confessed too. It's hard to see why he denies Benoir's murder. It would make it so much harder for Benoir's daughter. It's possible he is innocent of that crime. The Crown has closed the case so we'll probably never know.'

Bunch looked at Cecile, upright and serene, all alone in the front pew. 'It must be hard,' she murmured. She wondered why the woman had insisted upon taking her place there alone. *Yes, she's the only family he had but in her place I'd stretch tradition just a fraction. One needs a crumb of human comfort.* 'Bale was proud of the de Wit killing, odious little man,' she said at last. 'Then he tortured my friend. Why would he do that if he had nothing to do with the Prof's death?'

'Confronting outsiders had become an act of patriotic duty in his imagination. Had he murdered Professor Benoir he'd have confessed without a qualm.'

'You've told me more than once that you don't believe in coincidences. Bale was on the spot and he seems to like killing well enough.'

'Inured to death might be a better phrase. De Wit's murder was done on the spur of the moment whereas Benoir's murder seems a calculated act. And the poisons were quite different. Having access to one let alone two lethal chemicals would seem to be unlikely.'

'So the Benoir case should remain open?'

He sighed whilst he considered his reply. 'The official line is that Bale was most likely responsible for his death.'

'Yet Bale is adamant it was not him?'

'The Superintendent claims to be more concerned with rounding up the Italian residents now that Mussolini has thrown his hat into the ring with Hitler. But...' Wright sank a little in his seat as the Vicar caught his attention and frowned.

'And?' Bunch hissed at him.

'Benoir was under scrutiny,' Wright whispered. 'His death came at an opportune moment. It saves them some considerable embarrassment.'

'You don't think they may have done away with him?'

'It's only a rumour. We shall never know for sure.'

'Poor Cissy.'

'She is at least able to bury him.'

'True.'

They fell into silence as Reverend Day chanted the final words of the eulogy, of which, Bunch realised, guiltily, she had heard barely a syllable.

They all rose as Cecile walked down the aisle behind the casket containing her father's remains, Everett Ralph stepping adroitly into step at her side and the woefully short cortège fell in behind them to escort Professor Benoir to his final resting place.

Bunch remained puzzled as to why the woman had been so insistent on walking the path alone. *Or rather in the company of a comparative stranger, when she has a friend at hand.*

'It is what Papa would have expected,' Cecile had told her.

Bunch had known Cecile Benoir for a long while and she was confused by the distance that had grown between them in a very short space of time. She shook her head, feeling it unworthy to imagine such ill will toward a woman in mourning. Yet the certainty that something was seriously amiss would not go away. She adjusted the fine black veil on her cuvette hat and stepped out into the light, leaving the blessed coolness, in every sense, for the intense light of a summer afternoon.

The coffin bearers were manoeuvring their burden around the corner of the church and down the gravelled path toward the further end of the graveyard, coming to stand near the freshly dug grave. A small clutch of people from Perringham House had ranged themselves around Ralph and Cecile. *Like an honour guard.* Other than Bunch, no one had volunteered to attend from the farm, which was no surprise to anyone. *There's been no time for them to get to know her.*

Cecile tipped a few handfuls of soil into the grave, the dried clay rattling against the coffin lid in such a way that, to Bunch, it sounded like fingers drumming against it. The moment Cecile turned from the open grave Bunch went to offer a few words.

'There will be no funeral tea.' Cecile was apologetic. 'Hardly anyone here knew him. Perhaps, when this war is over, I shall hold a family memorial in France. For now, though,' she took Bunch's hands and leaned in to kiss both cheeks. '*Au revoir,* Rose … Bunch. Thank you for being my friend. I don't know how I shall ever repay you. I shan't ever forget.'

'You're leaving?' Bunch said.

'*Oui.* I've received my orders. The Colonel was good enough to delay them until after the funeral but I'm leaving Perringham House later this afternoon.'

'Already? Where to?'

Cecile glanced unconsciously toward Ralph. 'I … shall be away for a while.'

'Then write.'

'Not possible.'

Her reply was terse yet Bunch could not fail to understand the code. 'You're off to put those language skills to practical use,' she said.

'I cannot say.'

'Of course.' They knew each other well enough to know the rest without any need for further words. 'I shall miss you. Come back to us when you're done. Promise?'

'Promise.'

'I am so very sorry for what happened to your father.'

Cecile smiled ruefully. 'As am I. Despite everything.'

'Despite what?' An expression Bunch could not quite place passed over her friend's face and it occurred to her that there was no sign of emotion. Not a tear, or a sadness of any kind. She gathered Cecile into a hug. 'We shall find out who did this. I don't care what Wright says. I give you my word on that.'

Cecile drew back to look Bunch in the eyes. 'Leave it be,' she whispered. 'Please…'

'I can find the truth. I'm sure of it.'

'No.' Cecile gripped her shoulders, her nails digging in like a dog's bite. 'I know who was at fault.'

Bunch looked around them, not sure if she had heard correctly. 'There was someone else in the house?'

'*Non.*' Cecile's eyes darkened. 'Papa killed my mother. Did I ever tell you that?'

'What?' Bunch wondered at her sudden rise in tempo and lowered her voice. 'When? How?'

Cecile sneaked a glance around them. 'He broke her.'

Bunch cocked an eyebrow. 'I know he could be odd but surely he was not violent?'

'I don't mean he murdered her with bare hands though he may as well. He broke her spirit with his cruel mind. Nothing happened in our house that was not for his wish, nor our flight from Berlin in the dead of night. I did not think then, but it was all lies… I should have known that everything was made too easy. He became an enemy of France and he left me with no choice.' She dropped her hands away to her sides, looking Bunch calmly in the eyes as she waited for her words to sink in.

Bunch glanced back at Wright, waiting at a discreet distance. Had he honestly not heard any of this? She couldn't tell. '*Us?*'

Cecile took a step back to run her fingers down the side of Bunch's face and kissed the air, an erotic moue, reviving memories of long-ago nights. Walking backwards for a few paces more, Cecile blew Bunch a final parting kiss before turning to hurry after Everett Ralph.

Bunch watched her slip into the waiting staff car, knowing it was likely to be her last sighting of Cecile Benoir. She clenched her jaws against a swell of sadness, barely noticing that Wright had come to stand beside her.

'You heard all of that?' she said.

'Heard what?'

She eyed him suspiciously. He seemed genuinely not to have been listening. *A gentleman, as ever, allowing us a few last moments.* She felt she should tell what she had learned from Cecile, or thought she had, and changed her mind as quickly. *It's perfectly obvious where Cissy is going and what she will be asked to do. And what did she really say? When – if Cissy comes back, maybe then I shall ask.*

Wright moved toward the gates and on impulse, with only a smallest spark of guilt, she linked her arm with his. 'She was a tad cagey perhaps. But in her defence, she's been doing a frighteningly good job.'

END

Acronyms and Associations

FANY – First Aid Nursing Yeomanry. Later: Princess Royal's Volunteer Corps

WVS – Women's Voluntary Service. Later: Women's Royal Voluntary Service

RAF – Royal Air Force

LDV – Local Defence Volunteers. Renamed Home Guard in July 1940

ATS – Auxiliary Territorial Service, the women's arm of British army during World War 2

BEF – British Expeditionary Forces: troops sent to France in September 1939

MoD – Ministry of Defence

Min Ag. – Ministry of Agriculture

Min Food. Ministry of Food

Ag Labs – Agricultural Labourers

BUF – British Union of Fascists

FO – Foreign Office

Lowther's Lambs – The Royal Sussex Regiments: "Southdown Battalions" 1914-1920

Glossary

Sussex Dialect and Terms

Aah – yes; general term of agreement and/or approval

Aggy – peevish

Ampery – weak, in poor health

Atchety – bad tempered; tetchy

Bain't – have not; is not

Coombe – a downland valley

Downs – hills, specifically South Downs, which stretch from
        Eastbourne to Winchester

Dumbledore – bumblebee

En – catch-all for it, that, those, them, they, him, her, you, etc

Four-ale bar – public bar where beer was cheaper than in the
        saloon. So named from a time when the cheapest beers
        were sold at 4d (old pence) per quart

Frenchie – foreigner; person or thing from anywhere overseas
        (not just France)

Frith – young underwood/undergrowth, specifically that grow-
        ing by or under hedges, or along the edges of woodland

Hatchety – tetchy

Jigger – surprise

Lapsy – lazy

Maid – general term for a girl or a young (especially unmarried) woman

Moil – annoyance

Piece, A – an unpleasant person

Shaw – small wood, especially one that shelters a farmyard or building

Sheer-meeces – field mice

Shrammed – to be shivering with cold

Slabby – dirty, greasy, sodden

Sussex Trug – flattish basket woven from chestnut slats, used to carry garden produce, eggs, etc

Twitten – narrow alley or passage between two walls or hedges

Vanner – horse or pony (often piebald) used to pull a caravan

Vexatious – irritating; frustrating

Wapsey – spiteful

Windshaken – thin and/or puny animal

Wrap-over-pinny – cover-all apron, which is wrapped across the front and fastened with a small tie

Yapin – gossiping or indulging in general chit-chat

Yaffler – woodpecker; often used to denote a foolish or idiotic person

Thank you for reading this book. If you enjoyed it please do leave a review on the purchase site (Amazon, Waterstones, etc) or on your own blog. (Remember to let us know where to find it.)

Bunch Courtney and DCI William Wright will be back with you later this year with more crimes to be solved.

You can find out more about Courtney and Wright, as well as Jan Edwards and her books, at:

https://janedwardsblog.wordpress.com

https://thepenkhullpress.wordpress.com

Twitter   @jancoledwards
                   @bunchcourtney00

Facebook   Janedwardsbooks

Lightning Source UK Ltd.
Milton Keynes UK
UKHW040212120119
335404UK00001B/3/P